Praise for the national bestselling League of Literary Ladies Mysteries

"Logan has fun with this unusual story, intimate setting, and feisty characters, and readers will, too."

—*Richmond Times-Dispatch*

"This is one of my favorite series. What could be more fun than a mystery series that is about a reluctant book club? I love how the mysteries run parallel to the book the League of Literary Ladies are reading. Bea and her friends always rally together to solve the mystery—especially if the accused is one of their own. This well-plotted mystery will be a delightful treat for cozy mystery readers. I found I could not put this book down—I had to find out whodunit."

—MyShelf.com

"One of my favorite cozy mystery writers . . . What great characters Kylie Logan has created." —Fresh Fiction

"Kylie Logan has created a cast of characters with whom readers will feel invested, as their histories are played out throughout the series . . . The plot, a surprisingly complex one in this third of the series, never suffers from the focus on character development. Literature, the struggle of authors, and friendship among women make this an absorbing read— a spookily good book with an even greater mystery."

—Kings River Life Magazine

And Then
There Were Nuns

Kylie Logan

BERKLEY PRIME CRIME, NEW YORK

BERKLEY PRIME CRIME

An imprint of Penguin Random House LLC
375 Hudson Street, New York, New York 10014

AND THEN THERE WERE NUNS

A Berkley Prime Crime Book / published by arrangement with the author

ISBN: 978-0-425-28295-3

PUBLISHING HISTORY
Berkley Prime Crime mass-market edition / March 2016

PRINTED IN THE UNITED STATES OF AMERICA

10 9 8 7 6 5 4 3 2 1

Cover illustration by Dan Craig.
Cover design by George Long.

Penguin
Random
House

To all the teachers,
lay and religious,
who taught me to love learning

ACKNOWLEDGMENTS

After twelve years of Catholic schooling, it should have been easy for me to write about nuns. But when I started *And Then There Were Nuns*, I realized there was a whole lot I didn't know about convent life. I hope I've reported it honestly.

There are some familiar names in this book. Sister Liliosa was the principal of my elementary school, a formidable figure who struck terror into the heart of every child at Sacred Heart of Jesus. I'd like to think that there was another side of her and I wrote this Sister Liliosa to reflect that. Sister Francelle was my third-grade teacher, and I still remember her fondly. Sister Helene taught World History at my high school. She was an ancient woman with a brilliant intellect who not only awarded As, but A++s when she liked your work.

The other nuns are drawn from my imagination, but Mary Jean and Margaret . . . you know who you are!

As always, there are so many people to thank when a book is complete—my editor, Tom Colgan; his assistant, Amanda Ng; my agent, Gail Fortune. I have to include my family, of course, as well as my brainstorming buddies Shelley Costa, Serena Miller, and Emilie Richards. A shout-out, too, to Maureen Child, who listens to my ideas (and sometimes my rants and raves) via email every day and always offers sound advice.

To those readers who have asked, yes, South Bass Island is a real place. It is full of friendly people, fun restaurants, and not nearly the number of dead bodies that appear on these pages!

❖ 1 ❖

"There's a penguin on my front porch."

Truth be told, that statement doesn't sound any less crazy to me now than it did that early spring morning when I muttered it through a fog of sleep.

But then, it had been a long and interesting night, and since I'd just rolled out of bed, I couldn't really be certain that I was thinking straight.

I was pretty sure I wasn't seeing straight.

Just to confirm this to myself, I brushed my long, dark hair away from my face and rubbed my eyes. Nothing changed. From the doorway of my private first-floor suite at the B and B, I looked to my right and toward the foyer. There was a row of long, thin windows on either side of the front door, and the glass in them was as old as the house. Through those windows, the scene outside always looked as rippled as the waves that lapped against the Lake Erie shore beyond the tiny strip of rocks and grass just across the street.

Between the antique glass and the glare of the early morning sunshine reflecting off the lake, it was impossible to see clearly, but I knew this much—I'd come out of my bedroom to make a pot of coffee and I saw what looked like a penguin on my front porch.

Black head.

Torpedo-shaped body.

White at the front.

Outlined with black.

"Very large penguin," I mumbled.

"What did you say? There's a big peregrine on the porch?"

From back in my bedroom, Levi Kozlov sounded as sleepy and confused as I felt.

Yeah, that's right, Levi, the guy who I'd felt an instant attraction to the moment I met him. The one I swore I'd never get involved with because I'm convinced good relationships are all about honesty and for reasons I wasn't ready to divulge to Levi or to anyone else, I couldn't be honest.

We'd been dancing around our feelings, me and Levi, for months, taking two steps back for every one we took forward, weaving and bobbing and dodging every hint of intimacy like old pros.

That changed just hours before the penguin porch encounter.

Blame it on what I made the mistake of calling my "world-famous Bolognese" when I was chatting with Levi earlier in the week. Blame it on him for daring me to prove how good my pasta sauce was and me for taking him up on the challenge. Blame it on the fact that I didn't have any guests staying at the B and B and the soft glow of the candles on the dinner table and the dancing fire in the parlor fire-place. Heck, blame it on spring fever. Or just go ahead and blame it on plain ol' stupidity. Whatever the reason—the alignment of the stars, the overwhelming power of passion, the weakness of human nature—we'd finally stopped side-stepping each other the night before and finished the dance.

And yes, just for the record, Levi is as good of a dancer as I always imagined him to be.

All of which was incredibly exhilarating to remember.

None of which changed the fact that Levi and I had some serious talking to do.

After I took care of the penguin.

"Not a peregrine," I told him. "It wouldn't be weird to see a falcon on the island. This is a . . ." I had always prided myself on my good eyesight. In fact, I didn't need the glasses I'd chosen to hide behind ever since coming to the island and I'd left them on the nightstand next to the bed. I leaned forward and squinted. "Penguin. Definitely a penguin."

When Levi came up behind me, the temperature shot up a dozen degrees and my heartbeat quickened along with it. He wrapped his arms around my waist, propped his chin on my shoulder, and looked where I was looking, his bare chest brushing my terry-cloth robe.

"It's a nun," he said.

A wave of memory washed over me like the slap of a cold Lake Erie wave and I groaned. "The nuns! The nuns are coming to the retreat center today. Elias told me . . ." I spun around and raced back into the bedroom, collecting the clothing we'd discarded in disarray hours earlier.

"Not my socks, yours." I'd already scooped them up off the floor and I tossed them to Levi and found my purple panties and bra, then pulled on jeans and a sweater in record time. My shoes were . . .

When I didn't see them, I settled for what I could find; I slipped my feet into the fuzzy bunny slippers next to the bed. "Elias Weatherly, the guy who runs the retreat center. He said the nuns were coming today."

"Right." Levi had a blanket wrapped around his waist, and in the glow of the brilliant morning sun just peeking in my bedroom window, his chest looked as if it had been sculpted by an artist with a keen eye for both the gorgeous and the tempting. "You're helping with the food."

I raced to my 1930s-vintage dressing table and dropped down on the bench in front of it, the better to see myself in the mirror when I combed my fingers through my hair. "Yeah, but what I didn't tell you was that he called yesterday to tell me his mother-in-law was really sick over on the mainland, and I promised I'd help with anything else he needed. The nuns must have just arrived. They must need something." I whirled away from the mirror. "How do I look?"

A slow smile spread over Levi's face. Have I mentioned tall, golden-haired, chiseled chin? Oh, what that smile did to me! Before my heartbeat raced out of control and took my common sense along with it—again—I popped off the dressing table bench. I had every intention of heading for the door. I would have done it, too, if my conscience didn't prick.

"Look . . ." Feeling suddenly as awkward as I definitely hadn't been all night long, I scraped one bunny slipper against the carpet and stabbed my thumb over my shoulder in the direction of the front porch. "I need to take care of this. Then I'll make that pot of coffee and some breakfast. We need to talk."

He pursed his lips. "Talk. Sure. But not now." Levi reached for his jeans. "Twelve years of Catholic school," he said. "And I'm not about to let a nun know that we—"

"What?" My shoulders had already shot back before I could remind myself that the stance was altogether too confrontational. "You're having regrets?"

His head came up. "That's not what I said."

It wasn't and I knew it. I could have kicked myself for letting my conscience get the best of what should have been a punch-drunk morning of simmering smiles and sizzling shared memories. Damn conscience!

"No, it's not what you said," I admitted. "I'm sorry. I just didn't think you'd be leaving so soon."

"I've got a delivery coming in for the bar this morning, so I really do need to get over there." Levi sat on the bed to put his sneakers on. "But Bea . . ." He looked up at me through the honey-colored curl of hair that fell across his forehead. "You're right. We do need to talk. There are a few things—"

The doorbell rang.

"Penguin at the door," I said and heck, who cared if I was running away from whatever he was going to say or simply dodging what I knew I had to tell him, I spun around and raced out into the hallway.

With any luck, by the time I took care of the nun at my door, Levi would be out the back door and gone.

The thought stabbed at my heart and the memories of what had been a perfect night. Rather than dwell on it, I pasted on a smile, threw open the door, and came face-to-face with one of the most formidable-looking women I had ever seen.

I had been right about the body type. Stout and tapered. Like a hoagie sandwich. I had been right about the penguin similarities, too. The nun who stood at my door wore an old-fashioned habit, a black wool robe that touched the floor and was covered by a panel of creamy white. She wore a very shiny silver crucifix over that. Her head was covered by a black veil, her face was framed with a stiff white contraption I knew was called a wimple and covered her forehead and her ears.

She had dark eyes, thick lips, and the kind of eagle-eyed stare that my imagination told me had intimidated school-children for decades.

"Good morning. I hope we didn't wake you." Her smile was bright enough to rival the morning sunshine and, instantly, her forbidding face was transformed. If she was a teacher, I had no doubt she was a kind one. "I'm Sister Liliosa and this . . ." She waved a hand toward the stairway and for the first time, I realized there were two other nuns waiting there, both of them wearing much the same kind of old-fashioned habit as Sister Liliosa. "Sister Mary Jean," she said, gesturing toward a lean-faced, ruddy-cheeked nun. "Sister Gabriel." This nun was far younger than the other two. She didn't look at me when she was introduced. "And this is Sister Margaret." That particular nun had been stand-ing off to the side at the base of the porch stairs checking out the daffodils just peeking their heads out of the front beds. Her dress was black, too, but shorter than the ones worn by the other Sisters. Her veil was a simple square of black fabric, pinned back on her head to reveal a glimmer of silvery hair. She took the stairs carefully and stepped up to Sister Liliosa's side.

"Elias Weatherly told us we could contact you if we needed help," that Sister told me.

"Of course!" I stepped back to allow the nuns into the B and B and, one by one, they came inside and clustered in the foyer, Sister Liliosa nearest to me and the others lined against the wall. I closed the door behind them just in time to catch a glimpse of Levi's black Jeep backing out of the driveway.

An inglorious finish to what had been a splendid night and maybe I wouldn't have felt so disappointed if I reminded myself that it was bound to end this way.

"The others who were with us on the ferry this morning have gone on to the retreat center," Sister Liliosa informed me, shaking me out of my thoughts. "They rented golf carts down near the ferry dock. We thought . . ." The Sister slipped a quick sidelong glance toward Sister Margaret who, rheumy blue eyes wide, studied the stained glass window in shades of peacock, teal, and purple above the front door. "They dropped us here because we thought it might be best if we didn't ride all the way in an open golf cart." Another furtive look in Margaret's direction. "You know, with the morning air being a little brisk. We didn't want to take a chance of getting sick. Not when we've got such an exciting week ahead of us."

I had no doubt "they" weren't worried about anything at all except their elderly companion and I couldn't blame them. Sister Margaret was short and so stick thin, I was sure a stiff southern breeze could have blown her clear across the lake to Canada.

"You stopped here because you need a ride to the retreat center."

Sister Mary Jean grinned. "You're reading our minds."

"Could we be so bold as to ask?" Sister Liliosa asked. "Mr. Weatherly said we should contact you for anything we needed."

"I have to go over there today anyway," I told them, though I left out the part about how I'd been hoping it wouldn't be until later, long after the time Levi and I might have done a little more of what we'd been doing the night before. "I can bring over the salads I made for your lunches and that will save me the drive over at noon. Elias asked me to help with the food," I explained and headed into the kitchen for the salads that I'd already prepared and put in ten separate containers, one for each of the nuns who would be attending the week's retreat. I loaded the salads into carry bags and added the extras I'd packaged, cheese and ham and turkey, pickled beets and chopped hard-boiled egg and bacon bits, along with a variety of dressings. When I got back to the foyer, I put the tote bags on the floor and grabbed my jacket from the nearby coat-tree. "Elias was called away. His mother-in-law is very sick. Over on the mainland. The house that's being used as a retreat center—"

"Old and fabulous, from what we've been told," Sister Mary Jean said, and I caught the trace of a Southern drawl.

Fabulous. That's what I'd always heard, too. The lake-front home now officially known as Water's Edge Center for Spirit and Renewal had once been the home of wealthy island recluse James Scott Findley. Findley died right before I came to South Bass Island—about a year earlier—and in his will, he left the house to a nonprofit with the requirement that it be used as a retreat facility. All were welcome and since its opening, the Center had already hosted a group of rabbis and a meeting of Buddhist monks.

"Old and fabulous and still a work in progress," I told Sister Mary Jean, who'd already reached for one of the bags of food and hefted it up in her arms. "From what I've heard, the kitchen isn't exactly up to snuff. That's why Elias asked me to help with the food." I didn't add that the original plan was for me—or more likely, Meg, who helped with cooking for my guests—to prepare the meals and for Elias to come get the food every day and take it back to the center. That had changed when Elias went to the mainland. Now I'd need to schlepp the meals up to the center, but there was no use mentioning that and making the nuns feel guilty.

"Actually, I've been looking forward to checking out the house," I admitted instead. "Everyone says it's amazing, and when Mr. Findley lived there, no one was allowed near it."

"Oooh!" Sister Mary Jean shivered. "Sounds like something out of a gothic novel. I can't wait. You don't suppose it's haunted, do you?"

Sister Liliosa laughed and picked up the other bag of salads. "If it is, I think we can handle it, right?"

Sister Mary Jean nodded.

Sister Margaret, her eyes wide and her steps shuffling, mumbled something about extra prayers and angels.

Sister Gabriel didn't say a thing. In fact, when she followed the other Sisters toward the door and I stepped up behind her, she flinched and shot a look over her shoulder. Like she just remembered I was there, she offered a thin smile.

"No worries," I told her. "I'm not much for ghost stories, either."

"Things that go bump in the night?" From out on the front porch, Sister Liliosa's silvery laugh flowed through the house on the tail of a spring breeze. "There are ten of us at this retreat, remember. And if there's one thing I know for sure, it's never bet against ten nuns."

I stepped out onto the front porch just as Sister Liliosa stepped back to allow the other nuns to go down the steps ahead of her, and I would have followed right along if I didn't stop to shoot a dirty look at Jerry Garcia. Jerry? He's the cat that lives next door and loves to lounge (and do other less sanitary things) on my front porch. I glared at Jerry. Completely unconcerned and ever unrepentant, Jerry tossed his head and went right on doing his cat thing.

The momentary pause gave Sister Liliosa a chance to step in front of me. Her grin melted. "I hope you'll convey our apologies to that handsome young man who left here in such a hurry when we arrived," she said. "I'm sorry if we interrupted anything."

My jaw had already dropped when she gave me a wink and allowed her gaze to slip to my feet.

"He has your head in such a whirl, you're leaving the house in your bunny slippers."

It took me a couple of minutes to race back in the house and find my sneakers and put them on and a couple minutes after that—my SUV chockablock with nuns—we had already cruised to the other side of the island and were closing in on the retreat center.

This is not as much of a big deal as it sounds. South Bass Island, three miles from the northern shore of Ohio, is a scant four miles long and only a mile and a half wide. Bea & Bees, the inn I'd owned and operated for the last year, is just about in the center of the island, near to a downtown that bustles in the summer season and a harbor that teems with fishing and pleasure boats, parasailers and fun-in-the-sun types of every ilk. What used to be known as Findley House and was now Water's Edge was located on the western shore of the island not far from a place called Stone Cove Beach.

During the busy summer season, golf carts zipped up and down island roads along with vans and vacationers' cars, but at this time of year when the cottagers were just starting to think about opening their homes for the summer, things were still pretty quiet. As I navigated my way to the retreat center, I had a chance to appreciate the beauty of the island waking from its dreary winter doldrums and bursting into bloom. Yellow forsythia bushes brightened the landscape along with daffodils here and there that, just like mine, were just beginning to pop. I reminded myself to enjoy the peace and quiet while I could. Soon enough, the slow pace of off-season island life would quicken to the calypso beat of summer.

In the year I'd lived on South Bass, my curiosity had been piqued each time I'd driven by what used to be the Findley House. But then, the house and the man who'd once owned it had given rise to a thousand island legends that claimed everything from the fact that Findley was once a big-time mobster who was hiding out from his old associates to the belief that he had come to the island and locked himself away after a doomed love affair. I didn't know if any of the stories were true, but I did know that the setting was perfect for igniting any number of dark-and-stormy fantasies, from the windswept bluff overlooking the lake on which the house was built to the thick stand of trees that surrounded it so that even in winter when their branches were bare, it was nearly impossible to see more of the house than a glimpse of the slate roof and tall chimneys.

The entire property was surrounded by a tall iron fence, and I'd been told that when its owner was still in residence, the gates across the driveway had always been shut—and locked. Even my closest island friends, Chandra Morrisey, Kate Wilder, and Luella Zak—the other members of the book discussion group we called the League of Literary Ladies who had lived on South Bass all their lives—had never been inside the house. Now, I had a chance to get a first look and I confess, when I made the right turn from Catawba onto Niagara, my heartbeat quickened when the property came into view.

"Is this it? The place with the wrought-iron fence?" Sister Mary Jean was in the backseat and she leaned forward to peer out of the windshield. "When I said it sounded gothic, I never expected Dracula's castle."

Today, the gates were wide open and there was a new sign to the right of them that glimmered in the morning sunshine. It had a soothing blue background and gold lettering that said, "Water's Edge Center for Spirit and Renewal," and was crowned with an orange sun.

"That doesn't look scary at all," Sister Liliosa commented. "It's lovely. In fact . . ."

When we snaked up the driveway and rounded the last thicket of trees that kept the house from view, her words dissolved in a little hiccup of surprise.

As it turned out, Dracula would have felt right at home.

Water's Edge was Gothic Revival to the max, a hulking mansion built from blocks of stone that over the years, had weathered to the menacing gray color of a thundercloud. The house was three stories high and there was a tower at one end of it and leaded glass windows everywhere that winked in the morning sun like watchful eyes. Pointed arches, gingerbread tracery, a steep-pitched roof. Water's Edge had it all, including, at the back of the house, that stony bluff I'd heard so much about with its killer view of Lake Erie and stone steps leading down to a strip of rocky private beach.

We rolled up the circular drive, and I parked the SUV next to three golf carts piled with luggage, and no sooner was Sister Liliosa out of the car than the front door opened and six more nuns poured out of the house to greet the new arrivals. None of them was dressed as traditionally as the nuns who'd appeared at the B and B that morning. In fact, two of them wore short gray dresses and veils; the rest were in street clothes.

I stepped back and skirted the group so I could take the salads inside. The entryway just inside the front door was a massive room paneled with dark wood that smelled like years of history and lemon furniture polish, and I took a chance and followed the hallway beyond it past a dining room with views of the water and on to the kitchen where I stowed everything in a brand-new refrigerator.

It was the only thing in the kitchen that didn't look as old as the house, and with a glance at the massive old stove and another at the dripping kitchen sink faucet, I understood why Elias had asked for help with the cooking. Water's Edge was, indeed, a work in progress, but one quick look at the plans that had been left out on the counter under the windows that lined the far wall and I could tell that when it was done, it would not only be modern and utilitarian, but lovely as well. Elias planned a breakfast nook, a door that led out to the patio outside the dining room, and even space devoted to what must surely be the luxuries of retreat life: latte machine, bagel slicer and toaster, waffle maker.

For now, though, I would be forced to work within the confines of what was here, not what Elias had planned. Already convinced that whatever I'd bring for dinner would be individually packaged like the salads to allow for easier cleanup and taking it home for washing, I stepped back into the hallway just as the ten nuns streamed back inside, hauling suitcases and heading up the hand-carved mahogany staircase to the rooms that had been assigned to them for the week.

"Oh, this is going to be just wonderful," I heard one of them say. "The perfect week of prayer and reflection."

"Not to mention a little relaxation," another one of them commented.

"And if it warms up a little," someone else called out from the top of the stairs, "I'd like to catch a few rays out on the patio."

The rest of the nuns laughed and before I knew it, I found myself joining in.

Too bad my smile didn't last.

But then, it wasn't like I could help it.

Like everyone else, I froze when we heard a voice call out from one of the bedrooms.

"No! Oh, no!"

❖ 2 ❖

I was the closest to the stairs and I took the steps two at a time not only because I was curious, but because the way I figured it, it made more sense for me to check out the cause of the scared, wavering voice than it did for a whole bunch of nuns to. After all, I'd had some experience handling bad situations. There was the Chinese restaurant owner who'd been killed on the island just about a year before, whose body I'd found behind his front takeaway counter. And the handyman who'd been poisoned in Levi's Bar and the ghost hunter who was searching for our local headless ghost, and—

I told my imagination to shut down and the little panicky voice inside me to shut up.

Just because I'd been involved in a few murder investigations during my time on the island did not mean there were more to come. I was in a retreat center full of nuns, for heaven's sake, and nothing could be more benign than that.

This was all good advice, but it did nothing to calm the blood that was pulsing through my veins like a jackhammer by the time I made it to the wide landing at the top of the steps. There, I stopped for a second to catch my breath just as a couple of the nuns scampered up the stairs behind me. Up here at a wall of windows that looked out over the just-turning-green property that was all a part of Water's Edge, the hallway split in two, one portion of it on either side of the wide staircase. To my right—the back of the house—I found a nun in a short gray habit standing outside an open bedroom door, her suitcase on the floor next to her and her mouth hanging open.

"No," she said, and she probably wasn't talking any louder than she had been when we heard her in the foyer. The ceilings at Water's Edge were twenty feet high, and the wood-paneled walls were perfect for projecting and echoing sound. The Sister shook her head. "No, no, no."

I wasn't sure what was going on, but since I was Elias's surrogate of a sort, I felt responsible. I stepped up beside the nun.

"Can I help you, Sister?"

She turned wide, moist eyes my way. "I'm sorry to be such a bother. I'm—"

I put out a hand, the better to try to calm her and to relieve what was obviously a combination of terror and embarrassment. "I'm Bea and I'm helping out this week. What can I do for you?"

Color rushed into her cheeks. This nun was probably in her mid-forties and just a bit taller than me. Her veil was the same mouse gray as her habit, and like elderly Sister

Margaret's, it was short and simple and anchored to her rusty-colored hair with bobby pins. She stared at my out-stretched hand for a long time before she flinched and stuck out her own clammy hand.

"Sister Sheila Buckwald," she said. "From the convent of . . . of the Sisters of the Holy Spirit in . . . in Chicago. I need to settle into my room and . . ." She swallowed hard and licked her lips.

I leaned forward so I could look where she was looking and peeked into the room. It was wide and spacious and included a bed, a desk, a couch with a reading lamp next to it and a coffee table in front of it, and its own private bath. There was a window seat built into the far wall made of the same rich, dark wood that lined the walls of the foyer down-stairs and it was topped with leaded glass windows in dia-mond panes. Beyond the glass was a million-dollar view, a wide swath of blue lake as far as the eye could see.

Sure, the kitchen of Water's Edge was something of a fright, but if this was what each of the private suites was like, I could see nothing to complain about.

"Do you have a problem with your room?" I asked her.

"No. It's lovely. It's just that—"

"I could switch with you, Sister Sheila." One of the nuns who'd followed me up the stairs stepped up beside me. She, too, was wearing a short gray habit, but her veil was white instead of gray. Blond hair peeked from the edge of her veil and she had wide blue eyes and a broad, friendly face. She had the same rounded pear shape as Sister Sheila and was about the same height. "I'm Sister Catherine," she told Sheila. "You remember, we talked on the ferry."

Some of the panic drained from Sister Sheila's eyes and for a second, the look of terror on her face was replaced with a smile. "Of course." Her smile vanished in a wave of memory. "You sat next to me and you . . . you brought me a cup of tea."

"And I just put on the kettle downstairs." Sister Catherine wound an arm through Sheila's. "I thought maybe you'd like another cup and I know I'm dying for one. Until then . . ." Sister Catherine made a face. "I just put my suitcase in my room over there." She glanced to the other side of the stairs and the rooms that looked out over the front of the house. "The light isn't as good in that room as it is back here and my eyes . . . Well . . ." Just like I had, she peeked into Sister Sheila's room. "Any chance I could talk you into switching?" she asked.

As if the weight of the world had been lifted from her shoulders, Sister Sheila released a long breath of relief. "You wouldn't mind?"

"You'd be doing me a favor," Sister Catherine told her and she went to retrieve her suitcase at the same time Sister Sheila picked up hers. The way she hightailed it across the hallway, I couldn't help but think she wanted to get installed in the other room before Sister Catherine changed her mind.

"Well, what do you suppose that was all about?" I hadn't realized there was another nun around until I looked to my right and saw a middle-aged woman in jeans and a red sweater with a tiny gold crucifix pinned to it. She watched Sister Sheila's every move. "I guess I shouldn't be surprised. With Sister Sheila, it's always more of the same."

We stepped back out of the way when Sister Catherine went into what was now her room and closed the door behind her. "The same? Elias Weatherly told me the nuns who were coming here this week didn't know each other."

The nun in the red sweater twitched her shoulders and gave me a smile. Her hair was cut fashionably short and shaggy and was the wonderful sort of true silver some women are blessed with. It glimmered in the stream of light that flowed in from the windows at the top of the steps.

"We don't," she told me. "Well, most of us don't, anyway. Most of us never met until a few months ago. We were all invited to New York, you see, to receive grants from a philanthropic foundation for the work we do. There was even a fancy dinner where we were honored. We're from all different parts of the country and we never saw each other again until this morning at the ferry. But Sister Sheila . . ." She shot a look across the hallway and Sister Sheila's now-closed bedroom door. "Our paths have crossed a time or two over the years. I'm Sister Helene McMurty, and I'm involved in music ministry. So is Sister Sheila."

"Are all the nuns here musicians?"

Sister Helene laughed. "Oh, no! We each have a different charism. Charism, that's sort of the same as spiritual orientation. For instance, some nuns, like Sister Sheila and myself, are involved in music, though her calling is song and mine is dance worship. Sister Catherine Lang whom you just met, she runs a center for homeless women in Philadelphia, Sister Liliosa develops curriculum for schools that encourages nonviolence and the peaceful resolution of conflicts. Sister Grace Donovan . . . I don't know if you've met her yet, she's wearing an orange sweatshirt . . . she works with death row convicts, and Sister Paul drives an old school bus around Los Angeles to teach English as a second language to immigrant children. Charism. Each of us has a different charism."

"But you're all here together for the week."

Sister Helene nodded. "And it's going to be wonderful! Richard Ward Parker is going to be conducting the retreat. Ever hear of him?"

When I shook my head, she went right on. "Fabulous speaker. At least from what I've seen online. Truly inspirational, even if he is a Unitarian!" There was a twinkle in Sister Helene's eyes that told me she didn't hold this against Richard Ward Parker. "He's written a few truly incredible books that I've enjoyed. It's quite a treat to have a chance to meet him. It should be a wonderful week."

"So you're all from different cities and you all do different things." I thought this over for a second. "So how did you all get invited to this particular retreat?"

Sister Helene shrugged. "No one's ever said. As far as I can see, it must have been because of that article in the *New York Times* recently. You might not have read it."

I had, and now that she mentioned it, I remember being impressed with the details of the story. "It was about American nuns and how they're involved in social justice programs."

"Each in our own way," Sister Helene said. "Like I said, charism. After it was announced that we'd be awarded those grants, that's when the *New York Times* reporter interviewed each of us and wrote about the work we do. This week is our chance to learn from each other, to see how each of our own programs works, and according to the email schedule we all got, we're going to get started . . ." She pulled a smart phone from her pocket and checked the time. "We're supposed to have our first get-together in just a couple minutes. Any idea if Richard Ward Parker is here yet?"

I hadn't a clue, but after all the good things Sister Helene said about him, I was anxious to meet the week's retreat facilitator, too, and I didn't have much time. I had guests checking into the B and B that day and because of not-so-set-in-stone schedules, no idea what time they might be arriving. The nuns had come over from the mainland on the first ferry; I needed to get home before the second one docked. Fortunately, at this time of year—unlike during tourist season—the ferry ran infrequently and I had a few minutes to try to catch a glimpse of Richard Ward Parker, so I followed the Sister downstairs to the spacious living room where a few of the other Sisters had already gathered. The room had a marble fireplace that was taller than me and comfortable seating groups: a couch and three chairs in front of the hearth, another couch with chairs on either side of it over near the far wall, a few more comfortable easy chairs scattered around, a table near the windows that would be perfect for reading.

"We've got a couple minutes," Sister Liliosa pointed out, and in that time, the nuns who had been in their rooms drifted downstairs and got settled.

As someone had already mentioned, there were ten of them in all, three in traditional long habits and veils that covered their heads and ears completely, three in short dresses and half-veils, and the rest wearing street clothes that made me think that had I met them under any other circumstances, I never would have known they were nuns. As Sister Helene had explained, they all did different work. In addition to the English-as-a-second-language teacher, the death row missionary, the two music ministers, Sister Liliosa who was committed to nonviolence, and Sister Catherine Lang who ran the homeless shelter, Sister Mary Jean ran a food pantry in Lexington; Sister Francelle was the CEO of a company that produced religious-themed calendars, note cards, and gifts; Sister Gabriel (the young nun who was on my porch that morning) specialized in liturgy; and old Sister Margaret administered an urban garden in Pittsburgh and was committed to environmental sustainability.

The retreat hadn't even officially started and already, I

was impressed by the experience and dedication of the women in the room.

As far as I knew, no one had appointed anyone to be in charge—not officially, anyway—but it was clear from the start that Sister Liliosa just naturally fit the role. Considering the scope of the programs each of these women ran and their experience, that said a great deal about Sister Liliosa.

"Well, it's time to get started," she said, and when she stepped in front of the fireplace, the conversations around the room stopped. "Since there's no sign of Mr. Parker—"

Sister Liliosa's words were cut off when her cell phone beeped.

She reached into the folds of her habit and brought out the phone. "It's him," she told the group. "Or at least it's a text message from him."

"He's probably been delayed," one of the other nuns suggested.

"Or he's gotten lost trying to find the place."

Sister Liliosa checked the message and held up a hand. "Listen to this," she said, and she read the message.

"'Pick up your voicemail,'" it said. "'Put it on speaker.'"

She followed the directions and the next thing we knew, a man's voice—it must have been Richard Ward Parker—filled the living room.

"Good morning, Sisters! I hope you had a good journey to Water's Edge. I know you've had some time to look around the facility and I expect you're as impressed by what you've seen as I was when I visited there briefly earlier in the year. It's a wonderful place. I only wish I could be there to share the excitement of the week with you."

A murmur of surprise went around the room and apparently, Mr. Parker had expected this, because he paused for a moment.

"I'm sorry to pull the rug out from under you like this. I was looking forward to meeting each and every one of you. But you see, me not being there was part of the plan from the beginning."

Another buzz of conversation and surprise filled the room and someone had to warn the Sisters to "Shush!" so they could hear the rest of the message.

"You see, Sisters, rather than have me there to oversee each day and each retreat activity, the real purpose of this week is for you to design your own retreat. That's the whole point! You are intelligent, capable, and impressive women, and I know that working together, you'll come up with dynamic programming that will speak to your own individual needs much more effectively than anything I could come up with ever would. So I leave you with this—work together, form teams, plan and carry out the ideal retreat. Relax, enjoy, and feel renewed. Blessings to you all!"

For a few seconds after the message ended, the nuns sat in stunned silence.

But like I said, they weren't exactly wallflowers, and it is hard to keep a room filled with accomplished and efficient women down. It was time to leave them to it, but even before I was out of the room, Sister Liliosa was already looking over the assembly and I swear, I could just about see the wheels turning inside her wimple.

"Sister Francelle, Sister Margaret, Sister Mary Jean . . . you are all involved in sustainability and nourishment, not just of the body, but of the artistic soul. Why don't you three get together and see where your combined experience takes you, programwise. Sister Gabriel, I'm sure you can take care of our daily prayers." She glanced around the room. "Sister Catherine and Sister Paul and Sister Grace, you are out in the community daily, so I think your experience with social

programs and social justice will come in handy with organizing the agenda. If no one has an objection, I'll grab my laptop
and get the daily schedule down and be the point person.
That leaves . . ." Her gaze roamed the room and stopped on
Sister Helene, who was seated near the fireplace, then
skimmed over to Sister Sheila, who was standing in the doorway that led out to the hallway.

"We've got to have music," Sister Liliosa said. "And we've
got two of the best in the country who can be in charge of
that."

"In charge of music? With Sister Sheila?" Sister Helene's
voice was so sharp, I stopped in my tracks just as I was about
to head out of the living room and into the hallway. I guess
I wasn't the only one who realized how bitter she sounded
because just as I looked back over my shoulder at Sister
Helene, I saw color flood her cheeks. Her lips worked
silently. Her eyes narrowed. Finally, she drew in a deep
breath and got to her feet, her arms close to her sides, her
chin high, and her smile so tight, I waited for it to shatter.
"Actually, I was hoping to learn new skills at this retreat,"
she said. "So I think I'll leave the music up to Sister Sheila
and join the social justice crowd."

No one objected.

But if you ask me, no one in the room believed that bull
about learning new skills, either.

Especially Sister Sheila because Sister Sheila . . .

Well, from where I was standing it was impossible to see
clearly. But I swear, just as I looked her way, Sister Sheila's
hands curled into fists.

I got back home just in time.

Not for my guests, for the two dozen red roses that arrived

along with a card signed by Levi that said *Yes, let's talk. Tonight at the bar.* Considering that there wasn't any place on the island that sold flowers at that time of the year, I could only imagine he'd called over to the mainland and had someone with a boat make the very special delivery. I hope he gave the fellow a whopping tip.

I divided up the flowers in vases and put them in the parlor, the dining room, and each of the four guest rooms that would be occupied that night. No, none in my own private suite. But then, I didn't need flowers to remind me of what Levi and I had shared the night before. No more than I needed the quick stab of conscience that jabbed me every time I thought about the conversation there was no way I could avoid.

Let's talk. Tonight at the bar.

My heart in my throat, I practiced what to say a thousand times in a thousand different ways.

With a laugh, like the whole thing was a big joke and didn't Levi think it was as funny as I did?

With my expression serious and grim. (I tried it out in front of the mirror just to be sure.) Surely, he would understand if I tugged at his heartstrings.

I tried to go for down-to-earth and hard-nosed, too. Lay it on the line. Tell it like it is. After all, he'd understand if I just told the truth.

Right?

Lucky for me and the worry that pounded in my brain, I'd just gone through the scenario for time one thousand and one when my front doorbell rang.

I opened the door to find a middle-aged man of middle height and middle weight standing on the porch.

"Joe Roscoe." Since he had a beat-up briefcase in one hand, a stack of file folders in the other, and a two-foot-long cardboard tube tucked under his right arm, he nodded by way of introduction. Roscoe had nondescript brown eyes, hair the color of the stones along the beach across the street, and a face that was as bland as the khakis and beige jacket he wore. He juggled the file folders so he could wedge the tube under his left arm and shake my hand. "You've got a room for me."

"I do." I ushered him into the front hallway. "Suit-cases?" I asked.

"In the car." Joe set down the briefcase along with that cardboard tube. He held on to the folders. "Lots of other stuff in the car. Books and more files and such. You said there was a desk in my room. There's plenty of space to work, right?"

I nodded. "A desk in your room, and depending on what you're doing and how much space you need, there's a table down here in the parlor. The light's good and you can work in front of the fire." I pointed to the room directly to the right of the front door. "As long as you clean up when you're done."

Something told me this would not be a problem for Joe Roscoe. Though there was nothing flashy about him, there was nothing that struck me as haphazard about his appearance, either. His hair was neatly combed. His brown shoes were polished and the bows tied in precise, matching knots. That beige jacket of his was pristine, as if it had just come off the hanger at the department store.

"Family history," he said, confirming my opinion with an explanation that was quick and as efficient as I imagined Joe himself was. "I'm researching my genealogy and I've got ancestors who lived here on the island. I thought it would be better to do my research before the tourists showed up for the summer. You know, so I can get a better sense of what island life was like when my ancestors lived here."

"That sounds fascinating." I wasn't just blowing smoke

because he was a paying customer; I'd always loved research. "And we've got some lifelong islanders around here who may be able to help. Chandra Morrisey is one of them." I pointed out the window and to the left at the house next door, although I'd bet a dime to a donut Joe had noticed the house when he pulled his car into the driveway. But then, it's hard not to notice Chandra's single-story, very purple house with its teal blue garage door, its yellow trim, and its orange doors.

And yes, just for the record, Chandra is just as colorful as her house.

"She and Kate Wilder there across the street . . ." I pointed toward Kate's house, catty-corner from mine. "I bet they'd love to help you. And there's Luella Zak, too. Luella knows all of the old-timers. Maybe some of them even know the people you're asking about."

"I doubt that." Joe hoisted his briefcase. "The family I'm looking for was here more than a hundred years ago. Still, it wouldn't hurt to put out some feelers, would it? Always good to make connections. Connections, that's what it's all about when it comes to genealogy."

I grabbed the key to Joe's room and led him up the stairs. "There's the historical society, too," I suggested.

When I threw open the door to his suite, he stepped in and looked around. He didn't so much smile as bow his head, as if to indicate that yes, this would do just fine. "I've talked to the historical society people," he said, setting his briefcase on the bed. "Any number of times. They've been great. I'm eager to get settled and get to work, and this . . ." Joe set the cardboard tube on the desk in front of the windows that overlooked the side of the house facing Chandra's. "Perfect," he said. "I've got plenty of room to spread out. Breakfast—"

"Is at nine," I told him. "Tea is laid out in the dining room at three. The rest of the day, you're on your own."

Joe rubbed his hands together. "On my own. I like the sound of that. I can't tell you how anxious I've been to get here and get started."

I left him to it and got back downstairs just as the doorbell rang again.

My second guest had arrived, a thirty-something named Tyler Stevens. Tyler was short, broad, and had hair the color of a newly minted penny. Tyler's blue eyes were set close together and his cheeks were pudgy. A redheaded Pillsbury Doughboy with a smile to match.

Unlike buttoned-up Joe, Tyler was dressed more casually: jeans, sneakers, a blue sweatshirt with a drawing of a cardinal on it. The cardinal was the state bird of Ohio. I could see that Tyler—who'd told me that he was from Massachusetts when he called for his reservation—had come prepared. Like Joe, he had his hands full. This time with camera equipment.

"Birds," Tyler said as if he was reading my mind and answering the question I hadn't had time to ask. "I hear this is a stellar place for birding. Say, you haven't seen any Kentucky warblers yet this spring, have you? It's a little early in the year, I know, but I've heard from fellow birders that there have been some seen in the area and I'm really anxious to get pictures of Kentucky warblers."

My blank expression must have been all the answer he needed because Tyler raced right on. "Small songbird, yellow underparts with an olive green back. It's got black sideburns down the side of its face and throat and a yellow stripe all around its eyes, like glasses. Its song sounds like *cheery, cheery, cheery.*"

"No warblers," I was sorry to tell him.

"Scarlet tanagers?" Excited expectation wavered through his question.

"Sorry."

"Well . . ." His sigh was enough to tell me that, disappointed or not, Tyler would soldier on and continue his quest for warblers and tanagers. "I can't wait to get started and it's early in the day and the weather is perfect and the light is good. I'll get my bags unpacked and then I'll head out."

I showed him to his room, gave him all the same instructions about tea and breakfast that I'd given Joe, and left him to it, congratulating myself as I headed back downstairs. I might have to have "The Talk" with Levi later that day, but until then, there was no use fretting about it. I could prepare dinner for the Sisters at Water's Edge and take heart in the fact that the B and B I'd opened just a year earlier was thriving. I'd followed my dream and made a success of it, and no matter what happened with Levi, no one could take that away from me.

I headed into the kitchen to gather the ingredients that Meg—the woman who did most of my cooking and who also happened to be Luella's daughter—would use to prepare muffins for the Sisters' breakfast tomorrow, and while I was at it, I got to work on dinner for the nuns. I'd already decided on individual meatloaves, garlic mashed potatoes, grilled veggies, and brownies for dessert and I'd just gotten the little metal meatloaf pans out of the cupboard and set them on the kitchen counter and counted them just to be sure there were ten of them when out of nowhere, a chill like the icy fingers of death snaked across my shoulders. I flinched, my hand slapped one of the meatloaf pans, and it went flying and landed on the floor with a clatter.

As I retrieved and rinsed the pan, I reminded myself that feelings of dread had no place at Bea & Bees and certainly nothing to do with Water's Edge and the nuns who were staying there. It was early spring. I was bound to feel a chill now and then, I told myself. There was nothing to worry about.

Good advice, right?

At least I thought so at the time.

Too bad I listened.

Because when it comes to a little spring chill versus apprehension, I should have learned by now.

Dread always wins out in the end.

❮ 3 ❯

Of course, at the time, I wasn't thinking about any dread but the dread I was feeling at the thought of the upcoming conversation I had to have with Levi.

But even that had to take a backseat to the tasks that kept me busy the rest of that Saturday afternoon. I had more guests checking in, librarians from the mainland, all of them friends of our island librarian, Marianne Little-john.

The four women, all in their mid-fifties (Marianne's age), arrived by the three o'clock ferry, each of them with stacks of books they wanted to read and share, notes on books they'd already read that they wanted to discuss with one another, and lists they wanted to exchange: favorite books, favorite authors, favorite series. Marianne had told them about our book discussion group and, of course, they were plenty interested.

"What book are you reading now?" a pleasant, round-faced woman named Angela asked practically before I had her and her roommate, Bette, settled in the suite at the front of the house.

I explained that it was my turn to pick a novel for this month and I'd chosen George Eliot's *The Mill on the Floss*, but since we hadn't had our first meeting to talk about it, I didn't know how the others felt about my selection.

"Stuffy." Bette wrinkled her nose. "Can't force readers to read any of the old classics. Too stuffy for most people. The stories move too slow. The situations aren't anything like the real world today. Our patrons try to read books like that and they get bored. Then they stop reading altogether."

"Murder." Angela pointed at me in a knowing sort of way. "That's what people really want to read about. Murder and lust and—"

"Greed and jealousy!" Bette chuckled. "All the things that make the world go round. Find a story with a good ol' murder mystery and—"

"No thanks." I had already given them their room keys and I backed out of the room—and away from their suggestion—as quickly as possible. "Been there, done that. And when we did read a mystery—"

"That's right." Bette's dark eyes shone with excitement. "Marianne told us. You read Christie and then had a mystery here on the island. Just like in *Murder on the Orient Express*."

"Not taking that chance again," I told them both, though I didn't bother to mention that even when we steered clear of whodunits, murder still had a way of rearing its ugly head when the League of Literary Ladies was around. "In the last few months, we've read *Pride and Prejudice* and *A Christmas Carol* and *To Kill a Mockingbird* and *A Tree*

Grows in Brooklyn. We have been blessedly murder free since back in the fall when we read *The Legend of Sleepy Hollow* in honor of Halloween."

"Marianne told us about that, too," Angela informed me. "Imagine, a headless ghost!"

"Which is all he was. Imaginary," I told them and reminded myself. Even if I was sure I'd seen the specter the night we solved a murder and unraveled an eighty-year-old death to boot. I shook away the thought and the chill that settled on my shoulders. "Classics. Only the classics. That's all we're reading from now on. No more murders."

"Well, there's a drowning in *The Mill on the Floss*," Angela informed me. "Maybe you haven't read that far yet. There's an awful lot of water around here and—"

This was not something I wanted to think about.

I reminded the ladies about tea and breakfast and left them to their literary pursuits and I got back downstairs and into the kitchen. I'd just put a plate of cheese and crackers out on the counter when Chandra came in through the back door.

"All set to help!" Chandra whisked off her purple ruana and draped it over the back of one of the high stools set up next to the black granite breakfast counter. "Ten nuns to feed and plenty of cooking to get done. You ready to get started?" Chandra had eyes the color of the lake on a stormy day and she widened them and gave me a look meant to be as innocent as a lamb. "Or are you still too tired? After all, with the way Levi left here so early this morning . . ."

I groaned. Bad enough I had to face Levi later that day. I didn't need Chandra of all people (who couldn't keep a secret and never wanted to, anyway) spreading stories of my love life all over the island. "He stopped by to pick something up this morning," I said, lying with the same wide-eyed innocence.

Chandra batted her eyelashes. "He was here last night."

They didn't need it, but I straightened those ten small meatloaf tins. "For dinner."

"His Jeep was parked in your driveway all night."

I cursed myself for not realizing that the world's nosiest neighbor was bound to notice. "He left and came back this morning," I said.

"He did not!" Chandra could only maintain her aplomb for so long. She jumped up and down and giggled like a teenager. "He was here. All night long. Details, Bea. I need details!"

As soon as I realized I'd allowed it to escape, I wiped the smile off my face. Lucky for me, I didn't have time to do anything else; Luella and Kate arrived.

"I can't believe we're cooking for nuns." Kate scurried through the kitchen and gave both Chandra and me quick hugs. She'd brought a shopping bag along from a pricey all-organic grocery store over on the mainland, and she swung it up on the countertop. "Whole wheat bread crumbs, brown eggs, and gluten-free ketchup made with cider vinegar."

Chandra made a face. "We're trying to feed them, not bore them to death."

Since Kate knew Chandra was kidding, she merely smiled.

"I still think you should let Meg handle all the meals." Luella must have just come from her boat. She was wearing tan Carhartt overalls and she peeled out of them and down to her jeans and sweatshirt. "It's an awful lot of work, cooking for ten. I ought to know. My Joe, he came from a family of ten and we used to have them all over at our place for Thanksgiving dinner."

"We're not doing anything as complicated as Thanksgiving dinner," I reminded her.

Chandra tipped her head and tried for a lah-dee-dah Scarlett O'Hara accent. "We simply don't have the energy."

I shot her a look.

Like I expected that to work?

Chandra tossed her sleek blond bob. St. Patrick's Day was long gone, but she'd decided she liked the emerald green streaks she'd added to her hair for the occasion. She must have touched them up since last I saw her; the green stripe on her bangs winked at me in the sunlight. "Go on," she said, obviously talking to Kate and Luella and just as obviously, ignoring the glare I shot her way. "Ask Bea what she was up to last night."

"What Bea was up to last night is Bea's business." I tried to sound logical and reasonable. Honest. But with the burden of my upcoming talk with Levi weighing heavy on my heart, I couldn't help myself. I snapped. And snapped at Chandra while I was at it. "Maybe we'd all be better off if we worried a little more about cooking and a little less about sticking our noses where they don't belong."

Chandra winced as if she'd been slapped. Kate and Luella looked at me in wonder.

I stayed strong. Or at least I pretended to by going to the fridge and taking out ground beef and the onions I'd chopped the night before.

"Meatloaf," I said, slapping the ingredients on the counter. "We need to make meatloaf."

It was Chandra's turn to straighten those meatloaf pans. Kate grabbed the onions. Luella took a big mixing bowl out of the cupboard and as soon as she had it on the counter, I plopped the ground beef into it.

It probably was no more than a couple seconds, but the silence that filled the room felt like it lasted a lifetime.

Finally, Chandra cleared her throat. "I have news," she said, and I gritted my teeth. If she was going to try to bring up the subject of Levi again, I really would lose it.

Instead, she reached in her pocket, pulled out a single sheet of folded paper, and smoothed it out on the counter.

From where I was standing I could see it was a drawing of some kind.

Chandra gave the paper a pat. "I'm putting in a pool," she announced.

The stiffness went out of my shoulders when I realized she'd actually surrendered on the subject of Levi. That is, until I realized something else.

I closed in on the drawing that showed a long rectangle representing Chandra's house, circles representing the trees on her property, and a square that stood for the patio just outside her back door.

"You don't have enough sun for a pool," I said. "Unless—" The reality of the situation dawned on me and I froze, my finger poised over the drawing and the shape on it that represented the inground pool. "Unless you put the pool right on my property line."

"You're right, it is the only place with enough sun," Chandra said. She brushed a finger across the drawing. "Too shady on the other side of the house. And the garden is here and I'm not going to disrupt that, or the patio." She tapped a finger in the center of the pool. "That leaves here. This spot. It's the only one that will work."

I exchanged looks with Kate and Luella and saw that they were thinking exactly what I was thinking. Utterly surprised, I waited for Kate to speak up. She was, after all, Kate. I knew she would.

"That's going to be mighty inconvenient for Bea's guests," Kate pointed out. "It will be harder for them to park."

"They can pull up farther into the drive." Chandra was completely unconcerned. "Or they can park along the road."

"When Bea's guests sit on her front porch, all they're going to see is you in your pool," Luella added.

Chandra's smile was tight. "I hope they like my orange bikini. If not . . ." She shrugged. "Well, they can just look the other way."

"But—" I swallowed the rest of what I was going to say because, really, I had no idea what words might tumble out of my mouth and I didn't want to take the chance of going off half-cocked. At least not until I had a chance to think about the bombshell Chandra had just dropped.

"That's not the only improvement I'm planning on making."

I snapped out of my thoughts and saw Chandra poke a finger at another portion of the drawing, at a spot almost directly in front of her door—directly across from Kate's house. "A driveway light." Chandra tap, tap, tapped the drawing. "Right here. Isn't that a good idea? There aren't many lights on the island and no streetlights outside of downtown. This will make my house easier to find for the people I do crystal and tarot readings for. And it will help you out, too, Bea," she added with a look my way that clearly said I should be grateful she'd thought of this. "When you have guests coming after dark, you can tell them to look for the light and it will help them find your place next door."

"The light . . ." Kate whipped the drawing off the countertop so she could give it a more careful look. "Your landscape designer needs a little more practice," she said. "The whole drawing is out of proportion. The way it is, that light looks—"

"Really big. It is!" Chandra cooed. "He found me an old street corner gas lamp and he's refitting it for electricity. So yeah, it's bigger than a regular lamppost might be, but it's going to look terrific. Don't you think?"

A muscle twitched at the base of Kate's jaw. "It's going to be bright."

"That's the whole point," Chandra reminded her.

"But that light is directly opposite my bedroom window and—"

Chandra plucked the drawing out of Kate's hand and folded it in quarters. "You'll get used to it," she assured Kate, who did not look at all convinced. "Just think of the romance of the whole thing, that light glowing through the darkness, all night long."

"All night long." Kate grumbled the words under her breath.

Before she could say more, I put a hand on her arm and told her with a look that we'd put our heads together later and talk about these latest unneighborly developments.

Big surprise, Kate actually followed my advice. Her lips pressed together, she sprinkled bread crumbs on the ground meat, and I went to find a big spoon to mix the meatloaf mixture.

"Ten nuns, huh?" Big points for Luella, she tried her best to relieve the tension with a little small talk. "Are they nice women?"

"Very nice," I told her. "And really impressive. They do all kinds of interesting things. There's one who runs a food pantry and another one who works at a shelter for homeless women."

Luella nodded. "Nice."

"Any that are interested in animal rights?" Chandra asked.

Kate, Luella, and I stared at her in wonder.

"What?" Chandra had taken the eggs out of the shopping bag and set them down on the counter but she took one look at them, and as if in solidarity with unborn chicks everywhere, she hooked her fingers together behind her back and raised her chin. "I've had a revelation," she announced. "About the sanctity of all life. You'd think nuns would think that, too."

"Not about eggs, I don't think." I grabbed the eggs, cracked them into a bowl, and whisked them.

Kate harrumphed under her breath. "Does that mean you're becoming a vegan?" she asked Chandra.

"I might." Chandra thought this over while she crunched a cracker.

"You probably can't eat those, then," I told her, pointing to the bit of cracker left in her hand. "I bet there's some milk in them, and milk is an animal product."

"And you definitely can't eat the cheese." Kate scooped the platter off the counter and set it down out of Chandra's reach.

"I said I might." Chandra finished off the last of her cracker and wiped crumbs from her lips. "Besides, I'm not so much worried about cows and chickens and animals like that. I'm thinking more about fish."

Luella had been stirring the meatloaf mixture and her hands froze, mid-mix. "You haven't been talking to those crazy PAFLE people, have you? I saw them on the island last week, protesting down near the marina. People Against Fishing Lake Erie. Imagine a bunch of nonsense like that."

"Maybe it's not nonsense," Chandra suggested. "Maybe they've got a point. After all, they say that overfishing—"

"Overfishing my eye!" With the big mixing spoon, Luella gave the meat mixture a slap. "Those of us who depend on fishing for a living know a thing or two about being responsible. More than a bunch of bleeding hearts who think fish should swim free and never get caught."

"Swim free and never get caught." Chandra's voice was dreamy. "I like the sound of that. I'll suggest it as a slogan at our next meeting."

When she gritted her teeth, Luella's jaw just about snapped. "Next meeting of—"

"People Against Fishing Lake Erie, of course." Chandra's smile was bright. "They've started up a new chapter here on the island. I'm the secretary."

In the great scheme of things, it is a good thing that itty-bitty meatloaves cook faster than full-size ones.

It meant Kate, Luella, and I didn't have to keep our tempers in check and our tongues under control for long while we finished cooking.

Which didn't mean I didn't notice that Luella peeled the potatoes with a whole lot of gusto and chopped them with mighty whacks.

Or that Kate didn't scrub the carrots a little more fiercely than was absolutely necessary.

At the risk of being accused of not being self-aware, I will admit that I mixed up a batch of brownies with all the fury of a woman possessed, plopping them into the pan to bake and trying not to think how when each scoop of batter hit, the sound reminded me of a body flumping into a swimming pool.

And Chandra?

Well, that's the weird thing. Because Chandra—queen of the warm and touchy, empress of the empathetic, and princess of let's-get-it-all-out-in-the-open-and-talk-about-our-feelings—hummed a little tune and scampered around the kitchen helping out and acting for all the world as if there was nothing wrong.

Weird.

And an hour into the melodrama, I told myself not to get my knickers in a twist.

I kept the thought in mind while we packed ten individual dinners, sliced the brownies and put them on a serving platter, and grabbed a bag of extra dark roast Colombian coffee just in case one of the nuns was (like me) partial to a morning cup with a little extra jolt.

Thus supplied, we loaded my SUV and headed for Water's Edge.

"You really didn't have to come along," I said, more to break the icy silence than because I thought it mattered. "I could have delivered the food myself."

"We said we'd help. We're helping." Next to me in the front seat, Luella folded her hands in her lap.

"And I'm dying to see the house." From the backseat, Chandra leaned forward. "Think they'll let us explore?"

"Why, want to root through the attic and look for another streetlamp?" Kate's question was acid.

"Oh, no! One is plenty!" Chandra twittered.

Luella and I exchanged looks just as we drove through the gates of Water's Edge. After that, the three of them were too busy gawking to say a word.

"All these years, and I've never been here." Luella shook her head. "It's impressive."

"It's gorgeous," Kate said when we pulled up in front of the house. "This is the place you should have bought as a bed-and-breakfast, Bea."

"Except it wasn't for sale then," I reminded her. "And it's kind of spooky."

Then again, Water's Edge was nice and secluded and if I lived here, I wouldn't have to worry about a swimming pool practically in my front yard.

As soon as we parked, the front door opened and Sister Catherine and Sister Francelle and Sister Paul spilled out of the house, eager to help us carry dinner inside.

"We've got the table set," Sister Catherine said. In the last of the late afternoon light, her gray habit made her look ghostly. "It's so nice of you to spoil us this way."

"Not a problem," I told her. "Have you gotten everything organized for the week?"

"Almost," she assured me, leading the way into the dining room where elderly Sister Margaret was already seated at the table, a glass of wine in front of her.

"Time?" she asked, and when Sister Catherine nodded, Sister Margaret rang the little silver bell near her plate.

A minute later, we heard the sound of footsteps on the wooden floor overhead and on the stairs and nuns filled the dining room.

Sister Catherine, and Sister Margaret, and Sister Helene, and Sister Paul. Sister Liliosa and Sister Grace and Sister Mary Jean and shy Sister Gabriel and Sister Francelle and—

"Where's Sister Sheila?" someone asked.

"Well, we can't say grace and get started until she shows up." Clearly disappointed, Sister Margaret plumped back in her chair and just for good measure, rang the bell again.

As one, we listened for the sound of Sister Sheila's footsteps on the stairs.

And heard nothing.

"Sister Mary Jean . . ." Sister Liliosa looked her way.

"Why don't you run up to Sister Sheila's room and check on her. It's been a long day, she probably fell asleep."

Only she hadn't. Sister Mary Jean came back to report there was no sign of the missing nun in her room.

"I'll check the rest of the upstairs." Luella started out and no one stopped her.

"And I'll look in the kitchen and such," Chandra said.

"Is there a basement?" None of us were sure, but Kate headed off to find out.

"I'll check outside," I told the nuns. "Maybe you should start eating. So the food doesn't get cold."

"That's why God invented microwaves," Sister Liliosa told me, getting out of her chair. "I'll take the front yard."

"We'll go around the side." Sisters Francelle and Paul started off together, and the other nuns scattered, too.

I followed a group of them as far as the back patio, and when they headed into the rose garden, I started down the stone steps that led to a small strip of sand bordered by huge boulders that poked out into the water, creating a natural pier. By now, the light was fading fast, and I squinted into the gloom, watching the white puff of surf as it hit the beach, listening for any sounds above the pulse of the water that would tell me Sister Sheila was around.

Nothing.

I finished walking the beach and clambered up onto the boulders. From this height, I could see farther, but to my left was the beach I'd already explored and to my right, nothing but a border of scraggly trees that bent back toward the land, as if they'd spent years trying with little success to keep out of the way of the wind that flowed over the lake from Canada.

I hopped a crevice where water lapped the stone and

stepped farther onto the rocky outcrop. Here, there was water on either side of me, the waves gray now that the last of the sun skimmed the horizon to the west.

Gray.

I guess that's why I almost didn't see Sister Sheila.

Her gray habit blended with the waves where she bobbed, arms out to her sides and facedown, in the water.

It was a drowning.

And this wasn't even *The Mill on the Floss*.

❖ 4 ❖

"You found her, huh?"

Hank Florentine's voice snapped me out of my thoughts. Which wasn't a bad thing, really, since what I'd been thinking about was the way Sister Sheila's face looked when the police arrived, fished her out of the water, and brought her lifeless body to shore.

Pale. Like a fish.

Ashen. Like her gray habit.

Dead.

Her eyes staring, her mouth open in a little *o* of amazement, as if she knew her life was slipping away and she couldn't believe it was actually happening.

I shivered, and it wasn't until I did that I realized that sometime while I was lost in my bleak thoughts and replaying the moment of finding Sister Sheila over and over in my head, someone had draped a blanket around my shoulders.

I had no doubt it was the paramedics, who even as I watched zipped Sister Sheila into a body bag and loaded it onto a gurney.

"Found her? Yeah." I glanced to my left and up. Hank was taller than me by far, a broad man with a square jaw, a bullet-shaped head, and a buzz haircut. He was also the chief of police and in the year I'd lived on the island, our paths had crossed on a number of investigations. Though he'd never come right out and say it because he was as hard-nosed and steely as any cop I'd ever met, I liked to think that in that time, he'd come to value my opinions and my judgment and to trust my instincts when it came to murder.

Which—I reminded myself in no uncertain terms—this was not.

I watched the paramedics wheel Sister Sheila away. "She missed dinner."

"She's going to be missing a lot of dinners." Hank barked out a noise that was half laugh, half grunt of disgust. "Sorry," he said. "Police humor." He, too, had his gaze on the paramedics as they accordianed the legs of the gurney down so they could carry the stretcher with Sister Sheila's body strapped to it up the stone steps. "Never had a nun die here on the island," he mumbled.

"The others are sure to be upset." I glanced up the steps but from where we were, it was impossible to see more than the lake in front of us—the water as dark as a blackboard now that the sun was down—the strip of beach where we stood, and the rocky bluff at our backs. I couldn't tell if any of the nuns waited on the patio. "They just got here today."

"For a retreat."

I nodded, then realized that in the gathering gloom, it was just as impossible for Hank to see me as it was for me to see to the end of the rocky pier where I'd stood when I caught sight of Sister Sheila's body bobbing in the water. "For a retreat without a facilitator," I added.

"So ten nuns show up here, they're left high and dry by some big-shot speaker who's supposed to keep them busy for a week, and one of them ends up dead?"

"That's pretty much it." I glanced again toward the rocky outcropping and remembered how I'd had to step carefully when I walked to the end of it. "She must have been walking on the rocks and slipped."

"Must have."

"And if she hit her head—"

"We can't know that. Not until they do an autopsy over at the coroner's office on the mainland. That won't happen until tomorrow earliest. If there's blunt force trauma—"

"That would mean she hit her head."

"Or someone hit it for her."

I can't say I was surprised by Hank's comment. After all, cops are cops, and if there was one thing I'd learned over the years, it was that cops always think the worst of people, at least when it comes to motives and such. Of course the first place Hank's mind went was to murder. That's what he was trained to do.

Still, the very idea of someone murdering a nun was so foreign, so *wrong*, that I protested instantly, "Why would someone—"

"Come on, Bea. You know better than that. People have their reasons for killing. And victims, sometimes they have reasons for getting killed."

"But certainly not a nun!"

Hank turned toward the stairs but he didn't start up. "Nuns are people, too," he reminded me. "What did you know about her?"

I shrugged and while I was at it, I tugged that blanket

tighter around myself. The sun had slipped below the horizon and it was cold there on the beach. "I know her name was Sister Sheila Buckwald and she was from the convent of the Sisters of the Holy Spirit in Chicago. She was a musician. At least that's what one of the other nuns told me. I met her when I brought a carload of nuns over here this morning and we talked for maybe a minute or two. That's it. She was a stranger to me. Most of these nuns, they are even strangers to each other."

"A house full of strangers, huh?" There was no way he could see the house from where we stood, but Hank looked that way.

"Well, except for Sister Helene and Sister Sheila," I said, remembering the earlier conversation I'd had with Sister Helene. When Hank shot me a look, I explained, "They apparently knew each other somewhere along the line. It doesn't mean a thing."

"It might."

"They're nuns."

"And more likely to confide in a woman than they would be in me."

I knew what he was asking and I'd like to say I had to think about it, the way any rational person would. But I also knew that I felt responsible. Oh, not for Sister Sheila's death. There was nothing I could have done about that. But for the comfort and care of the nuns. After all, I'd told Elias Weatherly I would assist in any way I could.

Helping Hank figure out what happened to Sister Sheila, that was the least I could do.

"I'll talk to them," I promised him. "I'll ask some questions."

"And you know I'll do the same thing, but my questions will be official and yours—"

"I know the routine," I assured him. "Chat them up. Get them talking. If they all knew each other, it would be different. But ten strangers—"

"Ten people who say they're strangers."

"Ten *nuns* who say they're strangers," I reminded him and really, I couldn't help but shake my head in wonder. "Do you trust anyone?" I asked Hank.

He didn't even have to think about it. "Nope."

"This time, you're going to find out you're wrong." I was sure of it.

"And you're going to help me. You're going to talk to them all."

I nodded and Hank nodded back. It was as much of an agreement as we needed, and as much of an acknowledgment as I'd get from him that I'd helped him unravel a couple mysteries before.

We were at the bottom of the steps now, and I looked up the bluff to where the paramedics were setting the gurney on the patio. "They're going to be awfully upset," I said, but when we got back to the house, I realized I should have known better. We were dealing with powerhouses—determined, intelligent women fueled by their commitment and their faith. By the time Hank and I walked in, the Sisters were assembled in the living room, and they were doing more comforting—of Luella and Kate and Chandra and the cops who waited there with them—than they were looking for consolation.

Sister Francelle and Sister Paul had made coffee and were passing steaming mugs of it around the room. Sister Liliosa had somehow gotten ahold of a bottle of sherry (I wondered if she traveled with it) and she found liquor glasses and filled them, then insisted each of us take one. Sister Margaret's lips moved silently while her fingers worked over the rosary beads in her hand. The rest of the nuns—except for Sister Gabriel, who was sitting in the corner weeping quietly—had taken those little meatloaves and carved them up for cold sandwiches, and when she took one over to him, I heard Sister Grace tell one of the young cops that he really had to eat, that his job was important and that he couldn't afford to let his energy flag.

"I know this isn't a good time." Hank stepped to the center of the room and I couldn't help but think that no matter how many times he'd given this speech or one similar to it, he'd never been surrounded by nuns when he did. He looked around a little uncertainly, his gaze staying just a little longer on Sisters Helene, Francelle, Paul, and Grace, as if he was trying to tally their street clothes with the fact that they were nuns. "I need to ask you all a few questions."

"Of course." Sister Liliosa took a sip of sherry. "We said a prayer as soon as we heard what happened. Now we can all settle down . . ." She glanced around the room. "Of course we'll help in any way we can."

"Good." Hank rubbed his hands together, and the Sisters took their seats. "So which of you saw Sister Sheila last?"

"I switched rooms with her," Sister Catherine said. "But that was much earlier today. Right after we got here."

"And it was weird, wasn't it?" I hadn't been asked to contribute my two cents, but by the way Hank stepped back when I stepped forward, I realized I had his permission, and his respect. I didn't want to jeopardize either, so I treaded carefully.

"When we arrived," I told Hank and Chandra and Luella and Kate and any of the Sisters who might not have been paying attention to the incident, "Sister Sheila went up to her room and she seemed quite upset."

"That's right," Sister Mary Jean said. "You all remember . . ." She looked around the room. "Most of us were down here and we heard her from upstairs."

"What did she say?" Hank asked.

"Something like 'Help!' or something like that," Sister Paul said.

"It was 'No,'" I said because I remembered it clearly. "She was upstairs in the hallway," I explained to Hank, "but the acoustics are really amazing in here, what with all the wood. What Sister Sheila said was, 'No. Oh, no!'"

"And what was she talking about?" Hank waited for more.

I guess it wasn't the answer he'd hoped for because when I shrugged, he let loose a little sigh of frustration.

"I went upstairs and found her standing outside her room," I said. "The door was open, her suitcase was on the floor next to her. I looked into her room and Sister Catherine and Sister Helene . . ." I glanced their way. "They came upstairs, too. I didn't see anything wrong with the room. Sister Catherine, you've been in there all day. Is there a problem with the room?"

"It's perfect. Better than perfect." A smile lit the nun's broad face. "It's as clean as a whistle and I've got a comfy bed and a waterfront view."

"Sister Sheila couldn't have known about the comfy bed, or even the cleanliness of the room," I mumbled, more to myself than to the group. "She hadn't even walked into the room yet. She opened the door and dropped her suitcase and stopped dead." (Yeah, bad choice of words, but no one seemed to hold it against me.)

"What did she see?" Hank asked.

"Just that gorgeous view," I told him. "The entire far wall of the room is windows."

"Sister Sheila didn't like the water." The comment came from Sister Catherine and, interested, we all turned her way to hear more just in time to see her take a sip of sherry and set down her glass. "I didn't know her," she said, by way of explanation. "I never met her until we were all in New York. But on the ferry ride over this morning . . ." Sister Catherine gathered her thoughts, running her fingers over the folds of her short gray habit. "Not two minutes into the ferry ride, I saw Sister Sheila standing at the railing of the ferry. She was as pale as a ghost . . . sorry . . ." She cringed. "She was ashen, and she was shaking like a leaf."

"Cold," Sister Margaret said. "It was cold on that boat."

Sister Catherine shook her head. "It was chilly, yes. But this was so much more than that. Sister Sheila wasn't cold, she was terrified."

"Of the water?"

When I spoke, Sister Catherine turned to me. "I think so. I went to the little coffee bar on the ferry and got her a cup of tea and I did my best to get her talking. You know, to take her mind off the boat ride. Even so, when we docked, I thought she'd fall to her knees and kiss the ground. She was that relieved to be back on dry land."

Sister Liliosa finished her tiny bit of sherry and cradled her glass in her short, thick fingers. "So when she saw that her room looked out over the water . . ."

"Yes, that's exactly what I thought when I realized she wouldn't walk into the room," Sister Catherine said. "It seems a little . . . well, a little over-the-top. I mean, to be afraid of the water even when you're on land. But I think we've all met people with phobias and we all understand that no matter how hard they try, they can't control them. Irrational fear."

"That's exactly what I saw in Sister Sheila's eyes this

morning," I said. "And when you said you'd switch rooms and she knew she could look out her window at the Water's Edge property all week instead of at the lake, she was thrilled."

"So the woman was afraid of the water." Hank made a note of this in a little pad he pulled from his pocket. "Does anyone else know anything about her?"

Automatically, I glanced Sister Helene's way. "You and Sister Sheila are both musicians. You said you knew her."

"Just in passing," Sister Helene said.

"But you wrote that wonderful song together!" Sister Paul shot up in her chair. "'Living Bread.' That was you and Sister Sheila, wasn't it?"

When she spoke, Sister Helene's shoulders were stiff. "I wrote the music. Sister Sheila wrote the lyrics."

"It's a nice song," Sister Margaret said.

"It's not like we were sitting shoulder-to-shoulder at the piano," Sister Helene told us. "The whole thing was done via email."

I took Sister Helene at her word. After all, she was a nun. But that didn't mean I'd forgotten her comment earlier in the day when Sister Sheila wouldn't walk into her lake-front room.

More of the same.

Sister Helene said Sister Sheila's behavior was more of the same.

To me, that meant she knew more about Sister Sheila than she was willing to admit.

"We did all have lunch together." Sister Francelle spoke up. She was a tall, slim woman and in her jeans and a baggy white sweater, she looked more like a college student than the CEO of a successful religious gift company. "Sister Sheila joined us in the dining room. And the salads were delicious, by the way, Bea. We appreciate you making them for us."

A few of the other nuns nodded.

"Did Sister Sheila say anything at lunch?" I asked them. "Anything about taking a walk on the beach this evening?"

Sister Liliosa got up so she could set her glass on the table near the fireplace and when she was done, she clutched her hands at her waist under the white wool panel at the front of her habit. "Before lunch we broke into groups and planned the week's activities. After lunch, we decided that we could all use a little quiet time and that we'd start into our actual retreat tomorrow. Some of the Sisters decided to explore the property."

"There's a greenhouse!" Sister Margaret's smile was angelic. "Imagine having the luxury of a greenhouse!"

"A few of us went down to the beach then," Sister Paul told us. "We asked Sheila to join us, but she said she was going to her room to read. I don't know about the rest of you . . ." She shrugged. "That's the last time I saw her."

"Me, too." The comment was echoed around the room.

"So that's it?" He obviously knew he'd gotten all he was going to get because Hank tucked that little notebook of his back in his pocket. "Anybody have contact information?"

I wasn't surprised when Sister Liliosa spoke up. "I have a list upstairs," she said and started that way. "All our emails, all our cell numbers. There's a list of emergency contacts, too."

She was back in a few minutes to give the list to Hank, but she didn't sit down. "We said a prayer earlier," Sister Liliosa said, "but if we're done here, I think we all need a quiet time of reflection. You'll excuse us?" she asked Hank.

He nodded. "Of course. If any of you think of anything else—"

"We'll certainly call," Sister Liliosa assured him.

"And if you find anything—"

"We won't touch a thing," Sister Paul told him. "We all watch *CSI*. We know the rules."

After Hank and the two young cops left, Luella, Kate, Chandra, and I went into the kitchen to clean up.

"Terrible." Luella shook her head while she collected containers and rinsed them at the sink.

"Awful." Heaven forbid Kate would let anyone know she could actually be a softie. When she loaded tote bags, she turned away from us to wipe a tear from her cheek.

"Horrible." When it came to emotions, Chandra wasn't nearly as tightly wound. A big, fat tear slipped down her cheek and she sniffled. "Imagine, dying so far from home, surrounded by strangers. What a terrible thing to happen. And what a terrible accident."

Sister Sheila's death was all those things—terrible, awful, horrible. And what an excuse I had for delaying my talk with Levi that evening!

The thought struck out of the blue, and shame on me for letting it get the better of me and transforming my expression. When I realized I was smiling, I looked around and saw my friends staring at me, their jaws slack.

"What?" I asked. Classic defensive comeback, I know. "What's wrong?"

"You thought of something," Kate said. "Something to do with Sister Sheila?"

"You know something," Luella suggested. "Something about the way she died?"

"Or you're thinking about someone." Chandra dangled the words like a fish on a hook that she'd never use now that she was the secretary of the local People Against Fishing Lake Erie chapter.

I didn't rise to the bait.

"It's nothing," I assured them all. "I was just thinking—"

"About last night."

Chandra's words floated in the air and for sure, she expected me to snatch them up and provide some kind of explanation that would satisfy the curiosity clearly etched on Kate and Luella's face.

I didn't give any of them the satisfaction.

Instead, I ducked into the living room long enough to let the nuns know that I would be back first thing the next morning with breakfast.

"And is there any way . . ." I don't think Sister Liliosa had a shy bone in her body, but she pulled a face when she asked for the favor. "Church. We need some way for all of us to get to Mother of Sorrows for ten-thirty Mass tomorrow. Mr. Weatherly said he'd take care of it and now—"

"No problem," I assured the nuns and really, it wasn't. I could have breakfast out for my guests at nine and still have plenty of time to get over here and collect the Sisters for church. "I'll pick you up at ten. That will give us plenty of time."

"Time?" Sister Margaret hadn't moved from the chair where she'd been sitting when Hank interviewed the nuns. She turned a confused look on me. "Is it dinnertime already?"

With a little wave of one hand, Sister Liliosa told me not to worry about it.

"Thank you," she said to me before she turned to the other nuns and said, "Now let's gather together and pray for the repose of the soul of Sister Sheila Buckwald. Sister Gabriel, you are our liturgist. I'm sure you can suggest appropriate prayers."

From her place in the corner near the fireplace, Sister Gabriel looked up when she heard her name. Her eyes were swollen. Her nose was red. Tears streaked her face.

And when I backed out of the living room and gathered up a couple of the bags of containers and such that Kate and Luella and Chandra hadn't been able to handle and joined them outside at my car, a little voice inside me said that it was touching to see so much empathy in such a young woman.

That is, right before another little voice told me it was also odd that a woman like Sister Gabriel—who, except for having dinner with her in New York, had never met Sister Sheila—would be so upset by her death.

It was the same voice that stopped me in my tracks and made me turn around and take another look at the hulking mansion, the voice that said it was plenty weird for a woman who was afraid of the water to take a stroll down a rocky pier into the lake.

❈ 5 ❈

The next morning, Tyler Stevens was in my dining room before I had a chance to put breakfast on the table.

"Coffee?" I asked even though I'd just walked out of the kitchen and I knew it was still brewing. "You're a tad early and everything isn't ready, I'm afraid."

"Coffee? No. No time." Tyler checked the heavy gold watch he wore on his right wrist. He had a camera in one hand and another on a strap looped around his neck and for the first time, I noticed that his suitcase was out in the hallway at the bottom of the steps.

"You're leaving?" I can be excused for being surprised. For one thing, Tyler had reserved his suite for the entire week, and for another, in the year that I'd owned and operated Bea & Bees, I'd never had any complaints. Not about the house, not about the food, not about the value guests received for their money. My rates weren't cheap, but then,

I wasn't looking to pack the house with college kids on party weekends.

I swallowed down the tight ball of panic in my throat. "Is something wrong? With your room? With the house? Because—"

"Oh, no! No, no." Tyler's face flushed as red as his hair. "The house is great. It's terrific and the coffee . . ." He took a deep breath and let it out slowly. "It smells heavenly. I just . . ." He checked his watch again and scurried out to the hallway and, curious, I scrambled behind him.

"The ferry leaves in twenty minutes and I know I've got plenty of time because there can't be much traffic at this time on a Sunday morning, but still, I don't want to be late."

"But Mr. Stevens!" He already had his hand on the doorknob and he looked at me over his shoulder and cringed.

"Forgot. Sorry. I forgot." He dug in his pocket, came out holding a wad of cash and pressed it all in my hand. "This will cover last night and the other nights I had reserved. I'm so sorry to be leaving you high and dry like this, but I've got to get going."

He opened the door and stepped outside. It was a chilly morning and yesterday's sunshine was lost behind a heavy haze that turned the sky ghostly white. Considering what had happened at Water's Edge the night before, the weather seemed appropriate, the clouds a funereal pall. I shook off the thought and followed Tyler down the stairs and over to where he'd left his rental car in the driveway.

"You could at least tell me what's going on," I said while he loaded his suitcase in the trunk. "If there's a problem—"

"Problem? Oh." The high color drained from his cheeks. "I'm so sorry. I've been in something of a state ever since I got the call a little while ago. The house . . ." He looked over my shoulder at my hulking turquoise Victorian with its purple and cream-colored gingerbread trim and the fabulous brickwork chimney that hugged the outside of the house all the way from the first floor to the rooftop.

"The house is great," Tyler slipped into his car and set both cameras on the passenger seat beside him. "The island is wonderful. I was downtown for dinner last night and it's charming and everyone was so nice and so friendly. But I got a call from my friend Tim this morning, you see, and he tells me there have been warblers sighted. Warblers in Sandusky. I didn't see a one here yesterday and I can't take the chance of missing them completely." He started up the car and slowly backed down the driveway.

"Will you be back?" I called to him.

Tyler put on the brakes long enough to open the window. "That all depends on the warblers, of course."

"Of course," I found myself saying as I watched him pull away.

"Morning!" My second surprise of the day came when Joe Roscoe sauntered up the same street Tyler drove away on. He waved and called out again, "Breakfast ready yet?"

"Just about," I assured him and waited until he joined me on the slate sidewalk that bisected the lawn and led up to the front steps. "You're up and about early."

"I love it." He grinned and hoisted that big cardboard tube of his to secure it under one arm. "Maps," he said when I glanced at the tube. "I'll show you later. I've been able to plot out a couple of the early family homesteads. I was just checking things out and thinking about my ancestors and how they were probably up with the sun every morning. They fished, you know."

"A lot of people around here do."

"Noble profession." Joe stopped to stow the tube with

his maps in it in the backseat of his car. "My guess is it's also the reason they ended up leaving the island and relocating to Michigan. Ended up working in the car factories there. Every last great-grandfather and great-uncle and great-aunt. Hard to make a living fishing and there's nothing like a regular paycheck. I guess my ancestors liked life to be predictable and dependable."

"Don't we all!" When a gust of wind buffeted us, I chafed my hands over the sleeves of the green sweater I wore with black pants. "So you're finding the information you need?" I asked Joe Roscoe.

"Like I said, I've checked what I know against modern maps and checked those against the old ones." He glanced toward the car and that cardboard tube. "Things are starting to come together. I spent some time at the cemetery yesterday. It really . . ." We climbed the steps and he stopped at the top and turned to look out over the water. It was an eerie shade of gray that morning, and I'd lived on the island long enough to know that the whitecaps that knocked one into the other and slapped the shoreline meant that bad weather was on its way.

"It's one thing to poke around online and in dusty archives and find your ancestors' birth certificates and marriage licenses and such. But standing at their graves . . ." His voice clogged at the last word. "It's really something," he whispered. "It really makes me feel humble."

"Humbled and chilly." I hadn't grabbed a jacket when I scrambled outside after Tyler Stevens, and the cold seeped through my sweater. I shivered. "I've got coffee ready." At least I hoped it was by now. "And there are muffins and fruit and I've got just enough time to whip up some scrambled eggs."

"Sounds perfect." Roscoe held the door and I stepped

inside ahead of him just as the four librarians scrambled down the steps.

"Good morning!" they called out.

"Coffee smells fabulous," Bette said.

"And after sitting up all night yakking, we need all we can get," another of the librarians commented.

"Any mysteries on the island since we've been asleep?" Angela asked.

I bit my tongue. It was not fair to start anyone's morning with talk of dead nuns and drownings. Besides, Joe and the librarians, they'd hear the story soon enough. All it would take was a visit downtown. I knew the South Bass grapevine was already busy and the news was all over the island by now. In fact, I'd already had a voicemail from Levi before I got back from Water's Edge the night before. He'd heard the news and knew I was busy. He understood why I hadn't stopped at the bar and said we'd talk another time.

Oh yeah, that gave me something to look forward to.

I sloughed the thought aside and instead of telling my guests about Sister Sheila and destroying their good moods, I invited them all to sit down at the dining room table, served the muffins and fruit Meg had come in the evening before to prepare, and scrambled a couple dozen eggs. Once I'd served those, I told them I had to get moving. I had nuns to collect and get to church and since my SUV wouldn't hold them all, Kate had offered to help.

By the time the two of us, the two vehicles, and the nine nuns arrived at Mother of Sorrows church, a sharp wind had kicked up, and it whistled through the bare tree branches. Sister Catherine and Sister Margaret needed to hang on to their half-veils when they scurried inside the stone church, and even Sister Liliosa's formidable habit was no match for the wind. Just before she walked through the double doors under the stone arch, the wind lifted her skirts and I caught a glimpse of sturdy ankles, sensible black shoes, and what looked to be handmade and very cute knitted socks in shades of black, gray, and white.

Waiting in the car for an hour made no sense, especially with the weather being what it was. Neither did going home only to have to turn around and come back to pick up the nuns. Kate and I held back until all the nuns were inside, then slipped into the church behind them and found seats at the end of the row of the pew where Sisters Francelle, Paul, Margaret, and Gabriel sat. The other nuns sat in the pew directly in front of ours.

Thanks to the weather, there was little traffic on the island and it had taken us no time at all to arrive at the church. It was still early and obviously, the parish priest knew the nuns were coming. He welcomed them and he and Sister Liliosa put their heads together. I had no doubt he'd heard about Sister Sheila's death, just as I had no doubt Sister Liliosa and her companions would be sure to do something at the service in honor of Sister Sheila's memory.

As churches go, Mother of Sorrows is small and intimate, a lovely little oasis of quiet and beauty on an island that can—at least at the height of tourist season—be all about the food and the drinks and the music and the nightlife. According to Luella, who was a member of the church, the building had been constructed in 1928, and I breathed in the stillness of the years and the lingering scent of incense and burned candles and took a look at the windows, like transparent mosaics, on either side of the church. After the events of the night before, this bit of calm and quiet was exactly what I needed and I counted my breaths, listened to my heartbeat, and closed my eyes.

"Sister Gabriel."

Sister Liliosa's voice was hushed, but still, my eyes flew open just in time to see her turn to look at the young nun seated at the end of the pew. "Father would like your input. About today's liturgy."

Sister Gabriel didn't budge. In fact, she didn't even look at Sister Liliosa.

"Sister Gabriel?" The older nun tried again. This time, she crooked her finger and the rest of us seated in the row leaned forward to see what Sister Gabriel was up to.

What she was up to was crying. Beneath her black wool habit, her chest heaved, and by the way the light shone on her face, I could tell it was stained with tears.

Sister Liliosa's expression morphed from understanding to stern. "The liturgy, Sister Gabriel? Father thought it would be best if we chose today's prayers and readings and we're depending on you to make suggestions."

"I . . . I . . ." Sister Gabriel's voice broke. "I'm not sure I can."

"It would give you comfort," Sister Paul suggested in hushed tones.

"And it would help us out," Sister Francelle reminded her. "If we're each supposed to contribute to the success of the retreat   "

Sister Gabriel pushed forward on the slick wooden pew, and I thought she was going to stand up and get a move on. At the last second, she froze and slid back. She buried her face in her hands. "I can't."

"Poor thing." Next to me, Sister Francelle shook her head. "She's so very upset about what happened to Sister Sheila. Went right to her room after you left last night and I heard her in there sobbing. But then, she's young and she hasn't yet accepted that everything that happens, it's all part of God's plan. She will. Someday, she'll understand. Until then . . ." Sister Francelle got to her feet. "I can help with the readings," she offered.

"And Sister Helene is the perfect person to choose the music." Though her voice was light, I couldn't help but notice that when Sister Liliosa turned away from Sister Gabriel, a muscle jumped at the base of her jaw.

A couple of the other Sisters got up, too, and went to the front of the church where a gorgeous fresco that featured a cobalt blue background and a glorious angel crowned the altar.

They got to work choosing prayers and songs and readings and slowly, the church filled with worshippers. It felt wrong to turn around and ogle the crowd, but I listened to the sounds of their footsteps, sharp against the church floor, and the whispers that turned into a buzz when parishioners realized the nuns were in attendance.

"Everybody okay?" Luella took a seat in the pew directly behind me and Kate, leaned forward, and gave me a poke. "Everything under control?"

"I'm not sure." I glanced down the row of nuns, each of them praying quietly, and toward Sister Gabriel. "Awfully upset," I mouthed.

"Young."

It seemed to be everyone's excuse for Sister Gabriel's reaction to the death of Sister Sheila and for all I knew, they were right.

That didn't keep me from thinking it was also a little over-the-top.

Especially for a nun.

By the time I went back to Water's Edge to deliver lunch (Meg's excellent chicken salad, egg salad for those who might be vegetarians, loaves of fresh bread, fruit, and an assortment of Meg's home-baked cookies), the stiff breeze had turned into a howling wind that battered the SUV. The lake was whipped into a fury of whitecaps and waves, and I found myself thinking that Tyler Stevens was a lucky man; no doubt that first ferry of the morning would be the only ferry off the island that day. I wondered if warblers went out in bad weather and wished him happy bird hunting on the mainland.

I arrived at the retreat center and got everything inside, slamming the door on the wicked wind just as Sister Gabriel came out of the living room. She had her phone in one hand and an eye on the window.

"They're not saying it's going to last, are they?" It wasn't until she closed in on the window and peered outside that I realized she was talking about the storm. "I mean, it's going to clear up anytime now, right?"

I had checked the weather app on my phone before I left the house and I could see that Sister Gabriel was looking at the same one. She knew what I knew. "Not supposed to get better until later in the week," I told her.

"But it's got to." Sister Gabriel stopped just short of stomping one foot against the floor. Her mouth twisted. Though it was hard to tell, what with the wimple that covered her forehead and ears and the heavy veil that topped it all off, she looked to be a pretty woman. She had clear blue eyes and skin that was bright and rosy. There was a dusting of freckles across her nose and cheeks, like specks of cinnamon sugar. "If the weather stays like this . . ." Grumbling, she turned from the window and crossed her arms over her black habit. "If it doesn't get better, the boats won't run, right? I mean, like the ferry. What happens then? How do you people here on the island get your mail? And your food? And, you know, packages and such?"

"It's never been so bad that we've been without for more than a week or so," I assured her. "Even in winter, our mail is flown in along with supplies from the mainland."

"But what about deliveries? If something's supposed to be delivered the next day and—"

"Expecting something?"

She lifted her chin. "I didn't have room in my suitcase so I sent some books from home. I'd hoped they would get here in time for me to have them for the retreat."

It was my turn to look out the window. "I'm no meteorologist, but I've seen weather like this on the island before. It will be at least a couple days until the ferry can run again and bring over the delivery trucks."

"A couple days." When Sister Gabriel mumbled, she sounded more like a petulant teenager than a nun. She turned and stomped away. "I can't wait a couple days."

I almost offered the use of my library back at the B and B. It was extensive, after all, but then again, it didn't include any religious or inspirational books and I had no doubt that's what Sister Gabriel was looking for. Instead of worrying about it, I went into the kitchen to get the food unpacked and then delivered to the dining room. I was nearly done arranging apples and grapes on a big serving plate with a brightly painted chicken on it when my phone rang.

"Bea."

So much for polite chitchat. But then, I didn't expect much else from Hank.

"News from the mainland," he said.

My hands stilled above the little bunches of grapes I'd set along the perimeter of the serving dish. "From the sound of your voice, I'd say it's not good news."

"She was hit on the head, all right." Hank didn't need to say which *she* he was talking about. Instantly, an image of Sister Sheila popped into my head. "The coroner says the injury was perimortem."

I gulped down the sour taste in my mouth. "You mean—"

"Hit from behind and dumped into the lake. There was water in her lungs. She went into the lake alive."

I hadn't realized my knees gave out until I plunked into a nearby chair. "Murder."

"Looks that way."

"But who would murder a nun?"

"That's our job to find out."

Somehow, I knew Hank wasn't talking about himself and his department. *Our job.* He wanted my help.

"I'm at the retreat center now," I told him, automatically lowering my voice, though in a house the size of Water's Edge, I knew I didn't need to. The place was massive, and the only other person I'd seen since I arrived was Sister Gabriel.

"Good. See what you can find out, but don't tell them what we know. Not yet. Maybe our murderer will get a little too comfortable and careless and let some information slip."

I glanced toward the kitchen door and the dining room beyond. "You can't think that any of the other nuns—"

"I don't know what to think. And neither do you," Hank snapped. I didn't take it personally. Like I said, Hank was Hank. "Not yet. Not until we do a little digging."

I knew he was right, but really, I couldn't keep my gaze off the door or get rid of the picture inside my head—nine nuns seated at the table, waiting for lunch.

"But they're nuns," I whined.

He puffed out a breath. "I know they're nuns. What difference does it make? I'm not saying one of them actually killed Sheila Buckwald. I'm saying that they were all on the premises and somebody might have seen something.

Or heard something. Somebody might not even realize that they know something important. We need to talk to them and since you're right there . . ."

"Sure. Of course." I ended the call and tucked my phone back in my pocket. "Of course I'll talk to them."

It's not like I was reluctant to get to the bottom of what had turned into a mystery with a nasty twist. I'd interviewed suspects before. Plenty of them. Still, there was something about trying to elicit information from unsuspecting nuns that felt a little unscrupulous. The thought pounding through my head, I served lunch and I was all set to duck back into the kitchen to get my story straight and my questions sorted out when the nuns insisted I join them at the lunch table.

I took an empty seat at the far end of the table with my back to the windows and it wasn't until I sat down that I realized it was where Sister Sheila would have been seated.

"It's all right." Sister Grace was to my left, and she patted my hand. But then, she worked with death row inmates. I had to think she was more comfortable with the Grim Reaper than the rest of us.

"So . . ." Sister Liliosa took a heaping helping of chicken salad and passed the platter on to the nun next to her. "Any word from the police?"

"They wouldn't call me if there was an update." Since that made perfect sense, no one disputed it. "I wouldn't be surprised, though, if Hank didn't stop in again. He's pretty thorough."

"Needs to be in his job." Sister Liliosa grabbed two pieces of whole wheat bread.

"Such a terrible accident." Sister Grace said what everyone but me—and maybe the murderer—was thinking.

"So important to remember what we have and to be thankful for it every day," Sister Paul added.

And so it went. After a few minutes, the conversation drifted away from Sister Sheila and to the retreat and what the nuns had planned for themselves for the week. Not that Sister Sheila was forgotten. Her name was mentioned when the nuns bowed their heads and said grace before they ate, and when one of the Sisters suggested that some time be set aside each day to reflect on Sister Sheila's life and her contributions to her convent and her community, the suggestion was met with overwhelming enthusiasm.

For my part, I was reflecting on something else, that hint of discord I caught between Sisters Sheila and Helene.

I waited until lunch was done and Sister Catherine was helping me clear away the dishes before I dared to broach the subject.

"I suppose Sister Sheila's family has been notified," I said, trying my darnedest to ease into the subject.

Sister Catherine nodded. "A mother and father somewhere outside of Chicago." She had a pile of plates in her arms and she closed her eyes and lowered her head. "How terrible for them to get news like that. Sister Sheila's life held so much promise."

"You mean because of her music." Oh yes, I could sound plenty innocent when I wanted to and realizing it, another stab of guilt prodded my conscience. "That song someone mentioned, the one she and Sister Helene wrote together . . ."

"'Living Bread.'" Sister Catherine nodded. "It really is beautiful."

"But I get the feeling . . ." I wasn't sure how long I could pull off the wide-eyed-innocent routine so I laughed, as if I couldn't help myself or contain my curiosity and I was actually embarrassed because of it. "Every time someone mentions Sister Sheila or the song, Sister Helene practically bristles."

Sister Catherine added a few more plates to the stack in her arms.

"Could it be there was bad blood between them?" I ventured. "Since I've heard that none of you know each other well, whatever they felt for each other, it must have been because of the song. It was their only connection."

Sister Catherine looked over her shoulder toward the open dining room door and the empty hallway beyond. As lunch was being cleaned up, the Sisters decided they would take an hour to rest, then meet in the living room to hear Sister Margaret talk about her urban gardening program. Right now, all was quiet at Water's Edge.

"There's talk," Sister Catherine said and flushed a deep pink. "More like gossip and I shouldn't even mention it but now that Sister Sheila's dead . . . well, maybe it's not important at all now, or maybe it's more important than ever. You see, there was some sort of copyright dispute. Over 'Living Bread.' I hear Sister Sheila was adamant about her convent earning all the copyright money because she wrote the lyrics to the song. And Sister Helene, she wrote the music and of course, she wanted her share of the profits for her convent. At least that's what I've heard and I was thinking now that Sister Sheila's dead, I wonder if all the money will automatically go to Sister Helene. And really, I shouldn't have even mentioned it. It was small-minded of me to bring it up."

"Not at all," I assured her. "You never know what might turn out to be important."

"You mean, in a murder investigation."

It was on the tip of my tongue to lie and tell her I didn't know what she was talking about, but really, I thought more of Sister Catherine than that.

I looked away. "Like I said, you never know."

We finished cleaning up and washed the dishes in silence,

and I told the nuns I'd be back later with dinner. They protested—of course they protested—saying that the weather was too bad and they could make do with what was left over from lunch, but I lied and told them that Luella, Chandra, and Kate were already over at my place getting pot roasts ready. It wasn't like I was looking forward to venturing back out in the nasty weather that evening, but now that I knew what was going on between Sister Sheila and Sister Helene, I had plenty more questions to ask.

A copyright dispute.

Nuns or no nuns, it sounded like motive to me.

❧ 6 ❧

"So of course, Hank wants us to check things out."
I'd just finished filling in Luella, Kate, and Chandra with the facts. Murder. Sister Sheila had been murdered. While I packed containers of pot roast and roasted vegetables in tote bags, I gave them a few minutes to process the information, knowing that, like me when I'd heard the news, it would take them a while to try to make sense of it.

"Who would murder a nun?" Luella asked exactly what I'd asked Hank when he told me about the coroner's report.

"And why?" Kate wondered.

"I doubt Hank wants *our* help." Chandra's scowl didn't jibe with her sunny yellow top embroidered with twinkling sequins. "*Your* help, Bea. He wants your help. And I'm surprised a man that pigheaded and stubborn would even ask for that."

Have I mentioned that Hank and Chandra were once married?

In fact, Hank was Chandra's ex number two (there had been another after that), and though I knew for a fact that the two of them got together now and again in a very friendly way, anytime they were outside the bedroom, the old antagonism reared its ugly head.

I reminded myself of this, just like I reminded myself that for reasons none of us had yet to figure out, Chandra seemed to be trying her hardest to get a rise out of all of us. I wasn't willing to give her the satisfaction, so I kept my voice light and level.

"Of course he wants all of us to help." I finished packing dinner and went over to the countertop where Luella had left two of the amazing pies—cherry and apple—that Meg had baked for us that afternoon. "He knows we wouldn't have gotten to the bottom of the couple mysteries we've helped him solve if every one of us didn't contribute."

Kate's eyes shone with excitement. "So what do you want us to do?"

"For one thing, don't tell the nuns it was a murder." I made sure I kept my eyes on Chandra when I said this. Of all of us, she was the one who was most likely to get caught up in the excitement of the investigation and forget that for now, Hank had asked us to keep the secret. "Other than that, I guess what we need to do is talk to the Sisters. I thought if we got to Water's Edge a little early this evening . . ." I checked the clock on the kitchen wall. "If we leave now, their afternoon retreat session should be over. They were planning on a little quiet time between that and dinner."

"A little quiet time we can fill." Luella rubbed her hands together. "At least we know none of them will be out walking the beach."

As if we needed the reminder, rain pelted the windows and as one, we all glanced that way.

"Nasty." Kate shivered.

"At least it's not cold." I am not usually a Pollyanna, but facts were facts. Just a year earlier, we'd all been trapped on the island—with a killer—by a freak spring snowstorm. "And actually, the weather might work in our favor. If the nuns are stuck inside—"

"They'll be looking for something to do," Kate commented.

"And they'll be a captive audience." Luella slipped on her slicker and grabbed for the tote bags.

"I'll take Sister Helene," I told them, poking my arms into the sleeves of my raincoat. I flipped up the hood. "If no one has any objections. Since Sister Catherine confided in me about her dispute with Sister Sheila, it will be easier for me to keep the facts straight."

They all nodded in agreement.

"I'm thinking I can start up a conversation easy enough," Chandra announced. Her version of rain gear was yellow rubber boots—she poked her feet into them—along with a purple trench coat and matching umbrella. "I'll start with that Sister Margaret, the one who knows so much about gardens. I can get her advice as long as I'm at it. I was thinking of expanding my herb garden. You know, all around the pool."

Did I grit my teeth the moment that last word was out of Chandra's mouth?

I must have, because Kate shot me a look.

I bit back the comment I was all set to make about herbs and chlorinated water and how I had a feeling it was a bad mix. "From what I saw of your plan," I said instead, "the pool is going to be so close to my driveway, I doubt if there's room on that side for herbs."

"There's a little room." Chandra had obviously thought this through. "As long as your guests are careful where they walk."

Careful. When they didn't know where my property line ended and Chandra's began.

And they were carrying suitcases.

And anxious to get checked into their rooms.

This time it took my biting the inside of my mouth to keep me from snapping out a comment.

"I'm sure Sister Margaret can help you," I said and I don't think I was imagining it; Chandra really did look disappointed that I hadn't been sucked into the fight she was trying to pick.

When Chandra went to the door ahead of us, I exchanged quizzical looks with Luella and Kate.

Luella shrugged.

Kate made a face and put on her Burberry coat.

We all headed outside and met our four librarians just as they were hurrying into Marianne Littlejohn's car out in my driveway.

"Heading to dinner!" Marianne called out from the driver's seat over the sound of the roaring wind. "You want to join us?"

"Water's Edge." As if it was the only explanation I needed, I lifted the tote bags I was carrying.

"We're going to talk books!" Angela was just about to get into the backseat and she grinned. "You ladies would love it."

"I have no doubt." I also had no doubt I was going to be soaked through to my bones, so I waved a quick good-bye and raced to the SUV where the other Ladies of the League were already inside.

At the other end of our journey, we pretty much repeated the process: gather the bags, race to the door. Inside, we dripped on the slate floor of the entryway for a minute before anyone even knew we'd arrived.

"You're early." As luck would have it, it was Sister Helene who came down the stairs. She had a coffee mug in one hand and when she went into the kitchen, I gave my friends a wink to tell them to have at the other nuns and fell into step beside her. While Sister Helene made coffee, I unpacked dinner.

I'm not much for small talk, so I couldn't help but cringe when I said, "I hope the weather hasn't ruined your Sunday."

"Not at all." Sister Helene added cream and sugar to her mug. "There's nothing like staying inside in front of a roaring fire on a day like this. And the storm . . ." She twitched her shoulders. "Well, it seems in keeping with the mood, doesn't it? We're trying to stay positive and to keep busy, but no matter what else we're talking about, it seems Sister Sheila's name always comes up."

"It's only natural. We all need to process our grief."

"That sounds like something one of us should say to you!" Sister Helene filled her mug with coffee and took a small sip. "It's easy to talk about things like faith and trust in the Lord. But when it comes right down to it and someone you know has had her life cut terribly short, well, it's a little harder to walk the walk than it is to talk the talk."

It was a remarkable thing to admit, and I told Sister Helene I admired her for her honesty.

She waved away the compliment. "If we can't be honest, then there's no use saying anything at all, is there?"

Exactly what I'd been thinking.

"Speaking of which . . ." I'd just put the pies out on the

island in the center of the kitchen and I nudged them so they were perfectly in place. "I noticed that you and Sister Sheila didn't get along."

Sister Helene was wearing jeans and a navy hoodie with a kangaroo pouch at the front, and she set down her mug and tucked her hands in the pocket. "I told you, I hardly knew her."

"But you wrote a song together."

"I told you about that, too. We worked via email."

"What you didn't mention is that there's been some dispute over the distribution of the royalties."

I wouldn't have blamed her if she told me to get lost. It is, after all, exactly what I would have done if someone was so bold as to suggest what I was clearly suggesting.

Maybe nuns are made of better stuff than the rest of us; Sister Helene leaned back against the counter and met my steady gaze with one of her own.

"You don't think Sheila's death was an accident," she said.

"Like I said this afternoon, no one knows yet. And even if the police did—"

"We're nuns, but that doesn't mean we're naive. Or stupid." Sister Helene never looked away. "Whatever the police claim, you don't think Sister Sheila's death was an accident. You think she was murdered. And you think I had something to do with it."

"Did you?"

Her smile was tight. "Sheila Buckwald's songs are all about the glory of God and praising the Lord. Her life was anything but. Oh, don't think I'm just spreading lies and rumors," Sister Helene added. "The truth is the truth and like I said, there's no use talking at all if we're not going to be honest with each other. The truth is, there's a great deal of money at stake. Not that either of us would have seen it personally. My share of the royalties was earmarked for my convent, just as Sister Sheila's was for hers. While we're all loyal to our orders and the Sisters we live with, it's hard to imagine any of us would kill just to bring a few more dollars into the convent till."

"Sometimes motive goes deeper than that. For some people, money isn't nearly as important as status. Or recognition."

"You think I wasn't recognized for my contribution to 'Living Bread'?"

"I know you were. All the other nuns here know you wrote the music. That tells me it wasn't any big secret."

"It doesn't tell you—" I guess Sister Helene heard exactly what I heard, the way her voice sizzled with anger. She bit back the words and took a minute to compose herself. "Unlike Sister Sheila, I saw that the dispute between us was unhealthy and un-Christian. I saw that it was doing nothing but bringing grief to each of our convents. I didn't come to Ohio empty-handed. I brought along a contract relinquishing all my claims to the royalties from 'Living Bread.'"

Sister Helene went on even faster than I opened my mouth to ask what she was talking about.

"It's not worth it," she said. "It's not worth the strife or the aggravation or what it was doing to my blood pressure. I brought all the legal paperwork with me and Sister Sheila signed it soon after we arrived. I assigned all my rights from 'Living Bread' to her. So you see . . ." Sister Helene snatched up her coffee cup. "It makes for a really good story. Lies and jealousy and bitter artistic rivals. But it's a nonstarter. I didn't kill Sheila. Not for the money and not for any other reason."

And with that, she marched out of the kitchen.

"Well, she looked like a thundercloud." Kate poked her head into the room a moment after Sister Helene left it. "You made her mad."

"I made her think I was an idiot who didn't have all my facts straight," I grumbled. "Did you find out anything?"

She shook her head and reached for the stack of dinner plates I took down from the cupboard. "They're from all different parts of the country, from all different convents. None of them knew each other well."

"Except for Sheila and Helene." Thinking this over, I tapped the toe of my sneaker against the ceramic tile floor. It didn't take me long to come up with a plan. "Everyone in the dining room?"

Kate nodded. "Except for Sister Margaret and Chandra. There was some talk of thyme and parsley."

I rolled my eyes. "What do you suppose she's up to?"

Kate knew I wasn't talking about Sister Margaret. "She's clearly lost her mind. Did you see the size of that lamppost she wants to put outside her house? When the light's on, it will blind me. And destroy the atmosphere of the neighborhood. You think Chandra would know that."

"She's got to know it, just like she's got to know that a pool on my property line . . ." Just thinking about it made me feel as if my head would pop off. "I can't imagine what's going through her brain."

"Nothing right now but talk of herbs and more herbs." Luella joined us in the kitchen and picked up on our conversation. Her mouth twisted. "At least we know she won't be adding fish fertilizer to her garden!"

"She's acting crazy." Kate checked to make sure the door was closed before she made the pronouncement. "She's always been nuts, but now she's even more nuts."

"It doesn't make any sense." I shook my head, then

brushed my dark, curly hair out of my eyes. "And I suppose right now, it doesn't matter. We have a more serious problem on our hands."

Kate and Luella knew I was right, and I filled them in with what I had in mind. As soon as we were sure all the nuns were in the dining room, they'd serve dinner and I'd scoot upstairs and look through the Sisters' rooms. All my friends had to do was keep the nuns talking to cover up any sounds I might make. And to make sure they all stayed at the table.

When Chandra finally joined us—excitedly chatting about fennel and marjoram and something called licorice flag that Sister Margaret told her would be ideal for wet soil—and they ferried pot roast and veggies into the dining room, I stayed behind and counted to ten, realizing as I did that I did not have the steely constitution of a burglar. Especially when it comes to burgling nuns.

I counted to ten again just to try to calm my suddenly racing heart, then because I knew I was wasting time, I held in a tight breath, ducked into the hallway, and hurried up the stairs.

The steps creaked. Of course they creaked. The house was old. The stairway was made of wood. At the first noise, I cringed, then froze, but when the buzz of conversation I could hear from the dining room never lagged, I kept right on going.

At the top of the stairs, I stopped long enough to get my bearings.

I knew which room was Sister Catherine's because it was the one I'd looked into the day before when Sister Sheila refused to walk into it. And I knew which room belonged to Sister Sheila—I glanced across the hallway—because it was the one Sister Catherine walked out of when they decided to switch.

Though I knew the police had already been through it, I also knew I had to satisfy my curiosity. Before I worried about Sister Helene's room, I'd check out Sister Sheila's.

I flicked on the light and glanced around. Like the room she'd refused to enter, this room was spacious and inviting. There were bookcases against the right wall and windows opposite the door that looked out over the circular driveway at the front of the house. To my left was a bed and a desk and beyond that, a door that led to the bathroom.

Sister Sheila's suitcase was still on the bed, still packed as it must have been the afternoon when she decided to take a walk on the beach before she got settled. I ignored the stab of poignancy and closed in on the suitcase so I could shuffle through the contents.

Another veil.

Underwear.

Nightgown.

Toiletries.

There was certainly nothing remarkable to be found in Sister Sheila's few possessions, and I turned away from the suitcase so I could concentrate on the desk. There, right on top of it, was the contract Sister Helene had told me about.

I've had some experience with contracts and to me, this one looked pretty standard. Just like Sister Helene had said, in it she surrendered her rights to "Living Bread" and to all royalties resulting from the sale and use of the song.

I paged through the rest of the contract and saw nothing unusual.

Well, except for the one clause near the very end.

I read over it twice just to be sure that it said what I thought it said, and I thought about how right Sister Helene had been when she told me that just because she was a nun didn't mean she was dumb or naive.

What she was, apparently, was a little forgetful.

Or a really skilled liar.

Because though Sister Helene had been right about the contract and walking away from her royalties, what she'd failed to mention was this one niggling little clause.

See, the contract stated that there was one way for Sister Helene to resume receiving the royalties, and to get all the previously earned royalties assigned to her, too.

That was on Sister Sheila's death.

« 7 »

"So there's a dead nun, huh?" Joe Roscoe asked the question around the bite of cranberry pancake he'd just put in his mouth. "Everybody's talking about it," he said by way of responding to my surprised look. He washed down the mouthful of breakfast with a slug of coffee. "At least they were when I went downtown for dinner last night. Not surprising on an island like this. It's got to be real news."

"It is news, and it's very sad." I'd just carried a Georgian porcelain tureen heaped with fresh strawberries and kiwis into the dining room and I set it down on the table. It was just a bit after nine and the librarians weren't down yet so at least right now, the spread was all for Joe. Then again, I'd found four empty wine bottles in the kitchen trash when I got up that morning along with a pizza box, a used-up carton of Ben & Jerry's Hazed & Confused, and a couple dozen wrappers from those little Dove dark chocolates.

Something told me the librarians might be moving a little slow that Monday morning.

"So what's the story?" Joe sopped up the syrup on his plate with his last bit of pancake, then stabbed another flapjack from the serving platter and slathered it with butter. "Folks down at the restaurant where I ate said you were sure to know all the details. They told me you're a detective."

"I'm a B-and-B owner," I pointed out, then felt I needed to explain. "There were a couple little mysteries on the island last year," I said, purposely avoiding the word *murder* because I didn't want to freak out a guest or give the island a bad name. "I helped out a little. That's all. That doesn't make me a detective."

"That's not what I heard about you." Joe poked his fork in my direction. "I hear you're as sharp as a tack and pretty good about getting to the bottom of things."

"Just like you." How's that for a slick way to change the subject? I made sure I smiled when I sat down, poured myself a cup of coffee, and said, "Genealogists are detectives, too, aren't they? You're always searching for clues that will lead you somewhere and when you solve one mystery, you move on to the next one."

Thinking about it, he pressed his lips together. "You're right."

"That's all I've been able to do. Just think about things and offer some suggestions to the authorities. It was nothing. Besides . . ." I remembered what Hank had said about not revealing the whole truth about how Sister Sheila had died to the nuns and figured the same advice applied to laity. "Nobody said Sister Sheila's death was any kind of mystery. She fell into the water and drowned. It was an unfortunate accident."

"I'll say." Joe reached for the fruit and heaped strawberries and kiwi on his plate. "And this Sister Sheila . . . Everybody's talking about her, but nobody's got much when it comes to details. Was she a young woman?"

I thought about the last time I'd seen Sister Sheila—the last time I'd seen her alive. "Forties, I'd say, though I'm not very good when it comes to guessing people's ages and the whole habit and veil make it even harder than it would be if she were wearing street clothes."

"Short? Tall? Skinny? Plump?" Joe obviously liked to get his facts straight. Not surprising for a man whose passion was delving into family history. "What kind of woman was she?"

"I only met her once," I told him. "She was a little taller than me, a little rounder. She seemed . . ." I couldn't say *terrified*, not without having to explain. "She seemed nice. And like all the nuns, I'm sure she was looking forward to a week at Water's Edge. Then just like that, her retreat—and her life—was cut short. It makes you appreciate how fragile life can be."

"Amen." Joe raised his coffee cup in my direction. "So those other nuns, they're staying on at the retreat?"

"No reason they shouldn't," I said, and wondered if they would once they learned the truth about the circumstances of Sister Sheila's death. "I think they find a great deal of comfort in each other's company."

Nodding, Joe took another bite of cranberry pancake. "That retreat place, some old geezer at the bar was telling me about it. He said it used to be the home of some big shot."

"So I hear. He was dead by the time I moved to the island, and the house was empty until it was turned into the retreat center."

"Interesting old house?"

It was a natural question from a genealogist. "Big, rambling. Looks like something straight out of a gothic novel. But the inside has been updated and it's warm and inviting."

"Big enough that each of those nuns has her own room? There are what, like ten of them? That's what the folks at the restaurant said, anyway."

"There *were* ten of them," I reminded him. "And yes, each of them does have a private room with a private bath. Which tells you something about the size of the house. It's quite an impressive place."

"And it has views of the lake. That's what the geezer said. He said that when that rich recluse or whatever he was lived there, no one was allowed near the place, but that sometimes, they'd take their boats out and take a gander at the house from the water. It's near the nature preserve, right?"

"No, no." I stirred my coffee and took a sip. The coffee I brewed for my guests was a tad less strong than the pot I kept in the kitchen for myself, but still, it was tasty and the hot coffee felt good going down on a morning that was just as rainy, raw, and windy as the previous day had been. "Water's Edge is on the other side of the island," I told Joe. "North of the ferry dock and the old lighthouse."

"Any idea when it was built?"

"Not a clue," I admitted. "But I bet the folks at the Historical Society could tell you. Maybe the house was here when your ancestors lived on the island."

"I'd like to find out. And I'd love to get a look at the house if you don't think anyone would mind. Maybe my great-grandfather helped build the place. He was a carpenter."

I set my cup on its saucer. "I thought your ancestors fished."

For a second, Joe was confused, but the truth dawned on him and he chuckled. "Well, they all fished. Just like I told you the other day. But during winter, they had to have some trade to get them by. Great-grandpa Roscoe was a carpenter and I hear he did fine work. If there was a mansion being built, I'd like to think he had a part in it. Wouldn't that be something, standing in a room he helped build or looking at a wall he paneled."

I had no doubt he was right, but there wasn't a chance to talk about it. Four sleepy-eyed and a little worse for wear librarians stumbled into the room.

"Good morning," Angela said, and winced at the sound of her own voice. "Is there coffee?"

"Lots of coffee." Carole was already filling four cups.

Bette took a sip of hers. "I think we're going to need more," she told me.

I wasn't about to argue. When I headed into the kitchen to brew another pot, I took my own cup with me and refilled it with the special extra-kick variety I liked so much. I'd just sat down on one of the high stools near the breakfast counter when the phone rang.

"Got some stuff you should probably know about."

"Good morning, Hank."

"What? Ah, yeah, good morning. Got some stuff you should probably know about."

I thought about what Joe had said, about the gossip around town that had me pegged as a detective. There was no use adding fuel to the fire by letting my guests see the chief of police making a house call. "Give me a few minutes to finish up breakfast and clean up and I'll come over to the station."

"No hurry," Hank told me. "Dead is dead. Nothing we do is going to bring that poor woman back."

*   *   *

Pancakes are pretty hard to transport, but I knew better than to arrive at the police station in the basement of the town hall building empty-handed. In spite of everything Chandra said about him (and oh, the things she said about him!), Hank was a valuable asset and an important ally. I brought him a container filled with fresh strawberries and kiwis and as long as I was at it, I grabbed one of the extra cinnamon raisin muffins Meg had made—and delivered for me—for the nuns' breakfast that morning.

He dug right in.

"Been making the usual inquiries," Hank told me, muffin in one hand and a spoon loaded with strawberries in the other. "Thought you said these Sisters, they didn't know each other."

"Well, they didn't. Not really. Not until they arrived here. Except for that dinner in New York a few months ago where they were awarded their grants, most of them had never met each other."

"But not all of them."

"Sisters Helene and Sheila. Yeah. Like I told you, Hank, there was a dispute over royalties and Sister Sheila and Sister Helene had a contract and—"

"Sister Sheila gets all the money. Only now she doesn't because she's dead."

"It just doesn't feel like a motive to me." I twitched away the cold chill that settled on my shoulders because, of course, to too many people, that would be plenty of motive. "Nuns don't fight about things like money."

"Maybe not." Hank put down his spoon long enough to grab a piece of paper and slide it across his desk to me.

I leaned forward for a better look. "Is that a copy of an—"

"Order of protection." He chomped his muffin and talked while he chewed. "Yup. A good old-fashioned restraining order. Issued two years ago against one Helene McMurty. *Sister* Helene McMurty."

"Let me guess . . ." I didn't want to be right. Maybe that's why my stomach went cold. "The restraining order was requested by Sister Sheila Buckwald."

"None other."

I looked over the paperwork. "Sister Sheila and Sister Helene used to live in the same convent in Chicago? No one bothered to mention that."

"Well, my guess is that Sister Helene doesn't want us to know."

"But she must have known you were going to find out."

Hank shrugged. "Who knows how a murderer thinks."

"Murderer?" The word choked me. "You can't possibly think that Sister Helene—"

"Like I said, who knows." This time, Hank's shrug was more extravagant.

"You talked to the judge who issued the order?" I asked him.

He nodded. "First thing this morning. She remembers the case, all right. Says it's hard not to remember when two nuns are going at each other like lady wrestlers in a Jell-O pit. See, it all happened after they wrote that song of theirs, the one Sister Helene claims was all done by email. Emailing from the same convent? I'm not sure I believe that. Anyway, Sister Sheila, she asked for the order of protection because she said Sister Helene was harassing her. Said Helene was stealing things from her room at the convent, that she stole music Sister Sheila had written, and that she followed Sister Sheila around and harassed her and wouldn't leave her alone."

"Which explains why when Sister Sheila saw her room

at Water's Edge and cried out, 'No! Oh, no!' Sister Helene said it was more of the same."

Hank didn't follow and I guess I couldn't blame him. When it came to theories, I was taking a leap of faith (no pun intended).

"We can't know the truth of it all," I told him. "At least not until you talk to the other parties involved and get the whole story. But to me, it sounds like maybe Sister Sheila was overreacting. Could she have been a little . . . paranoid? A little unhinged? I mean, really, why would Sister Helene need to steal music? She's a trained musician herself and everyone acknowledges the fact that she wrote the music for 'Living Bread' and that it's a beautiful song. She obviously has talent. So maybe what happened at that convent in Chicago, maybe it was a figment of Sister Sheila's imagination. So when Sister Sheila started acting crazy on the ferry and then again when she went to her room facing the water and caused a scene, it was only natural for Sister Helene to say it was—"

"More of the same."

It was my turn to nod. "Or maybe the whole thing is legit," I admitted with a sigh. "Maybe Helene really did have it in for Sheila. Which one of them . . ." I looked over the restraining order again but couldn't easily locate the information I wanted. "And Helene left the convent in Chicago."

"Yup. Moved to some convent in Phoenix and has been there ever since."

"Have any of the nuns there had problems with her?"

"Now you're thinking like a cop!" Hank wagged a finger at me. "Going to call and ask them, but it's a little early in Phoenix."

"You'll let me know?"

"Of course. And you'll—"

"There doesn't seem to be any use in talking to Sister Helene again," I said. "Not until we have all our ducks in a row. Until we have facts to back us up and can challenge her with them, all she has to do is keep lying. If she's lying. And if we find out there's no credence to Sister Sheila's claims, there's no use embarrassing Sister Helene."

"So you've got nobody to talk to today."

I told Hank he was right.

But in my heart, I knew he was wrong and believe me, with every step I took out of the basement police station and into my car, I could feel the inevitability of the situation settling inside me like a lead weight.

See, in all the details of the investigation, and all the sadness that rose in me when I pictured poor Sister Sheila floating facedown in the water, and all the anger I felt when I thought about how someone had knocked her over the head and left her in the lake to die . . .

In all the aggravation that bubbled up when I thought of Chandra lounging on an air mattress in her new pool, sipping a drink while my guests tiptoed around her parsley, sage, rosemary, and thyme . . .

Even with all that, I hadn't forgotten that there was one conversation I couldn't avoid.

It was time.

I headed to Levi's Bar.

"Hey." I swung my purse onto one barstool and hoisted myself up on another, the better to get a good look at Levi when he zipped out of the back room and slid behind the bar, a crate of newly washed glasses in his hands. "We need to talk."

"We do." He set down the crate and with barely a look

at me, started back the way he'd come. "But this isn't a good time."

Relief washed through. This wasn't a good time! I could put off our conversation. I could stall and dodge and delay and—

If not now, when?

How much longer could I live with the block of ice in my stomach when I thought about what I had to do?

"It's got to be now," I said and realized that in the moment I'd thought about it, Levi had hurried back into the kitchen. I slid off the barstool and followed. It was still early, and the bar was empty.

"It's got to be now," I said, meeting him coming back out of the kitchen just as I was about to go in.

"Broken pipe." He had another plastic crate of glasses in his hands and he looked up and over his shoulder back into the kitchen. It was the first I noticed that the tile floor was covered with water and the last drip, drip, drips of it dribbled from a spot in the ceiling that was dark and wet. "Luckily I turned off the water in time, but something's broken in my kitchen upstairs and I've got a major mess on my hands."

It was a mess. Water covered the stainless steel counters where Levi's small but efficient staff prepared salads. It soaked the grill where his cook, a young and eager guy by the name of Dan, took care of the burgers and the chicken sandwiches and the other items on Levi's excellent, but simple, menu.

Three loaves of bread in their plastic wrappers floated by on the couple inches of water on the floor and I snatched them up and tossed them into a trash can.

"You don't have to help," Levi said. "Dan's on his way in and I called a couple of the waitresses. They're going to get here as soon as they can."

"Which might not be soon enough to save much of anything." I waded into the water and told myself that I might as well get to work because there was no use griping after it had already lapped up to my ankles and flowed into my sneakers. There was a squeegee nearby and I grabbed it and raked it over the floor, then grabbed a mop so I could soak up what I'd collected. I wrung the mop out over a bucket Levi had near the grill and made another pass.

In the meantime, Levi took another crate of glasses to the bar. When he returned, he saw that there were a couple bags of hamburger buns out on the counter, and realizing that they were soggy, he sighed and tossed them into the trash. "Really, I can't make you work like this. You're getting all wet and—"

"And you were right. You know, a few months ago when you said that story I told Chandra and Luella and Kate about how I'd been married back in New York to an older guy named Marty and how he died and left me enough money to open up the B and B . . ." I leaned on the long handle of the mop and stopped long enough to take a breath, but let's face it, now that the words had started tumbling out of my mouth—and started easing my conscience—nothing was going to stop me. "What you said then was that you knew the story wasn't true. You were right. That whole story, it was all a lie."

Levi was about to grab a rag and start sopping up the water on the countertops and he froze and turned to me.

"I know it sounds silly," I blurted out. "I mean, the part about how I invented this whole past for myself, but you see, I had to. Or at least at the time, I felt I had to. I was overwhelmed by my life and by everything that was happening to me. There was this stalker back in New York, see—"

"That must have been terrifying." His face was stone, but a muscle tensed at the base of Levi's jaw.

"It was, but I handled it, and the guy's in prison and so it's all taken care of. But that was sort of a wake-up call, see. It made me realize how valuable privacy is and how I was never going to get any. Not with who I am and with what I was doing."

I expected questions and didn't get any, and that was fine by me. I was on a roll, and I kept on going like a Soap Box Derby car on a steep incline.

"That's why I was avoiding you. Or at least why I've been trying to avoid you since I met you last year." I'm not the shy, retiring type, but heat flooded my cheeks. "That didn't really work, did it? I did all the avoiding I could. And I told myself about a million times it wasn't fair to start any sort of relationship with you because I wasn't being honest with you and that . . . well, I don't know about you, but I think that if you can't be honest with somebody, a relationship is pretty much doomed from the start. And I didn't want that with you. I wanted something more. I wanted something good. And I knew if I had to lie to you—"

"Did you lie? To me?"

Finally, a question, and it didn't take me more than a moment to consider it.

"Look, the other night . . ." Even the cold water that covered my feet and tickled my ankles couldn't stop another wave of heat from flashing through me. "Friday night was really great, and I'm not just talking about the sex. I had fun making dinner for you and it felt . . . I dunno . . . I guess it felt *right* sitting in front of the fire with you, sharing a meal. I really, really like you, Levi, and that's why I knew I had to talk to you. So you know what's really going on. And it's not like I'm ashamed of my past or anything, it's just that when I moved here, I wasn't sure how people would react if they knew the truth, and I'd just come off the whole stalker thing, and I just wanted to be me. Just Bea. And I didn't want anybody to have any preconceived notions or any expectations or anything, and I didn't like the thought that anybody would be checking into the B and B just to get a gander at me and maybe pick my brain because that's what usually happened back in New York. Agents and publishers and producers and directors and reporters . . ." Just thinking about it made my heart flutter. And not in a good way.

"Once I told Luella and Kate and Chandra the story about Marty the antique dealer back in New York, well, it just kind of took on a life of its own. And I figured it wouldn't matter because nobody else ever had to know the truth. But of course, I was wrong. Because they need to know the truth."

"You haven't told the League of Literary Ladies?"

I shook my head. "I wanted to tell you first. And when I leave here I'm going to stop and see each one of them and tell them the truth. And I'm sorry I lied, but heck, I didn't know who I was going to meet here on South Bass. I didn't know I was going to make such good friends. And I certainly didn't think I was going to fall in love."

Had I really said that?

I sucked in a breath and stared at Levi, but if he realized the enormity of the words that had just fallen from my lips or the fact that I didn't even know what I was going to say until after I said it, he didn't show it. His face was a mask.

"I'd like to think the truth isn't going to make any difference." I managed to stammer out to cover for my confession. "I'm still me and you're still you, and who we are and what we do now or used to do isn't going to change that.

But I'm sorry about not telling you the whole story from the start. I really am. I just couldn't have known how I'd feel about you or if I could trust you."

Now that the big moment was here, I found myself at a sudden loss for words. I swallowed down the sand in my mouth. "I really am Bea Cartwright," I said. "That part is the truth. But I'm also—"

"FX O'Grady, the famous horror writer."

Levi's words were punctuated by the ping of water dripping from the counter and splashing onto the floor. Or maybe the sound I heard was my clattering heart.

"You knew," I gasped.

"I told you I thought we needed to talk, too." He shifted from one foot to the other with a splash. "See, I kind of had the same sort of scenario going on. I wanted to tell you something, wanted to since the day we met. But I wasn't allowed."

"By your conscience?"

"By my contract."

I had no idea I'd gripped the mop so tight until I looked down and saw that my knuckles were white. "What are you—"

"Jason Arbuckle."

What he said made no sense, and I shook my head to clear it. "Jason Arbuckle is the name of my attorney. Are you telling me—"

"I'm telling you that when you announced to Jason that you were giving up your writing career and moving to the back of beyond, he was pretty surprised. You've been on the bestseller lists for years and you've had movies made from your books. And a couple TV series. There's a musical playing on Broadway based on one of your short stories. And he couldn't believe you were walking away from it all. He's a good attorney, Bea, and a good friend to you. He was worried about you. That's why he contacted me. See . . ." Levi scrubbed his hands over his face.

"After that stalker incident, Jason was more worried than ever about you, and truth be told, he thought you'd gone off the deep end, what with wanting to give up the good life and move to Ohio. We—Jason and I—have a business agreement. I'm just playing at being a bar owner, Bea. I'm really a private detective. Jason hired me to move to the island to keep an eye on you."

⫷ 8 ⫸

Let me make one thing perfectly clear—I am not and never have been a violent person. Sure, the books I wrote under the pen name of FX O'Grady were all about blood and gore and things that go bump—and do worse—in the night.

But those are just fiction. Just figments of an imagination that has been called both brilliant and warped by various and sundry reviewers and critics.

Those stories are not me.

I say all this by way of explaining that what happened there in the flooded kitchen of Levi's Bar once he'd announced that he was a private investigator was not premeditated. Before I ever realized what was happening, and long before I could have stopped myself even if I had, I raised that mop and whacked Levi over the head with the wet, sopping business end of it.

Then I marched out of the bar.

It was a grand exit, sure enough, and would have carried a lot more oomph had I not splish-splashed my way to the door.

A minute later I was in the car and already feeling bad about resorting to physical violence.

But not bad enough to apologize.

Ever.

I started the car and held the steering wheel in a death grip.

While I had spent a year with my conscience eating away at my composure and making it impossible for me to acknowledge my feelings for Levi, he'd spent a year knowing the truth and toying with me anyway.

I thought back to the way he'd kissed me one hot summer night.

And the way that right after, he said it was a mistake.

Now I knew why. I was a job to him, nothing more. I was a gone-off-the-reservation prima donna (at least that's what I imagined Jason Arbuckle had told him) who needed a babysitter.

That little kiss was a mistake?

I could only imagine what Levi thought about what we did on Friday night.

True to my word, I talked to each of the Ladies of the League individually that Monday. They were astounded to find out I was the mysterious author whose picture was never in the back of any of her books, who refused TV interviews, and who avoided movie premieres like the plague.

They were impressed, too, by my literary résumé, and Chandra came right out and said I must be the richest person she'd ever met. I had no doubt she was right. They were amazed that I could give up the condo in New York overlooking Central Park and the glare of fame and the adoration of millions of fans.

And guess what?

Every single one of them—Luella and Kate and even Chandra—said she understood.

"But here's what I don't get."

Just when I was thinking about what had happened earlier in the day and getting all sentimental about the benefits of friendship (especially in light of Levi's betrayal), Chandra pulled me out of my thoughts. All four of us were in my kitchen getting dinner ready for the nuns. Tonight's menu featured ribs that Meg had come in earlier in the day to start roasting as well as fresh broccoli, new potatoes, and a bowl heaped with salad greens and dressed with the most marvelous vinegar, oil, and herb concoction this side of Gramercy Tavern.

"Why write a book if you don't want to be famous?" Chandra asked.

I ripped butter lettuce into bite-size pieces and added it to the bowl where Kate had already mounded diced avocado. "All I ever wanted to do was teach English at a university," I told them. "That's why I decided to get a PhD." Of course that wasn't the whole explanation and I knew they'd never settle for it. I grabbed some red leaf lettuce, pulled apart each leaf, and put that in the bowl, too.

"I was out with a bunch of other grad students one night and we were all moaning about how poor we were," I told them. "I don't know who suggested it, but someone said we should have a contest to see which of us could write a book and get it published and make some money that way."

"No wonder you know so much about literature." Luella

was in charge of dicing carrots, and she tossed a piece into her mouth. "You've got all that schooling."

"Not really," I admitted. "I never finished grad school."

"Because you sold your first book," Kate said.

I nodded. "My other friends, they wrote some really interesting stuff, but let's face it, we were all engrossed with the academic side of things. Studies of manners in Jane Austen novels do not sell. But a spooky story about a vampire king and his minions . . ." Even though I'd had years to get used to the idea, it still struck me as crazy. I shrugged. "The idea just popped into my head one night and so that's what I worked on. It took me almost a year to finish the book, but it found a publisher and it sold pretty quickly and I was offered another contract right away. I quit grad school and never looked back."

"So you're like really somebody." Chandra sighed. "A famous somebody. I wonder if people would pay to come over to my house so they could get a look at you."

I froze, mid-lettuce-tear. "Just because I told the three of you doesn't mean the world has to know." I had, of course, pointed this out to Chandra earlier in the day, but with Chandra it never hurts to reinforce a point. Especially when she's talking about people paying to see me.

"She's here for privacy," Luella reminded her.

"And she told us her secret because she trusts us," Kate said. "If we betray that trust, we betray a friend."

"Well . . ." Chandra glanced away. "I already told Jerry."

Jerry Garcia was her (bad, horrible, terrible) cat. "I'm pretty sure Jerry can keep a secret," I told her.

Chandra looked relieved. At least for a moment. Then her brows (bleached the same color as her hair), fell low over her eyes. "Do you think that's what happened over at Water's Edge? That someone betrayed a friend?"

"You mean Sister Sheila." I gave the salad a final toss and covered the bowl with plastic cling wrap. I shrugged. "It doesn't look like Sheila and Helene were ever friends."

"Or they were." Luella spooned roasted new potatoes into the bowl we'd carry them in. "If they started out as good friends—"

"It would make things uglier when they had a falling-out," Kate said. "Like for instance if Chandra was ever stupid enough to let people know who you are and let them pay to get into her house so they could see you." Leave it to Kate not to mince any words. She added a withering look at Chandra to the statement, just to make sure Chandra got the message. "Just imagine how angry Bea would get, being betrayed like that. And no one could blame her. That's the kind of thing that destroys a friendship. In this case, it would destroy three."

"All right! I get it!" I certainly hoped Chandra did. She put a few dozen of Meg's amazing white chocolate cranberry cookies into a container. But not before she grabbed one and munched it down. "I was only kidding about making people pay to come see Bea. But not about the swimming pool or the streetlamp," she added quickly just as she headed to the door. "The streetlamp and the swimming pool . . . I'm as serious about those as I am about People Against Fishing Lake Erie."

I felt sorry for the nuns, and not just because one of their number had been murdered.

That Monday evening, the weather was still awful and while I had no doubt they were being truthful (could nuns not be?) when they told us how much they'd gotten out of a day of prayer, contemplation, and discussion, I couldn't help but think that the chance to get outside and get some fresh air would have done them all some good, too.

The strain showed most on Sister Gabriel, who was pacing the front hallway when we arrived that evening, barely got down more than a couple bites at dinner, and asked—more than one time in my earshot—about that package of books she was expecting and why it hadn't arrived yet.

The waves that pounded the beach where I'd found Sister Sheila's body should have pretty much told her that.

After dinner, the Sisters insisted on helping with cleanup, but hey, if nothing else, the Ladies of the League could be just as determined as a group of supercharged nuns. We shooed them into the living room for their evening scripture reading and proceeded to pick up, wash up, and clean up. By the time we were done, so were they, and we heard some of them drift upstairs. Sister Helene sat down at the piano in the first-floor library, and the strains of Chopin and Brahms drifted into the kitchen.

"You're distracted." Kate slipped between me and the kitchen island with an armful of rinsed containers that she dumped into a tote bag. "What's wrong? Because I don't think it has anything to do with you telling us your big secret. We're all over it and you know, I think it's really pretty cool, especially if you let me tag along on some trip to Hollywood and meet a few hunky leading men."

I gave Kate a smile and wondered if she knew how close she'd come to the truth with that leading man comment. I pictured Levi in the un-leading-man-like way in which I'd last seen him, his hair sopping and a look on his face that clearly said he'd been bushwhacked.

Much like I'd been when he told me what he was really doing there on South Bass.

"Nothing's wrong," I assured Kate and didn't quite convince myself. "It's just been a long day."

Kate slid a look toward the kitchen door and the rest of the house beyond. "And we've still got suspects to interview."

I shook my head. "We've done all that. It's not getting us anywhere. I feel so . . ." I pulled in a breath and let it out with a sigh that mingled with the sweet notes of the Chopin etude that floated through Water's Edge. "I feel helpless. There's something we don't know. Something we're missing."

"That's why they call it a mystery," Kate told me.

"And that's why there's no use all of us hanging around. Not if there's nothing to accomplish here tonight." I glanced toward Chandra and Luella, who'd just come into the kitchen after putting out dessert. Luella had an early morning meeting down at the marina where she docked her fishing charter boat, so she'd driven to Water's Edge because she thought she might want to leave early. "Why don't you all go home with Luella," I said as if they were following my train of thought and knew what I was talking about. They didn't, so I explained. "It's just dessert plates and coffee cups left to clean up. I can do that."

"You're sure?" I could tell Luella was grateful because she headed right for the door. "Because if you think it's too much trouble to handle by yourself—"

"No trouble." One hand on Kate's shoulder and one hand on Chandra's, I shooed them toward the door where Luella waited. "I'll give it another hour, clean up, and get out of here. What could be simpler?"

They called out their good-nights to the Sisters still on the main floor when they left, and I closed the front door behind my friends. I was just going to go into the kitchen to wait when Sister Catherine waved me into the living room.

"Come sit by the fire!" When I did, she handed me a cup of coffee and a plate with two of the white chocolate cranberry cookies on it. "We came to this retreat to get closer to the Lord," she said and grinned. "If somebody doesn't start sharing this food with us, the only thing we're going to get closer to is needing to attend Weight Watchers' meetings!"

"How are things going?" I asked her.

She patted her stomach. "You mean aside from the extra poundage?" Her smile dimmed. "We're doing all right. Sister Liliosa heard from Sister Sheila's parents today."

I could imagine their grief and it ate at my heart. "Did they offer any help? Had they talked to Sister Sheila? Did they know anything about—"

"Why anyone might want to push her into the lake?"

When my jaw went slack, Sister Catherine laughed. "Nuns gossip. Just like everyone else. And around here . . ." We were alone in the vast living room, but Sister Catherine looked around, past the light thrown by the flickering fire and into the shadows beyond. "Everyone has a theory."

I didn't want to look too eager so I took a bite of cookie and washed it down with a sip of coffee. "Want to share?"

Sister Catherine drew her golden brows down low over her eyes. "Well, I'm not sure Sister Margaret even understands that Sheila's dead," she confided. "I mean, she does. Off and on. Sister Margaret is a real dear and she's done more for the urban and community garden movement than anyone in this country, but she's a little scattered."

"I've noticed."

"And Sister Mary Jean and Sister Paul and Sister Francelle . . . well, from what I've heard, they're all convinced it was an accident. I guess they weren't paying attention to all that stuff we said about Sister Sheila being afraid of the water, huh?"

"You were paying attention."

Sister Catherine took the statement as the compliment it was meant to be. "I thought it was strange right from the start. But then, I saw her on the ferry. I knew how terrified she was."

"And that was the first you'd met her. I mean, except for that dinner in New York?"

"The dinner was the first time most of us met each other."

I felt like I'd been through it a thousand times, but I had to make sure I was right. "Except for Sister Sheila and Sister Helene."

Sister Catherine nodded. "And Sister Gabriel, of course."

I must have looked like Levi did when I whacked him with that mop because Sister Catherine grinned. "You didn't know? About Sister Gabriel?"

I thought about the nun who was so eager for that shipment of books. "I know she's young and that she has about zero patience when it comes to the weather."

"And you should also know that none of us ever met her before we arrived at the ferry to come to the island. She wasn't at the dinner in New York. She was sick that weekend."

I wasn't sure this bit of information was significant, but I tucked it away in my mental notebook.

"Do you suppose that means anything?" Sister Catherine asked before I could decide if it did.

I told her as much. "If anything, it seems to make her even more of an outsider."

"With even less of a motive." Sister Catherine's shoulders drooped. "I can't believe we're even sitting here talking about murder. It's . . ." She shivered.

"Wrong."

"And sad."

"And I'd love to get to the bottom of it."

Sister Catherine's blue eyes shone in the light of the fire. "I thought you might be helping the police."

"Am I that transparent?"

"Hey, I run a shelter for homeless women. A lot of the time, the women who come into Elizabeth's House—named after St. Elizabeth of Hungary—the women who show up on our doorstep aren't usually inclined to share the details of their lives. Over the years, I've learned that I can find out a whole lot by watching and listening. Just like watching the way Sister Sheila acted on the ferry told me she was afraid of the water. And when that policeman came here to talk to us, I saw the way he deferred to you. He let you talk. He let you ask questions. I can't imagine he affords that privilege to many civilians."

"You can say that again!" I finished my coffee and went around the room, picking up the cups and dessert dishes the other nuns had left behind. "If you hear anything—"

"Of course I'll let you know." Sister Catherine moved to the door. "Good night."

Sure that I had all the plates, cups, and saucers, I headed into the kitchen.

And stopped dead in my tracks right inside the door that led in from the dining room.

The back kitchen door flapped in the wind and streams of rain blew in from outside.

"What on earth!" I deposited the dishes on the countertop and took the chance of getting wet (I did) so I could race over and put my shoulder to the door to shut it.

I tossed my head to cast off the raindrops that had settled there, turned around, and—

"Oh!" Sister Gabriel was right behind me.

"Sorry." She didn't look especially contrite. Or at least not as contrite as a nun should look when she's being contrite. She leaned a bit to her right to see the door behind me. "I just thought I'd—"

"Go outside?" It sounded crazy until I saw the pack of cigarettes in her hand.

She had the good sense to blush. "Even nuns have bad habits," she said.

"Bad habits." I laughed. "That's a good one."

It actually took a moment for Sister Gabriel to get it. Her smile was light and quick. "Were you leaving?" she asked me.

"I will be in a minute. As soon as I get the last of the dishes cleaned up."

"But you were shutting the door."

"Oh, that." I hurried to the sink and ran the water so I could rinse the dessert dishes. "I wasn't going anywhere. I walked in here and the door had blown open."

"Blown open." Sister Gabriel's voice was hollow, and I looked away from the dishes and over my shoulder at her and saw that her face was so pale, her freckles looked as if they'd been drawn on, careful dot by careful dot.

"I locked it," I assured her, getting back to work and rinsing the dishes. "I guess that just shows you how really strong a spring storm can be. At least it's not cold." I let the water out of the sink, rinsed my hands, and grabbed a towel to dry them before I turned to Sister Gabriel. "Why, last year at this time—"

The Sister was gone.

"So much for discussing the weather," I grumbled to myself and gathered up my jacket.

It was the first time I noticed something curious. The door

I'd found open was directly opposite the one that led into the dining room. That meant when I'd come into the room . . .

Thinking about it, I walked through the scenario again, going to the dining room door and from there, over to where I'd slammed the back door against the storm.

The threshold near the door was soaked, and that wasn't a surprise. The wind was fierce and my damp hair proved it; the rain was blowing directly this way.

But that didn't account for . . .

Just to be sure, I tipped my head and turned on the lights over the kitchen island.

"Wet near the doorway," I confirmed to myself. "And my shoes were certainly dry when I came into the kitchen."

No way that accounted for the wet footprints that glimmered in the light.

There were two of them and I bent down for a closer look. The footprints weren't small, like a woman's definitely would be. Or large, like you'd expect from a man. But then, they weren't well defined, either, just watery imprints that showed me that whoever had come and gone had probably done it quickly. Two steps away from the door and another footprint leading back to it and outside.

"You left in a hurry when you heard me coming," I mumbled, glancing at the door and the darkness beyond, almost afraid of who I might find looking back at me. Rain pelted my reflection. "Who are you? And what . . ." A chill snaked up my back. "What were you doing here?"

❖ 9 ❖

When I opened my eyes on Tuesday morning and realized that the sun was shining, my mood soared.

At least for a split second.

Until I remembered Levi.

And Sister Sheila.

And those mysterious wet footprints inside the kitchen door at Water's Edge.

Never let it be said, though, that I am not a trouper. And a mighty stubborn one at that.

Though thoughts of Levi and Sheila and those footprints took turns rolling through my head, I refused to let any of them upend me. I threw myself into the day, reveling in the sunlight and, now that the winds had calmed and the waves were behaving, the silence.

Meg had offered to make quiche for my guests' breakfast and while she was at it, she made a couple for the nuns, too, and delivered them, to boot, along with the sandwich platters that would be lunch at Water's Edge. That meant I had the luxury of moving slowly that morning, catching up on paperwork, placing orders for some specialty foods from the mainland, goofing around on the Internet, and pretty much accomplishing nothing, since every time I tried to concentrate on an article or some silly quiz that promised to tell me what my old lady name should be or what color my aura was, I found my thoughts back on the misery treadmill: mysterious footprints, Sister Sheila, Levi.

By the time I had breakfast ready to serve at nine, I needed a major distraction and I found it by joining my guests in the dining room. Joe Roscoe would be staying for only a couple more days, and the librarians were leaving the next morning, so I did my best to leave them with a good impression, both of Bea & Bees and its owner.

The quiches (one bacon and cheese, one mushroom and spinach, and one traditional for the purists with nothing but onions, eggs, and Gruyere cheese) had just made their way around the dining room table for the first time when there was a knock on the front door and Marianne Little-john poked her head into the house.

I waved her into the dining room, pulled out a chair for her, and went into the kitchen for an extra plate and cup.

"You don't need to feed me," she twittered at the same time she took one piece of bacon-and-cheese quiche and another of spinach and mushroom. "I really just stopped by because . . ." She glanced at her librarian friends and Mari-anne's plump cheeks turned pink. "Well, we were talking last night at dinner—"

"And we know we're not professionals or anything. I mean, not like you," Angela put in.

"But all anybody here on the island can talk about is that nun who died," Carole said.

"And like I told Joe the other day . . ." Joe Roscoe was so busy chomping down his third piece of quiche, he didn't spare me a look, but I glanced his way anyway, just to include him in the conversation. "I'm hardly a professional."

"Hah!" This from Marianne, and I wouldn't have minded so much if she was just gossiping in front of her friends, but I'd already denied my detective tendencies to Joe and I hated to look like I'd lied. "She looks innocent enough," Marianne said in a stage whisper, pointing her fork in my direction so her friends couldn't fail to miss who she was talking about. "But there's more to Bea Cartwright than meets the eye."

I tensed, my fingers clutching the edge of the table, and prayed Chandra hadn't blabbered the secret I'd shared with my friends the day before and activated South Bass's version of the bush telegraph.

"She'd give Sherlock Holmes a run for his money," Marianne said, and I let go of a breath I hadn't realized I was holding. Looking like a liar in Joe's eyes was preferable to looking like what I really was, a bestselling author whose privacy would be ruined if word got out that she was living on the island. "She solves murders."

I glanced at Joe, who was chewing on a slice of apple.

"I only helped out the police a little," I said, my hands out, palms flat, to distance myself from the assertion. "It was nothing."

"There's no use denying it." Marianne waved away my explanation. "I told them all about it last night. Told them all about everything. That poor man who owned the Chinese restaurant who was killed there, and Richie, the handyman who used to help everyone out around here, and—"

"Like I said, it was nothing."

"Well, your nothing got us talking." The comment came from Bette, who of all four of the librarians struck me as the quietest and the most studious. She adjusted her wire-rimmed glasses on the bridge of her nose. "Marianne said you read Agatha Christie—"

"And that's when there was a murder at the Orient Express restaurant," Carole finished for her.

"And then you read Dickens and there was that whole crazy thing at the Bastille Day celebration." Remembering it made Marianne shiver.

"And then we hear you read Washington Irving's *The Legend of Sleepy Hollow* and Marianne told us"—Carole sucked in a breath of excitement—"you know, all about the ghost."

"Ghosts? Here on South Bass?" For the first time, Joe Roscoe looked up from his breakfast plate. "Any I'm related to?"

I doubted it, but I was grateful for the interruption and the change of subject, so I took his comment and ran with it. "I don't know if you've had a chance to meet Marianne Littlejohn yet," I told Joe and formally introduced them. "She's our island librarian and I'm sure she can help when it comes to genealogy. She's lived on the island all her life, haven't you, Marianne? If anyone knows anything about Joe's family—"

"Roscoe." Marianne tapped a finger against her cheek. "The name doesn't ring a bell. Where did they live?"

Since Joe had just stuffed his mouth with a huge chunk of quiche, he held up one finger to tell her to wait. He swallowed and took a drink of coffee. "Hard to say for sure.

They've been gone for close to one hundred years now. I've got some ideas and some leads, but nothing definite yet."

"Well, I'm sure we can find them. Plenty of people come here to do genealogy research. I'll check my files when I get to the library later. Maybe there's some family I've helped with research that's related to your family. That wouldn't be a surprise, would it? On an island this small, we're bound to find connections."

"Well, that would be just terrific." Joe pushed back from the table. "I'll stop into the library later and we can compare notes. For now . . ." He glanced toward the front windows and the sunshine that streamed over my lawn. "This weather is too good to be true. I've got to take advantage of it. If you ladies will excuse me, I'm going out to do a little exploring."

He was upstairs in a minute and back downstairs in another, that tube of maps of his under his arm, and he waved to us when he passed the dining room door and went outside.

"Nice man," Angela said.

"But we're not supposed to be talking genealogy, are we?" Joyce, the fourth librarian (well, I guess she was actually the fifth if I counted Marianne), leaned forward and lowered her voice. "We decided last night, ladies. About what we wanted to talk to Bea about today. Books. Books and m-u-r-d-e-r."

"Except no one's been murdered." I sounded as if this were actually true and congratulated myself. "And the League of Literary Ladies is steering away from any and all crime fiction. Like I told you, we're reading *The Mill on the Floss*. In fact, we were supposed to have our discussion meeting last night and we pushed it back to tomorrow afternoon because we were busy with the nuns. *The Mill on the Floss*. George Eliot. No murders."

"Of course there are no murders. That's because you're reading the wrong book."

When she announced this, Marianne was apparently ready for my look of astonishment. Her eyes glowing with excitement, she reached into her purse, brought out a paperback book, and slapped it on the table.

I had to lean to my right to see the title clearly.

And Then There Were None—I knew it was one of the most famous mystery novels of all time and like everyone else with half an ounce of interest in fine storytelling and an appreciation for a deucedly clever plot, I was familiar with the book and the movies based on it. Many readers considered it Agatha Christie's greatest masterpiece.

"We're not reading that," I said, and backed away as if somehow, that would protect me from remembering that in the book, ten strangers are called to an island where they are then murdered, one by one. "And no one's been murdered."

"Maybe not," Carole conceded. "But when Marianne told us about all the other murder investigations you've been involved in—"

"And then we heard that there were ten nuns," Bette said.

"It's only natural we thought of the book," Angela added.

"Especially since one of the nuns is already dead." Joyce clutched her hands to her heart.

"Well, nobody else is going to die. Not like in the book." There was no way I could be sure. There was no way anyone could be. But I wasn't taking any chances so I put as much distance as possible between myself and *And Then There Were None*. My voice rang with certainty and I scraped my chair back from the table. I couldn't stand the thought that a pall hung over Water's Edge and the wonderful ladies who were spending the week there. I guess that's why I was so intent on convincing the librarians—and myself—that the very idea was ridiculous.

My imagination barely in check, I cleaned up Joe's breakfast dishes and took them out to the kitchen, leaving the librarians to discuss their preposterous theory among themselves. Just as I pushed through the kitchen door, I reminded them, "There were nine nuns there when I left Water's Edge last night and I guarantee you, there are nine nuns there now. Nobody's going anywhere."

"There's no sign of her."

"And we've looked all over."

"It's like she's vanished."

"Disappeared." A click of the fingers. "Just like that."

Inside the front door of Water's Edge, I paused—tote bags in hand containing the burgers and hot dogs we would be grilling for dinner out on the patio now that the weather had cleared—and looked around in bewilderment at the nuns who surrounded me the moment I set foot in the house.

Their voices, tight with unspoken hysteria, overlapped. Their expressions were mixed with so much hope and despair and confusion that instantly, my heart started a rumba rhythm in my chest.

I took a deep breath and did what I imagined a thousand other people had done over the years when searching for a safe port in a storm.

I turned to Sister Liliosa.

She, it should be noted, had not been among those who surrounded me like flies at a picnic. Oh no, not Sister Liliosa! She had remained on the edges of the crowd of sisterly worrywarts and at my look, she raised her chin, clutched her hands at her waist, and stepped forward.

The crowd parted in front of her like the Red Sea when Moses showed up, and Sister Liliosa took full advantage. One glance from her and the nuns held their collective breaths.

"It's Sister Helene," she said quite simply. "We can't seem to locate her."

It took a moment for this news to settle inside my brain and no time at all for it to jump to conclusions.

Sister Helene.

The one Sister Sheila had a beef with.

The one Sister Sheila had taken out a restraining order against.

The one Sister who of all these Sisters had something to gain from Sister Sheila's death.

The only one who had a motive for murder.

Gone.

I resisted the urge to grab my phone and call Hank, but only because I didn't want the nuns to panic, or for Hank to realize I was really a rank amateur hiding behind a few clever deductions and a couple lucky guesses. I needed to keep my head and gather more facts before I got the police involved.

I kept my gaze on Sister Liliosa. "Tell me."

She was a woman who appreciated conciseness. She nodded. "Helene didn't join us for lunch this afternoon."

"And I doubt she misses many meals," Sister Francelle mumbled and an instant later when she realized she'd spoken aloud, she went pale.

"Before we get carried away . . ." It was probably too late for that, but I knew I had to try to calm down the Sisters. I broke loose from the group and marched into the kitchen, the nuns behind me in a line like so many ducklings. I unpacked the tote bags and set burgers and hot dogs and buns and potato salad out on the counter before I ever said another word, and when I was done, I looked from nun to nun—Sisters Francelle, Liliosa, Paul, Grace, and Mary Jean.

"Let's not get ahead of ourselves. When I left here last night, Sister Helene was in the library playing the piano. And this morning, you say she was at breakfast?"

A couple of the nuns nodded.

"Did she say anything either last night or this morning?" I asked. "About going out today?"

"I talked to her before I went up to my room to read last night," Sister Mary Jean reported. "We both said we hoped the weather would be better today and she said if it was, it would be a blessing to go outside and get a breath of air."

"Well, see, there you have it." I wished all mysteries could be solved so easily and every nun I had the audacity to even think might be a killer could be so easily cleared of suspicion. "Sister Helene left after breakfast and she went for a walk."

Sister Grace sniffed. "She missed midmorning prayer."

"And Sister Francelle's presentation on ethical corporate practices," Sister Mary Jean added. "Yesterday she told me she was looking forward to it."

"And there's a golf cart missing."

Sister Grace's comment caught us all off guard. As one, we turned to her and she shrugged. "Hey, when you work in prisons like I do, you sometimes think the worst of people before you can stop yourself. It's a failing I'm trying to overcome, but not always one I can resist. When someone said Helene had gone AWOL, I naturally checked out front. I'm not saying it's good news or bad news or that it means anything. I'm just reporting the facts. One of the golf carts is gone."

But it wasn't as simple as that, was it?

I edged into the conversation gently, careful not to ask any leading questions. "What do you mean, Sister? About thinking the worst of someone? Just because Sister Helene took out one of the golf carts—"

"Oh, come on!" Sister Grace included all of us in her grimace. "We need to stop pussyfooting around and say what's been on all of our minds. When you do what I do and you're around murderers all day, you sort of get a feel for these things. The evil, it's in the air like a vibe. You can't see it. You can't hear it. But you can feel it. It crawls along your skin and ruffles the back of your hair."

I don't think I was imagining it, we all twitched at the thought.

"The way that cop who was here was asking questions," Sister Grace said, "I pretty much figured it out from the start. Sister Sheila's death was no accident, was it? She was murdered."

I couldn't lie. Not even when a couple of the nuns gasped in horror and a couple more went pale. Not when all of them turned their collective gaze my way. "You're right, Sister. The police have determined that Sister Sheila was murdered," I told them. "She was stunned by a blow to the back of the head and shoved into the water. I'm sorry, I couldn't say anything sooner. The police asked me not to."

One by one, they bowed their heads in prayer and I joined them in the moment of silence.

It was broken by Sister Grace. "Maybe if the police had told us the truth from the start, we would have kept a closer eye on Sister Helene," she said.

Sister Liliosa's lips thinned. "You can't possibly think—"

"They knew each other," Sister Grace pointed out. "They didn't like each other. I'm not saying that means Helene is guilty, only that it's a possibility."

"A possibility we can't eliminate," I told them, "but not one we can be sure of, either. I'll call Hank and let him know that Helene is missing. Until then—"

I was about to suggest we search Water's Edge just in case Helene was still around the house, but I didn't have a chance. The kitchen door popped open and Sister Gabriel practically skipped into the room.

"Where is it?" she asked, and when her question was met with blank stares, she rolled her eyes. "My package. Catherine said my package was delivered a little while ago."

"Yes, it was," Sister Liliosa told her. She led the way out of the kitchen and we all followed along. "The delivery man left it right—" Sister Liliosa pointed to a table just inside the front door, a table that was empty.

"Well, it was here," Sister Liliosa said. "I saw him leave it."

"What d'you mean, 'was'?" Sister Gabriel's face looked especially red against her white wimple. "Are you telling me you lost my package? That someone took my package?"

"I'm telling you it was here and now it isn't." Sister Liliosa's voice was stone cold. "I'm sure if you ask around, you'll find out that someone was nice enough to leave it at your seat in the dining room or take it up to your room for you."

"Yeah, my room." Sister Gabriel lifted her skirt and raced for the stairs. "That's got to be it."

We heard her throw open her door and the clatter of her footsteps against the floor. We heard the word she barked out when she didn't find the package, too, and it was one that made a couple of the nuns' mouths drop open.

"A missing nun and a missing package." I wondered at the connection, if there was one, and thought about my original plan. "We've got a while before dinner. Why don't we each take part of the house and look around. Maybe Sister Helene came back and maybe she . . ." I had no idea what she might have done, but I played with the possibilities. "Maybe she fell out in the garden and got hurt. Or maybe she's asleep in the library. Before I call Hank, let's at least try to find her."

I didn't have to say it twice. The nuns scattered in all directions, some going outside and others heading to the far reaches of the house. Me, I went up to the second floor, but since Sister Liliosa was already up there making an efficient sweep, room to room, I knew she didn't need my help. Instead, I followed the corridor past the bedroom suites to the far end of the house where I found what must have been the servants' stairway in times gone by.

The door squeaked on rusty hinges, but I could see that someone had been this way, and recently. The dust on the stairway was smudged.

Careful not to step on them and disturb them any further, I followed the footsteps to the third floor and briefly looked into the empty rooms that once must have housed an army of household staff. There was another squeaky door here, and I tried the light switch at the bottom of the stairs.

Nothing.

I got my phone out of my pocket, turned on my flashlight app, and headed upstairs, again following the footprints in the dust.

The attic of Water's Edge was as big as a ballroom, an unending cavern of exposed timbers, screechy wood flooring, and bits and pieces of discarded household life. A wind-up Victrola, a dressmaker's dummy that startled me, a dresser, a chair, a few steamer trunks. My light didn't penetrate more than a few feet in front of me, making the objects look like crouching shadows, and I made my way toward them through a shimmer of floating dust motes. After I determined that I was alone, I trained the light on the floor and followed the smudges to a corner near the front windows where an old rocking chair sat next to a steamer trunk coated with so much dust, I knew it hadn't been disturbed in years.

There was a blanket tossed over the chair, and I yanked it away and coughed when a Vesuvius of dust clutched at my throat and stung my eyes, then bent closer to see the curious items that had been tucked beneath the blanket.

These were not old; they were clean, new, set on the chair as if someone wanted to be able to get at them quickly, and covered with the blanket to keep them from prying eyes.

A pair of jeans.

A black leather jacket.

A pair of Nikes.

And a box of hair color the Clairol folks called Dark Caramel Brown.

❖ 10 ❖

The last person I expected to show up with Hank was Levi.

I guess that would explain why I stopped dead halfway to the top of the stairway where I'd thought to welcome Hank and, instead, watched—sucker-punched and speechless—as he and Levi climbed the stairs into the Water's Edge attic.

"Thought Levi might be able to help." Hank's clipped explanation went along with the look he tossed over his shoulder at Levi, who was decidedly dryer than when I saw him last—and in worn jeans and a black-and-white short-sleeved shirt unbuttoned over a black T-shirt, every bit as delicious looking as I remembered.

I whacked the thought out of my head.

Delicious is as delicious does, and this Mr. Delicious had done me wrong. There was no way I was going to forget it, and there was no way I was going to let him forget that I wasn't going to forget it.

I set my shoulders and raised my chin. "I didn't know we needed help."

Hank's shrug was barely discernable in the gathering gloom. There was only one window in this part of the attic and it faced the back of the house. Through it, I saw the sun slip below the horizon in a fiery ball of Halloween jack-o'-lantern orange and on land, the sweep of flashlights as the other police officers Hank had brought along looked around the garden for any sign of Sister Helene. Hank, too, had a flashlight with him, and he turned it on and arced the beam all around. "Looks like nobody's been up here for about fifty years."

"That part of the attic, yes." I waved toward the expanse to my right where his shaft of light barely penetrated the inky shadows. "I looked around over there after I called you. There's no sign that anyone's been there. But over this way . . ." I led Hank to the chair and steamer trunk, sidling between him and Levi without so much as a glance at the man who had once been the man of my dreams.

And I'm not talking about Hank.

"You'll notice the footprints in the dust," I said, training my light—and my thoughts—that way. "Those . . ." I used the light to point them out. "Those are mine. You can tell because I've got boots on and they've got a little heel." I lifted one foot so Hank could see my boots were a match to the marks on the floor. "See, you can see the imprint of the sole of my shoe and the imprint of the heel. These other footprints . . ." I turned my light on them. "See how wide and flat they are? I'd say the person who made them was wearing sneakers or some other flat shoe."

"Probably." Hank took a closer look. "And they lead . . ."

"Right over here to this chair." When I called Hank and asked him to stop over at Water's Edge as soon as he could, I'd told him what I'd found, but even so, I backed up and let him have a look at the scene. I'd replaced the blanket so everything was exactly as I'd found it and I kept my eyes on him when he looked things over, even though I could feel Levi's gaze on me. It prickled over my neck and slid down my black sweater and back up again, landing on my face and staying there.

All the more reason for me to remain stone-faced and silent.

Hank pulled back the blanket from the chair, coughed, and waved away a cloud of dust. "Pants, jacket, shoes, hair color. They all look new."

"Exactly what I thought."

"Someone could have left that stuff here before the nuns arrived."

The comment came from Levi, and though I refused to spare him a look, I couldn't let it go by without a response. Especially since it was so far off base.

"The only other people who've been here since the retreat center opened were a group of rabbis, all men, and some Buddhist monks. Also all men if what Elias told me before the nuns got here is true." I aimed the comment at Hank and Hank only. "He said he was looking forward to having women in the house because he was anxious to get a feminine perspective on the renovations. I know what you're going to say." I held up a hand, not sure if I was telling Hank or Levi to put a sock in it, but knowing one of them was sure to speak up. "Elias could have easily left this stuff up here. But he has his own suite down on the second floor. If he needed clothing or hair color, why would he bring it up here?"

"He could have been hiding it from someone," Levi ventured.

"He lives alone," I countered.

"He might have been trying to surprise someone."

"Really?" For the first time, I dared a look at the man who'd been my lover such a short time before. As always, there was an invisible electrical current that ran between me and Levi. In the past, it had always crackled with unspoken attraction. That evening, it was more of the electric fence variety and it said *Keep Out* better than any sign.

Which was fine by me.

"That's kind of a stretch," I growled.

Levi set his mouth in a thin line.

I turned away and watched Hank poke through the items on the chair.

"You think one of the nuns left this stuff up here." Hank glanced at me over his shoulder. "Why?"

"It's a disguise, of course." Levi answered before I could. "Maybe that missing nun, that Sister . . ."

"Helene." My clenched teeth bit the name in half.

"Helene," Levi conceded. "If she killed Sister Sheila—"

I threw my hands in the air. "You told me not to tell anyone about the murder, Hank. Looks like you've been spreading the news yourself."

Hank stood up straight and cast an eagle-eyed glance from me to Levi. "You two want to tell me what's going on?"

I crossed my arms over my chest.

Levi stepped back, his weight against one foot.

Hank sucked on his bottom lip. "All right, then, you want to pretend everything is hunky-dory, that's what we'll do. But next time you two are in the same room together, remind me to bring a parka." His piece said and our reception to it colder than ever, Hank turned back to his work.

"Levi could be right," he said. "If this nun, Helene, is our murderer, she might have wanted to slip off the island and not let anybody know. A disguise would be just the thing."

"It would be. But not in this case." I picked up the box of hair color. "Dark Caramel Brown makes perfect sense. Sister Helene has silver hair and the dark dye would have covered that. But the clothes—"

"Nobody would look for a nun to be wearing jeans and a leather jacket," Levi cut in.

Aggravation bristled up my spine and shivered along my shoulders. I set my jaw. "Nobody would look for a nun to be wearing jeans and a leather jacket if the nun didn't dress in street clothes," I told him. "If you were paying attention to the nuns downstairs, you would have noticed that some of them wear traditional habits and some dress just like the rest of us. Sister Helene doesn't wear a habit."

Hank cocked his head. "Which means—"

"That she wouldn't need to not look like a nun because she already doesn't look like a nun."

"Well, that explains it," Levi grumbled.

And darned if I was going to ask what *that* was and what it explained.

Luckily, I didn't have to. Hank did that for me.

"Sent Levi over to the ferry dock," he said. "You know, to talk to Jayce."

"To ask if he'd seen a nun leaving for the mainland, now that the ferry is operating again."

It wasn't a question, but Levi nodded. "He said he hadn't."

It was on the tip of my tongue to point out that only men would make such a quick judgment without considering the fashion implications. Instead, I kept my voice level, even if my words did sting with unspoken criticism. "Because Jayce was thinking of a nun in traditional dress. No way he would have identified Sister Helene as a nun. She wore—"

The thought bounced around in my head and stopped so abruptly, it took my words with it. I stepped closer to the cache of clothing. "She wouldn't fit into these," I said, lifting the jeans so I could check them out. "Sister Helene probably wears a size twelve or a fourteen. These are eights."

"Which doesn't tell us anything about Helene McMurty, but does tell us these clothes aren't from our missing nun." Hank took the jeans out of my hands and checked the pockets and when he came up empty, he tossed the jeans back on the chair. "Maybe none of it means squat. Maybe—"

Whatever else Hank had to say, he was interrupted when someone called to him from the bottom of the stairs. "We've been through the whole house, Chief. No sign of her."

Hank grunted. "Missing nun. Dead nun. Clothes that don't belong to anyone." He stomped down the stairs. "I'd like to know what's going on around here."

Since I did, too, I started to follow him and would have made it if Levi hadn't put a hand on my arm.

I yanked my arm away.

"We need to talk," he said.

"We've already done that." As far as I was concerned, that was the end of it. I spun around and honestly, nothing on earth would have stopped me from going right downstairs.

Except when Levi said, "Bea," there was a catch of emotion in his voice. One I was powerless to resist.

I told myself not to be a fool and just for good measure, reminded myself not to forget it, and it was only after I was sure I wouldn't that I allowed myself to turn around.

"I didn't know what was going to happen. Not when I first talked to Jason back in New York and took the job,"

Levi said. "I only knew you by reputation. Famous author. Big star. Huge celebrity."

"I doubt the way to any woman's heart is to call her huge."

His smile came and went. Or maybe now that Hank and his flashlight were gone and the only light in the attic was from my phone, I was imagining the softening of his expression.

I wasn't imagining the voice inside my head that told me to keep mine poker-faced.

"Have you talked to Jason recently?" I asked Levi.

"You mean—"

"I mean since I fired him this afternoon." I will admit, the momentary look of surprise that crossed Levi's face was mighty satisfying. "It's too bad for him, really," I went on, "because that man's made millions thanks to me. Apartment in the city, house in the Hamptons, college for his kids. He didn't take the news well, but hey, I did my best to explain. You know, about how I don't take kindly to lies and betrayal."

It all sounded nice and tough. Just the way I wanted it to. But I knew I couldn't keep up the facade for long. Before Levi could detect any chink in my armor, I hurried down the steps and I never looked back.

I was moving so fast, I nearly rammed into Hank and the other police officer who were talking quietly at the bottom of the stairway.

"In a hurry?" Hank looked past me and up the stairs, but I guess Levi was as smart as I always thought he was because there was no sign of him. Hank dismissed the other cop with a nod. "Want to tell me what's going on?"

"Nothing's going on." I stepped around him and started down the hallway.

"You're not jealous, are you?" Hank asked. "I mean, because I brought someone else in on the investigation?"

The idea was so preposterous, I stopped and spun toward Hank. "What, you think I want to be the only amateur detective on the island?"

"Except he's not an amateur, is he?"

The full realization of what Hank said slammed into me like a freight train. I sucked in a breath and pressed a hand to my heart. "You know. About Levi. About how he's a—"

"PI. Sure." Hank nodded. "He came and told me. You know, as a professional courtesy. Right after he moved here to South Bass."

My breath caught behind a ball of outrage in my throat. For a year, I'd protected what I thought was an important and personal secret. Apparently, I shouldn't have bothered.

I tossed my hands in the air. "What, I should just take out a billboard over on the mainland? Maybe that would save us all a whole lot of time."

Hank shook his head. "I have no idea what you're talking about."

"I'm talking about you. About you and Levi and how you knew all along that he was sent here to—" I bit back the rest of what I was going to say, but only because I didn't know who might be behind the closed doors of the nuns' rooms. Sure, Water's Edge was built like a fortress, but I'd been talking pretty loud. No, actually, I'd been yelling. They all thought I was a prima donna? Well, maybe it was time I started acting like one. "Why didn't you tell me what he was up to?"

"Why would I?" Hank was so nonchalant about it, I could have screamed. "Besides, I couldn't say anything. Not without betraying a confidence."

I know for a fact that it is unladylike, not to mention uncultured, to snort. Like I could help myself?

"Betraying confidences seems to be the least of our worries."

"Well, I haven't. Not for a year," Hank said. "And I'm not going to start now. I mentioned that Levi was a PI because he told me that you knew. Otherwise, I never would have said a thing. As for what he's doing here on South Bass, if you know, you're one step ahead of me."

I darted a look over Hank's shoulder, but there was still no sign of Levi. "You mean you don't—"

"Know why he came here in the first place? I don't have a clue. He wouldn't tell me and as long as it's nothing illegal, I didn't pry. I do know he's helped me out with a little research now and again. You know, when Peter Chan died and again when ol' Richie Monroe was poisoned. But both times, you beat us both to the punch. Imagine," he chucked, "an innkeeper outsmarting two professionals."

An innkeeper.

I took comfort in the fact that to Hank, that's all that I was.

"I can tell him to back off," Hank offered.

"You can tell him—" Oh, it's not like I didn't know exactly what I wanted to say, it was just that the door of Sister Catherine's room opened and I bit back my words. "Do whatever you want," I told Hank and added a flip of my hands to emphasize the point.

"Uh, Bea . . ." Sister Catherine stepped out into the hallway and motioned to me. She glanced back into her room. "Can I speak to you for a minute?"

My heart pounded like the bass line in a heavy metal song, and I gulped down a breath to try to steady it and followed Sister Catherine into her room.

"I hope I'm not being a Nosey Norah." There was a single lamp lit on the table next to the desk, and in the light, Sister

Catherine's short gray habit looked as ghostly as Sister Sheila's had the night I found her in the water. "I really don't need anything. I thought . . . I thought maybe you needed an excuse to get away from that policeman."

I cringed and tossed my phone down on the desk near the wall-to-wall windows that had bothered Sister Sheila so much. Then I flopped into the nearest chair. "Sorry. I should have lowered my voice. I shouldn't have let my emotions run away with me."

"No worries!" She grinned. "And it's not like I don't think you can hold your own, it's just that—"

Her cell phone was on the desk, too, and it rang a celestial tone. Had I been in a better mood I wouldn't have thought, *Doesn't it figure.*

"Excuse me," Catherine said and answered the call.

The minute she did, her expression brightened. "Gram! It's so good to hear from you. How are you feeling?"

She paused to listen to the response on the other end of the phone, but only for a moment.

"No, it doesn't matter what I'm up to. You're what matters, and I asked first."

Catherine smiled over at me in a way that told me she was used to being indulgent to the person at the other end of the phone, and that she didn't mind it one bit.

"I've got plenty to tell you," she said. "But not tonight. You sound tired. Why don't I give you a call tomorrow afternoon after your doctor appointment. Will that work?"

She said her good-night and ended the call.

"Sorry." Sister Catherine set the phone back on the desk. "That was my grandmother."

"She's not well?" The moment I asked, heat rushed into my cheeks. "Now I'm being a Nosey Norah."

"No, really. You're not." She laughed. "It's nice of you to

be concerned. My Gram . . ." Sister Catherine cleared her throat. "Our parents died in a plane crash when we were kids," she said. "Gram raised me and my brother, Michael. We've always been really close. And now . . ." With her right hand, she made a quick sign of the cross over her forehead and chest. "I pray for her recovery, but right now, Gram's not doing well. Lymphoma." The very word made her wince. "We're trying to keep a positive attitude."

"That's all anyone can do." I got up, and figuring Hank had gone downstairs and that hopefully, Levi had, too, I moved to the door.

"And pray." Sister Catherine opened the door for me and let me step out into the hallway ahead of her. She was already out there when I realized I'd left my phone behind.

I ducked back into the room and I was just going to make a grab for the phone when something out in the garden caught my eye.

Not the cops. They'd brought flashlights with them and this figure moved through the dark.

I leaned closer to the window for a better look, but it was no use. The only thing I could see was a shape that was darker than the shadows as it looked up to the window where I stood then took off running.

≪ 11 ≫

What with seeing Levi again, having no choice but to fire the longtime attorney who I thought was also a personal friend, and wondering not only what on earth had happened to Sister Helene, but who (or what) I might have seen lurking in the garden at Water's Edge, it had been a long—and not a very good—day. All I wanted to do when I got back to the B and B that Tuesday night was grab a glass of wine and put up my feet. I would have done it, too, if I hadn't walked in the back door, gone into my suite to find my slippers, come back out, and—

"Mr. Stevens!" At the sight of Tyler Stevens in my parlor, I clutched my bunny slippers to my chest and jumped back at the same time he jumped off the couch.

"I'm so sorry. I didn't mean to startle you." He flushed a color that he, no doubt, would have compared to the crimson of a cardinal's wings. "I got here a little while ago and there was no one around. I waited on the front porch for a while, but there was this cat . . ."

His lips puckered and his gaze trailed toward the window and the porch beyond and even before he added, "I'm allergic and besides, that cat didn't seem very friendly," I knew he'd had an encounter with Jerry Garcia.

I looked toward the front porch, too, but there was no sign of the felonious feline out there now. "He lives next door," I explained to Tyler. "And he doesn't have any business over here."

"Exactly what I thought. Because you have great eaves, you know." Again, he glanced out the window and up, looking toward the porch ceiling and the gingerbread woodwork that edged it. "Perfect for nesting birds. If there's a cat around . . . well, the consequences could be ugly."

To tell the truth, I was more worried about Jerry peeing in my potted flowers.

"I shooed him away," Tyler reported. "But I came inside, anyway. I didn't think you'd mind."

"Not at all. But—"

"But what am I doing here?" Tyler grinned. "Warblers. It's always the warblers, isn't it?"

Apparently it was, but since he already knew that, it seemed a waste of time to point it out.

His smile disappeared. "There wasn't a one to be seen in Sandusky. But of course, the weather was dreadful, so I guess that's to be expected. Then this morning when it cleared, I thought I'd have better luck. Not so. I took a whole week off from work so I thought I should at least make the effort to make the time productive. This afternoon, I was checking one of the Internet sites that lists sightings, and lo and behold, someone here on the island just reported a

Geothlypis formosa, a Kentucky warbler! I caught the first ferry I could and if you still have my room open—"

"I do, and you paid me more than you owed me when you left so that's no problem."

Tyler rubbed his hands together. "Perfect! If breakfast is a problem tomorrow—"

"It isn't," I assured him. "I have other guests," I added, then went to get him a key.

Tyler marched upstairs just as the whole troupe of librarians was coming down. They lined up in front of me just as I slid my feet into my bunny slippers.

"Go ahead!" When she poked Angela in the ribs with one elbow, Marianne's smile was mischievous. "Ask her. I know this lady. I'm telling you, she won't mind."

I looked from librarian to librarian. "What am I supposed to mind?"

"Well, we hope you don't." Joyce stepped forward. "You see—"

"We were wondering," Carole said.

"If it's possible and not too much trouble," Bette added.

"If we could stay a couple more days." As if she was making a wish when she blew out her birthday candles, Angela squeezed her eyes shut, waiting for my answer.

I had gone from one guest—Joe Roscoe—to six in the span of just that many minutes, and I considered the implication, but only for a moment. "Of course!" I told the librarians and there were smiles all around.

Smiles were good things. Smiles helped wash away the tension that over the course of the last few hours had bunched in my shoulders and turned the muscles in my neck to a network of tightly cramped pain-makers.

"We're going out to celebrate." Marianne spoke up.

"Not that we just assumed you'd agree to let them stay. We figured if you didn't, we'd celebrate what a wonderful few days it's been."

"And if you did, we'd celebrate the fact that we can stay a little longer," Angela added.

"You'll come with us?" Carole asked.

I declined with the lie that I'd already eaten and watched them pile out of the house.

At the last second, Marianne turned around and stepped back into the entryway. She peered into the parlor. "Your Mr. Roscoe's not around, is he?"

As far as I knew, he wasn't, and I told her so without bothering to add that he wasn't *my* Mr. Roscoe.

"He didn't stop in at the library today," Marianne said. "No big deal, I'm sure he was busy. But I wasn't, not after toddler story hour. So I spent some time going over the history of the island's families. I hate to disappoint him. He seems like such a nice man. Would you tell him that I can't find any records of any Roscoe family? I'll keep looking. Tell him that, too, and tell him to stop in or give me a call and let me know some other family names. It never hurts to look at other branches of the family tree. I'm sure we'll have more success there."

I assured her I would give Joe the message and watched her scramble down the front steps to catch up with her friends and I will admit, when I closed the door behind the librarians, the first thing that came to my mind was the benefits of peace and quiet.

I forced myself to exhale a long, slow breath.

Peace and quiet. That's what I was looking for. As nice as they all were, I knew it was something I never would have gotten if I went out with the talkative librarians.

Especially if they insisted on talking about the parallels

between what was happening on the island and *And Then There Were None*.

I tried to work a kink out of my neck, but it was no easier doing that than it was to put aside the mystery of everything going on at Water's Edge. With that in mind, I poured a glass of Château Lafite Rothschild 1996 from a bottle Jason had given me as a Christmas gift a couple years earlier. I'd always thought I would share the wine with Jason and his wife, Amelia, but after our phone call earlier in the day . . . rather than dwell on the empty feeling that settled between my heart and my stomach, I grabbed my tablet and settled down on the couch in my suite and set the wine on the table where I could as easily reach it as I could enjoy the play of light against its gorgeous ruby purple coloring.

A sip of wine and a smile of appreciation for its incredible taste, and I was ready to get down to business.

The business, of course, was murder, and even though I didn't want to think about it, I couldn't help but wonder if the librarians were onto something.

Lucky for me, I'm a quick reader and I skimmed through the book, then found a movie version of *And Then There Were None* online. The old black-and-white flick had a happy ending that was not true to the book, but it gave me another look at the story and a better chance to make a mental list of what I was dealing with.

A remote island off the English coast.

A group of ten strangers brought there by a mysterious host.

And murder.

I knew that in Christie's book, each murder was planned and executed (even I cringed when the word popped into my head) to right a wrong. See, each of those guests on the island was guilty of a murder and each had sidestepped the long arm of the law for one reason or another. The man who invited them to the island was intent on finding . . . well, not revenge exactly . . . it was more like justice. He was judge, jury, and executioner, killing them off one by one.

Even another sip of wine didn't wash away the bad taste the thought left in my mouth.

"Not possible," I told myself. "It's not possible that the ten nuns are guilty of anything but being good people. And besides, nobody said Sister Helene was dead. If she's the one who killed Sister Sheila, then it makes perfect sense that she'd want to get off the island."

Wise words, but they did little to relieve the worry that settled on my shoulders.

Thinking, I tapped my fingers against the tablet keyboard and thought about the old movie I'd just watched and the book it was based on in relation to what was happening at Water's Edge.

Island.

Check.

Ten guests.

Check.

Mysterious host.

Check.

Or not.

Unlike the characters in the Christie mystery who'd been left in the dark about the reason they were invited to Soldier Island, the nuns knew exactly what they were doing when they came to South Bass. And they knew who they were supposed to be meeting here.

"Richard Ward Parker," I mumbled the name at the same time I thought about how in the book (and the movie), the mysterious host never appears. Instead, he leaves a recording that welcomes his guests.

A message.

Just like the one Richard Ward Parker had left on Sister Liliosa's voicemail.

The thought sent a tingle along my spine and I sat up so fast, those bunnies on my feet twitched. I positioned my tablet so I could more easily type on it, and the words I entered should come as no surprise.

Richard Ward Parker.

There were thousands of entries, but it seemed best to start with Parker's own website. I was met with a picture of a man with salt-and-pepper hair; a wide, friendly smile; and eyes the color of a South Bass summer sky. There was a short bio of Parker and a message from him that made even me— not religious in any strict sense of the word—feel all warm and fuzzy inside and infused with the promise of a better world.

There was also a tab that linked to his public appearances and, curious, I clicked on it and looked over his schedule.

Seattle just about a year ago.

Portland after that.

No mention of South Bass or Water's Edge or a retreat for nuns.

But then, when I clicked on Parker's blog tab, I could see why.

The page opened on a picture of Richard Ward Parker standing on a wide windswept plain. There were craggy, snowcapped mountains in the distance and a dome of sky above his head that was achingly blue and seemed to go on forever.

The blog had been posted that very day, and my heart suddenly beating double time, I scanned through it and scrolled down to check previous posts.

"Son of a gun," I whispered.

No wonder Richard Ward Parker had never made it to Water's Edge for the retreat.

He'd been on his own retreat for the last four months.

At a monastery in Tibet.

"Well, how could he be here on South Bass when he's in . . ." Doing her best to get the facts straight, Chandra shook her head. "He's in wherever it is he's in," she grumbled, looking down into the teacup she'd brought over to my front porch with her the next morning. I wasn't sure what kind of tea was in that cup of hers, I only knew that it was green and it smelled like a combination of fish and peanut butter.

When the next spring breeze whistled by, I made sure to lean back on the wicker couch so the scent of the tea zipped past me.

"He's in Tibet, that's where he is," I reminded Chandra. While I was at it, I grabbed my own coffee cup from the table in front of the couch and wrapped my fingers around it, enjoying the sensation of the heat against my skin.

"And you see what it means, don't you?" I was sure Luella's question was aimed at Chandra so I kept my mouth shut.

"If he's there," Kate pointed out, "he couldn't be here."

"Well, he's not here." Chandra was so proud of her reasoning, she smiled radiantly. "So it all makes sense."

It didn't. Not in Chandra's reality, and certainly not in mine.

I hauled in a breath, the better to try to explain so that she'd understand. "In that voicemail message, he said he'd checked out Water's Edge early this year. But he was already in Tibet, so he couldn't have. And he's still in Tibet," I told her, then before she could say what I knew she was going to say, I added, "And yes, he could have made the call from there, but that still doesn't explain everything. Richard Ward Parker had this trip to Tibet scheduled for a year. He's been living on some mountain for the last few months."

Chandra is not a stupid woman, but she is not as practical as some, and certainly not as down-to-earth as most. Like so many people with her airy-fairy outlook on life, she accepts people for what they are, and she assumes they're as open and up-front about their lives and their feelings as she always is about hers. I'm not saying that's a bad thing, just that sometimes, it doesn't hurt to be a little more hard-nosed. In Chandra's case that hardly ever happens, and it can sometimes take her far too long to come to grips with the fact that what she sees isn't always what she gets.

Her golden brows dropped low over her eyes. "So you're saying he didn't make that phone call? Someone else did?"

I was grateful I'd made that much of an inroad to her thinking, but I had to admit, "I can't prove it, not without listening to that voicemail Sister Liliosa received again so I could compare the voices closely, but I listened to a short inspirational message on Richard Ward Parker's website and I'd bet money that wasn't his voice we heard on the phone."

Inside at the breakfast table, my guests had just finished eating shirred eggs, fresh fruit, and thick, delicious pieces of oatmeal honey bread. Over at Water's Edge, the nuns' breakfast included the same bread and fruit along with slices of ham and, since Meg volunteered to go over there and oversee the cooking, poached eggs. Out on my front porch, I had served my friends bits and pieces of everything that was left over. Kate and I had bowls of fruit in front of us. Chandra had just finished a piece of bread smeared with apricot jam and she licked bits of jam from her fingers.

There was only one ramekin of shirred eggs left, and we'd all agreed Luella should have it since she had to work all day. When she left my house, she'd head to the marina and from there, out on the lake with a group of early spring fishermen.

Kate filled her spoon with strawberries and spoke before she popped them into her mouth. "So somebody else made the call."

Kate is never dense, but really, I could understand why she didn't catch on to what I was getting at. Even after having all night to think about it, I still thought my theory was a little bizarre. "Yes, somebody else made the call," I agreed. "But I'm saying there's more to this whole thing than that. I'm saying that I think Richard Ward Parker never had anything to do with any of this. Not the message, and certainly not the retreat."

Kate swallowed hard. "You mean—"

"Why would a man of his stature promise a retreat if he knew he wasn't going to deliver?" I asked my friends. "And why would he say he'd been to Water's Edge when he couldn't have been? He obviously never could have been planning to come here if he knew he was going to be in Tibet. Think about it. It makes no sense. The only thing that does . . ." Like I said, I'd had all night to get used to the idea. Still, I needed to take a deep breath to steady myself before I dared put the rest of what I thought into words.

"I think Richard Ward Parker was the bait," I said.

Bait was something Luella understood. She nodded. "You mean to get the nuns to come to South Bass."

My turn to nod. "Let's face it, being offered a week away from work is pretty flattering and pretty tempting for any-body. But these are not ladies who are used to shirking their duties. They wouldn't just fly in from all around the country for a week of fun and laughter. There needed to be some incentive. And from what I read about him online last night, Richard Ward Parker is about as big an incentive as there can be. He's a real mover and shaker in the world of spirituality and religion, a real inspiration, admired across denominational lines. Of course when they saw that he was involved—"

"They'd be dying to get here." Listening to her own words, Kate cringed. "You know what I mean."

I did.

"Another bad pun," I admitted, "but I have no doubt it was an answer to these nuns' prayers. An entire week with the man was an offer too good to refuse."

"So somebody was trying to make sure the nuns showed up here." Luella drummed her fingers against the rim of her ramekin. "And this someone pretended to be this Parker fellow, invited them all here, then said he couldn't make it but they should stay. Why?"

"Well, it's obvious why he left them the message that said he couldn't make it," I said. "Since Parker's in Tibet, the person who was pretending to be him had to have some kind of cover for why he wasn't here. As for the rest of it . . ."

Yes, I'd had hours to think about it.

Yes, I'd been over it a couple thousand times.

And yes, every time I worked through the problem, I did end up back where I'd started.

That didn't mean I was any more comfortable with the information I knew I had to share with my friends.

I shivered. "If you believe Marianne and her librarian friends, the reason the mystery person wanted the nuns all together is so he can kill them all."

I hadn't expected anything but openmouthed gasps so I wasn't surprised when I got them. I explained about *And Then There Were None*. I also explained why I wasn't exactly on board with the theory.

"Only one nun has been killed and it's already Wednesday, so really, I don't think there's anything to worry about," I assured them in a voice that sounded confident enough but didn't exactly convince me. Or the tiny tingle of apprehension that snaked through my bloodstream.

"Still, it seems mighty strange, doesn't it? There's a reason someone wants all these women in one place at one time. There has to be. Otherwise, none of it makes any sense." Thinking about it, I finished my coffee and made up my mind. "I'm going to go over there and hang out today, keep my eyes open, see what I can see. You don't mind if we cancel book discussion group for today, do you?"

I knew Luella wouldn't, and the way she waved away my concern told me so.

Kate frowned. "I'm not even halfway through yet. Next time, let's pick a book that's not as hefty. Something light and fluffy."

"And murder free!" Luella got up and hooked the straps of her Carhartt overalls over her shoulders. "Wish I could join you over at Water's Edge, but duty calls. Thanks for breakfast and the update."

Kate got up, too. "I need to get to the winery or I'd go along." She looked over to where Chandra was helping herself to another piece of bread. "Maybe Chandra—"

"Can't." Chandra popped out of her chair and took her bread with her. "The workers are coming over. You know, to take measurements for the pool. And the lamppost."

Kate and I exchanged looks, but though I was tempted

to get up and get in Chandra's face, I kept my seat. And my temper. Barely.

"You know, Chandra," I said, "we haven't had much time to discuss all this, but I think Kate agrees with me. What you're thinking about doing to your property isn't going to enhance the neighborhood."

"Neighborhood schneighborhood!" Chandra tossed her head and marched down the steps. "What are you going to do about it? Take me to court?"

❖ 12 ❖

As it turned out, I didn't have to make up an excuse for hanging around Water's Edge that day. By the time I cleaned up from breakfast and got over to the other side of the island, Hank was already at the retreat house. He'd just officially told the nuns that Sister Sheila had been murdered. Big points for the Sisters, they didn't let on that they'd already heard the news from me.

I was walking into Water's Edge just as Hank was leaving, and once he was gone and another prayer session conducted for the repose of Sister Sheila's soul was finished, I was greeted by a myriad of reactions, each tempered by strong faith and whispered prayers. The news was difficult to process, impossible to explain, and harder to understand—even the second time through. Sister Gabriel, the one I expected to see sobbing in a corner somewhere, raced out of the room while the last *Amen* still hung in the air. Tears stained Sister Paul's, Francelle's, and Mary Jean's cheeks. Sister Liliosa was a rock. Like I expected anything different? She suggested the nuns spend a quiet hour in reflection and, big surprise, no one argued with her. Once they scattered, I stepped from the hallway where I'd been waiting and into the living room.

"You were right," Sister Liliosa said. "Of course you were. It's not like I didn't believe you when you told us Sheila was murdered, it's just . . . well, this makes it all feel so much more real."

It seemed counterproductive to claim otherwise. "I sometimes help out Hank. Not with any of the really important details of a case, just with information. That's how I knew."

She pressed her lips together. "Knowing how she died makes it harder to come to grips with her death."

"I can understand that." It was a bright, warm morning, and someone had thrown open the windows that faced the lake. I couldn't help but think that Sister Sheila would not have been amused. I, however, didn't want to miss the opportunity to drink in the beauty of the day, especially since I hoped blue skies and lake breezes might counteract the ugliness of the subject we needed to discuss.

I moved closer to the windows and breathed in a scent I wouldn't have even recognized when I was living in that condo back in New York. Fresh water, fish, some very early blooming something. All of it kissed with spring sunshine.

"We need to find out what happened," I told Sister Liliosa.

"Exactly what I told all of them." She looked to the door where the nuns had just dispersed. "It's all well and good to say our prayers and think good thoughts, but we are, after all, women of action. Don't get the wrong idea, we're not looking for revenge. Just for answers. And justice."

Justice instead of revenge.

Exactly what I'd thought about when I read *And Then There Were None* the night before. "What we need to do is find answers," I told her.

"You mean about why someone would want to kill Sister Sheila. I know what Sister Grace thinks. And I have a feeling the police agree with her. Sister Helene's bed wasn't slept in last night, and Chief Florentine says there's been no sign of her on the island though they did find the golf cart she left in. It was parked downtown near the ferry dock. Everyone knows Helene and Sheila have been feuding forever. Do you think Helene could really have killed Sheila? That she's fled the island?"

I didn't mention the disguise in the attic because I still wasn't sure what it meant. "It's looking like a possibility. Do you remember where she was on Saturday?"

"Helene?" Sister Liliosa's brow furrowed with the effort of concentration. "We were all busy, of course, settling into our rooms. After a while, I remember that a few of the Sisters decided to take a walk and check out the property."

"Was Sister Sheila one of them?"

"I don't think so." Her dark veil stroked her shoulders when she shook her head. "Once she was settled in her room . . . the room she exchanged with Sister Catherine . . . once she was settled in there, I don't think I saw Sheila again at all that afternoon, though it's obvious she went down to the beach eventually since that's where you found her."

"And Helene?"

Sister Liliosa had broad, strong hands. She massaged the bridge of her nose with her index fingers. "Helene was . . . that is, she is . . . an unusual person. More artistic than the rest of us."

"Even more so than Sheila? Sheila was a musician."

"And a gifted one," Sister Liliosa said. "But I don't mean artistic in that way. What I mean is that Helene reminds me a lot of your friend, Chandra."

This I understood and I smiled to let her know it. "You mean a little fey."

Sister Liliosa's smile was surprisingly impish. "That's putting it kindly."

"But succinctly."

"Yes." She nodded. "Succinctly. And I don't mean to judge . . . I suppose I'm just more traditional than Sister Helene is. My idea of prayer is getting down on my knees and having a conversation with God. Hers is dancing. I'm not saying it's wrong—"

"Just different."

"Different. Yes." Sister Liliosa joined me at the windows. Outside the living room and dining room there was a wide flagstone patio that looked out over a vast vista of Lake Erie. The patio was bordered with beds where the first of the daffodils were peeking out of the soil and rose bushes waited to burst into bloom. There were benches scattered here and there around the patio along with the kind of café tables I'd seen at bistros in Paris. Sister Paul sat on one of the benches next to a fountain still swathed in heavy plastic and waiting to be set up for the summer. She was praying the rosary. Sister Catherine was on another bench against the back wall of the house where the patio was drenched in sunshine. She sat as straight as an arrow, her eyes closed, her hands on her knees, deep in meditation.

"On Saturday before dinner," Sister Liliosa said, "Sister

Helene mentioned that she was going to go down to the beach to dance in the last of the sunlight."

"The beach. Where Sheila was killed. Have you told Hank?"

Her nod was barely perceptible. "I didn't think it was important. Not until this morning. I mentioned it to him after he told us . . ." If her voice had broken, I wouldn't have thought any less of her, but I would have been surprised. Her jaw tensed. "Once we knew what really happened to Sister Sheila, I thought it was important for him to have all the facts. It might not mean anything." She slid me a look. "But it is a fact."

"And facts are all we have to go on. Facts and gut instinct."

"And faith."

I couldn't dispute this with her.

"If Sister Helene actually . . ." As strong a woman as she was, Sister Liliosa couldn't make herself say the words. She cleared her throat. "If she's the one the police are looking for, she's gone now."

"It looks that way. Helene killed Sheila. Helene left the island. It's one explanation."

"You think there's another?"

"If we knew for sure, we'd have all the answers we need. But I don't know . . ." Too antsy to stand still, I paced to the far side of the living room and back again. If there's one thing true about all writers, it's that we share overactive imaginations. Mine was on overdrive, searching for answers that would explain not only Sister Sheila's death, but what looked like a disguise in the attic, Sister Helene's disappearance, the person I'd seen hanging around the garden the night before, and those wet footprints inside the kitchen door the other night.

None of it added up.

"Could there be someone else?" I asked Sister Liliosa. "Could someone else have killed Sister Sheila?"

"You mean, another one of us?" Sister Liliosa sounded more bemused by the thought than she did surprised. "Isn't it bad enough that one of us is being accused?"

"It is. I realize it. I don't mean to be rude. But all the pieces just don't fall into place. Not for me, anyway. If we could look at things from a different point of view, maybe we'd find some answers."

She didn't agree, but she didn't shoot me down, either, so I gathered my thoughts and plunged on ahead. "It all makes me wonder," I said, "if there's more that connects the ten of you than those grants you received back in New York."

Sister Liliosa tucked her hands under the white wool panel that covered the front of her habit and when she did, the silver crucifix she wore glinted in the morning sunlight. "You're talking motive. Well, of course, you have to. No doubt, that's how the police are thinking, too. Sister Helene certainly had a beef with Sister Sheila. We all know that."

"We do. What we don't know is if anyone else here might have had a reason to dislike Sister Sheila."

I wasn't sure what I expected her to say. But instead of saying anything at all, what I got from her was stony silence.

And sometimes, silence speaks way louder than words.

"You know something."

Sister Liliosa raised her chin. "None of us lied when we told you we didn't know each other. Because we don't. Not well. But that doesn't mean our paths haven't crossed."

"In New York, at that dinner where you all received grant money for the work you do."

"Before that." Sister Liliosa drew in a breath and let it

out slowly. "Many years ago when Sister Helene was very young and was just considering her vocation, she visited a convent in Buffalo. Apparently, she liked what she saw because a few months later, she applied for the novitiate there. Novitiate, that's—"

"Sort of a training period. A time for the person to try out life in a convent or a monastery to see what it would be like."

She was pleased I knew even that much. "But it works both ways," Sister Liliosa pointed out. "It's also a time for the convent to decide if the person will be a good fit. Sometimes, things just don't work out."

I wasn't sure where she was headed with the story, but I had a funny feeling. "Are you telling me Sister Helene was let go?"

"I'm telling you she never got even that far. After the initial panel interview, it was determined that she wasn't the kind of woman the convent was looking for. Like we said, she's a little fey and she's never done anything to hide that fact. Not that there's anything wrong with musical talent. It's a gift from God, after all. But the Sisters of the convent of St. Mary of the Falls were more likely to go out at night and distribute blankets to the homeless than they were to dance for the glory of the Lord. They knew Sister Helene would never be happy there because she'd never feel she was serving God the way she should. They had no choice but to reject her application for admission."

"So you're telling me you met her back then? You were one of those nuns in Buffalo?"

"No, not me." Sister Liliosa lowered her head, and I could tell she was deciding if she should say any more. "It's not my secret to tell."

"But it might be important."

"Yes." She pressed her lips together. "It was Sister Grace," she said. "She was the chair of the panel that rejected Sister Helene. If you talk to Grace, she'll tell you the whole story," she added quickly. "She didn't really know Helene. Didn't even remember her until we all met back in New York. We've all changed over the years and names get jumbled. That's why you heard that none of us knew each other."

"But if Grace rejected Helene, it's not really a motive, is it? Sister Sheila's the one who's dead, and Sister Grace is just fine."

"Thank goodness!" Sister Liliosa raised her gaze heavenward.

It was an innocent enough look and a reverent enough comment, but something about it caused a shiver to prickle up my spine.

"What do you mean, 'thank goodness'?"

"I didn't mention it to Chief Florentine." Sister Liliosa put both hands to her chin. "Maybe I should have, but it seemed like nothing at the time and we hadn't been told about Sister Sheila's murder yet. I didn't think anything of it."

"And now?"

Remembering, she twitched her shoulders. "Sister Grace has the first room at the top of the stairs. When she walked out of her room yesterday morning, she hooked her foot on the edge of a throw rug that she swears wasn't in front of her door when she went to bed. She almost went down the steps headfirst."

My stomach froze.

Murdered.

One by one.

"It's not possible," I said, more to myself than to Sister Liliosa. "It must have been an accident."

"Yes, of course it was." She didn't look any more convinced than I felt. "And even if we did think it might be Sister Helene trying to cause more harm . . . well, no one's seen her, have they? The authorities are sure she's left the island. She couldn't have . . . She wouldn't . . ."

"She doesn't have it out for anyone else, does she?"

Sister Liliosa's face turned the exact color of her wimple. "You don't think Helene came to the retreat so she could do us all in, do you?"

"Do you?"

"Of course not. That's preposterous."

"As preposterous as thinking that Sister Helene might have killed Sister Sheila?"

Sister Liliosa drew back her shoulders and pulled herself up to her considerable height. "I'm not convinced of that, either. I don't care what you or the police say. It's one thing to play mind games and consider possibilities, but Helene is a religious woman. She doesn't pay back old wrongs by killing people."

"I hope you're right."

"Of course I am." She was so often, there was no doubt in Sister Liliosa's mind that it was true in this case, too. "I'm not even going to bring this up with the rest of them," she said in no uncertain terms. "I'm not going to have them looking over their shoulders, wondering if Helene is going to pop out of some shadow and come after them."

"Would she? Is there anyone besides Sheila and Grace she might come after?"

I guarantee that had she not been outraged by my question, Sister Liliosa would not have answered it. The way she was, she was so offended, she sputtered. "Well, Sister Catherine brought calendars her shelter produces to raise money and miscounted and Helene didn't get one. Maybe you think

Sister Helene might murder her. And Sister Margaret misplaced the ketchup on Sunday at lunch. Swore she used it, then couldn't find it. Sister Helene made no secret of the fact that she never eats sandwiches without ketchup. You think maybe she's so mad at Margaret that she might—"

"Sister Margaret." I'm not sure why the thought struck out of nowhere, but in my mind, I saw a mental image of the nuns gathered in the room when I arrived. I turned away from the windows, firmly ignoring the sudden cha-cha beat in my chest. "Sister Margaret wasn't here when I got here. She's all right, isn't she?"

Sister Liliosa's imagination firmly refused to go where mine did thanks to Marianne and her librarian friends. But then, I couldn't blame her. She was a woman of faith and commitment and so were her fellow nuns, and it was hard for her to come to grips with the fact that anyone was challenging that. She clutched her hands at her waist. "She's fine. Well, as fine as the dear old thing can be! She is a little flighty, in case you haven't noticed." Briefly, a smile relieved the somberness of Sister Liliosa's expression. "After Chief Florentine told us the news . . ." Remembering the moment, her smile dissolved. "Sister Margaret said she'd rather be alone in the greenhouse to pray, and none of us even thought to stop her. She finds strength in the soil. As much strength as she finds in her faith."

"Have you checked on her?"

"It was only a few minutes ago. You don't think—"

I didn't. Or at least I didn't want to.

It was clear from the way Sister Liliosa's mouth rounded with surprise that this was the first time her mind went to the place mine was trying so hard not to consider.

Thinking it through, she clamped her lips together, then said, "I told you what you're suggesting is impossible."

"I hope you're right."

But I couldn't escape the little voice inside my head, the one that told me that in a case like this, gut instinct might prove our most valuable ally.

Mine kept reminding me that elderly Sister Margaret had gone off to some out-of-the-way greenhouse on the property.

"I'm going to go see what she's up to," I mumbled, as if Sister Liliosa knew what I was thinking.

Apparently, she did. She pointed to the right, across the patio and past a stand of trees and a tangle of lilac bushes that would be glorious in just another month. "The greenhouse is over that way."

I followed her directions and found what I was looking for with no trouble at all. I found who I was looking for, too, and okay, I admit it, when I saw Sister Margaret quietly sorting through a pile of terra-cotta pots, I breathed a sigh of relief.

"Need any help, Sister?" I asked her.

My footsteps had been silent against the soft spring ground, but still, Sister Margaret wasn't startled by my arrival. "I can't find the fertilizer," she said.

It was warm outside, and even warmer once I was under the canopy of glass. It looked to me as if the greenhouse was of the same vintage as the mansion. It had a slate floor and iron ribbing that curled over our heads in a sort of Arabian Nights arabesque that made the building as beautiful as it was utilitarian.

I moved closer to where she stacked the pots, one on top of the other, first setting the stack to her right, then moving it to her left.

"What are you fertilizing?" I asked her.

"Fertilizing? At this time of the year?" She had clearly seen her share of novice gardeners in her time and Sister

Margaret turned a kind eye on me. "Too soon for that. Just trying to get these pots in order. They need to be cleaned, you know. No use re-potting into dirty pots. Spreads disease. Yes." She watched her own hands move over the pots before she glanced over at me. "Have you seen the fertilizer I ordered?"

I assured her I hadn't, and talked her into going back to the house with me to look for it. Before we were halfway there, she was so engrossed in studying the roses on the patio, she'd forgotten all about the fertilizer, and me.

"They're going to be beautiful when they bloom." Her back against the wall of the house, Sister Catherine opened her eyes and smiled at Sister Margaret.

"Bishop's Gate," Sister Margaret said, brushing a hand lovingly against the nearest rose bush. "Such a pretty pink. And that one . . ." She made a beeline across the patio. "William Morris, if I'm not mistaken," she mumbled. "Apricot. It's going to look lovely."

"She's a dear." Sister Catherine patted the bench and I sat down. "I hope when I'm her age, I'm just as interested in life and just as involved."

"I don't think there's much chance of any of you not being. I'm impressed."

She smiled. "You're not supposed to be impressed with nuns."

"Well, I'm impressed, anyway."

Sister Catherine grinned. "Well, stop. It's our job to be humble. And something tells me it's your job . . ." She turned so that she could face me on the bench. "You're helping the police, aren't you?"

"I'd like to if I can. If there's anything you can tell me . . ."

She glanced briefly at the house. "You were talking to Sister Liliosa earlier," she said, then held up a hand. "It's not like I was eavesdropping. Honest! But the window's open and voices carry."

"So you know what we were talking about."

She settled herself more comfortably on the bench and smoothed a hand over her gray habit. "I don't think Sister Helene is going to creep back here and try to off me because I forgot to bring her a calendar, if that's what you mean. Except . . ." The smile faded from her face.

I sat up. "You remember something?"

"Something that's probably nothing," she said.

"Or it's something and you should tell me about it."

"It's just that last night . . . well, it was late. A little after two in the morning. I woke up and I thought I heard something."

"Something? Or someone?"

"Someone, I suppose, because it sounded like footsteps."

I remembered the figure I'd seen in the garden and automatically glanced around. "Out here?"

She shook her head. "No. Upstairs. In the house. I'm sure of it. I thought it was someone just up and going to the bathroom, but you know we all have bathrooms in our suites and these footsteps, they came from out in the hallway. I suppose someone could have been getting up for a midnight snack."

"I suppose." I glanced her way. "Did you look to see who it was?"

"I got out of bed. And I listened for a few more minutes. And then I went to the door and—"

Whatever else had happened, I would have to wait to hear it because just as Sister Catherine was about to tell me what she'd seen, a piece of the stone facade of the house crashed down and landed with a thundering crash on the bench between us.

❰ 13 ❱

It wasn't planning, that's for sure, since it was impossible to plan for something that literally dropped out of the sky and nearly on top of me.

It certainly wasn't heroism, either, because I'm convinced that's all about courage and nerve and steely mettle and I am not made of any of those things.

It was instinct. Nothing more. Instinct and quick reflexes. Oh, and a whole boatload of good luck.

That was the only reason I realized what was happening the second before it happened and the only thing that explained how I was able to throw myself off the bench just in the nick of time and grab Sister Catherine so I could take her along with me.

By the time the echoes of the crash finished reverberating against the walls of the house and the dust settled and the reality of what had just happened registered in my brain, I was flat on the flagstone patio, Sister Catherine next to me, Sister Paul closing in on us, and Sister Margaret looking completely bemused when she bent over us and asked if we were all right.

Were we?

Carefully, I propped myself up on my elbows. My jeans were torn, and both my knees were bleeding. The lightweight jacket I wore over my T-shirt was bunched up and tangled around my waist. My face was pocked with tiny bits of shattered sandstone and my butt . . . if I had the energy, I would have winced, because my butt felt as if it had just had a too-close encounter with a too-hard patio.

Which it pretty much had.

I could tell by the way Sister Catherine sat up slowly and cautiously, testing out her arms and her legs with each tiny movement just like I did, that she felt the same way.

"Don't move. And don't try to sit up. Good heavens, don't sit up! You don't know if you have spinal injuries."

Sister Liliosa's command rang out from the living room window over on my left, and at the sound of it, both Sister Catherine and I flattened ourselves like pancakes on the patio. I actually would have laughed if I wasn't worried it would hurt too much.

A second later, we found ourselves looking up into the faces of the nuns who'd come running at the sound of the commotion and stood in a tight circle around us. Someone had thought to grab blankets and they draped them over us. Someone else wet washcloths and gently wiped away the debris on our faces, then draped the clothes over our foreheads.

"Chief Florentine is on the way," Sister Grace announced, and flashed her phone as if to prove it. "He's bringing the paramedics."

Bringing paramedics, Hank arrived in a wave of pulsing sirens and screeching tires, and after a few minutes of being poked, prodded, asked if we knew what day it was and what our names were and how much was two plus two, we were finally allowed to sit up.

"Come on." Before I could even think to get to my feet on my own power, Hank hooked an arm around my waist, lifted me, and carried me over to the nearest bench.

The nearest bench that hadn't been smashed to smithereens by a piece of falling stone.

I realized I was staring—at what was left of the bench where we'd been sitting and at the two police officers who walked around it taking pictures and making notes—and I tore my gaze away only to find myself face-to–oh-this-isn't-good-and-what-the-hell-is-going-on–face with Hank.

"This isn't good," he grumbled, his voice matching his thunderous expression. "What the hell is going on?"

I was lucky my brain hadn't been scrambled, but that didn't mean it was working at full capacity, either. Adrenaline has a funny way of flooding into all the places where logic and reasoning usually reside.

I glanced up at the top of the house and saw the place outside a third-floor window where a piece of the facade of the house about a foot wide and twice as long had fallen away. The gash was pale against the weather-worn stone, like a scar.

"It's an old house." My throat was raw and dry and my words sounded like they'd been smothered under the ton of stone dust that coated my clothing and tasted gritty in my mouth. "That's what happened, right? It's an old house. It needs repairs."

"You think?" Hank, too, studied the house.

"Did you—"

"Send somebody up there to look around? What do I look like, a rookie?"

My brain might have been scrambled, but I knew enough to keep my mouth shut.

It was just as well, because Hank propped his fists on his hips and turned back to me. "By the time we got here, there was nobody up there."

Under normal circumstances, I'd like to think that my intellect was quick enough to go wherever it was he was trying to lead. These were not normal circumstances. Adrenaline, remember. Not to mention shock. I guess one of the paramedics realized what was happening to me because just like the night I found Sister Sheila in the water, someone had come over and draped a blanket around my shoulders. It didn't do one single, solitary thing to calm the shaking that started deep in my solar plexus and radiated out like a supersized jiggle from the San Andreas fault, but it gave me something to hang on to. I clutched the blanket with trembling fingers.

"By the time you got here? This is not the time to speak in code, Hank. You'd better lay it on the line. Are you telling me you think there might have been somebody up there earlier?"

As if on cue, one of the cops who'd been sent up to the third floor hollered out to Hank and when Hank realized everyone suddenly had their eyes on the house and the cop who had that third-floor window raised, he shushed him with the wave of one hand and cocked his head, instructing the officer to get downstairs before he said another word.

With a nod, the cop agreed, and when Hank stalked off to meet him, I was darned if I was going to be left behind.

I threw off the blanket from around my shoulders and stood.

The world didn't gyrate.

At least not too much.

I gave it a moment to settle, refused the help of the paramedic who came running to offer me a hand, and one careful step after another, followed Hank to the door outside the kitchen.

"You shouldn't be here but as long as you are . . ." He shot me a look. "You need to sit down?"

"I'm okay," I assured him and surprisingly, it was nearly true. Oh, I'd have bruises by morning, that was sure enough. But nothing was broken, nothing was smashed (except the bench), and now that they were bandaged, my knees weren't bleeding nearly as bad as they had been. Already I was dreaming about the Jacuzzi jets in my bathtub. Aches and pains I could deal with. Compared to what might have happened . . .

From where we stood, I could see the entire patio and get a better feel for the scene of the accident. Sister Catherine, too, was up and moving now; she was on a bench on the far side of the patio surrounded by ministering nuns. The cops were done with their pictures and their measurements. They stood near the splintered wood of what used to be the bench near the house, waiting for further instructions.

"There's no use staring at it," Hank said. "Nothing's going to change."

"I'm just trying to get some sense of . . ." Of what? Even I wasn't sure, and I made as if to throw my hands in the air, realized both my shoulders felt like I'd gone a couple rounds in the ring with Ali, and gave up with a *humph* just as the cop who had been upstairs joined us outside.

He was a young guy with rosy cheeks and a gleam in his eye that told me he couldn't wait to impress the chief with news of what he'd found. He bit back his words when he saw me waiting with Hank.

"You might as well say it," Hank told the kid. "She's going to find out anyway."

"Sure, Chief." The young cop took out his phone and showed Hank a picture of what he'd found upstairs.

Hank chewed on his lower lip and stared at the phone, then handed it over to me.

"Footprints in the dust," I said. "Just like we found in the attic. This wasn't an accident. Someone was up there and pried away a piece of the stone."

Hank plucked the phone from my hand and gave it back to the young officer. "Get up there and make sure nobody touches anything," he told the cop. "I'll call the state crime lab and get them over here to process the scene." He waited for the kid to follow his orders before he turned back to me.

"So who was the target, you or that nun?"

Of all the scenarios that had raced through my head in the minutes since the accident, what he suggested wasn't one of them. I stammered what I wanted to sound like a protest, and when that didn't work, I gave up with a grunt. "Why would anyone want to kill me?"

The way Hank's eyebrows did a slow slide up his forehead was something I would have taken as an insult had I been feeling more like myself.

"I'm serious, Hank," I said.

"So am I." He checked to be sure we were out of earshot of anyone on the patio. "You're looking into a murder, aren't you? Maybe you've gotten a little too close to the truth."

"That Sister Helene killed Sister Sheila? Even if it's true, I can't see a nun trying to shut me up especially since I don't really know anything except that Helene's the only one who had a motive."

Hank slid a gaze toward the patio. "Well, if it wasn't you this person was after, then maybe it was her."

"Sister Catherine?" My gaze automatically went over to the bench where Catherine sat with the nuns all around her. "She's young, she's smart, she's energetic. She runs a shelter for homeless women. You can't think someone would want to kill her because of that, can you?"

"Plenty of abusers look to get even with the women who walk out on them."

"So you think some scumbag came all the way here from Philadelphia to kill the nun who runs the shelter? Even I think that's a little far-fetched, Hank. Besides, that might explain why someone would want Sister Catherine dead, but it doesn't explain Sister Sheila's murder."

"Which brings us back to Helene McMurty."

I made the mistake of rubbing my hands over my face and got a mini-exfoliation in the process thanks to all the grit on my cheeks that had mixed with the water from the washcloth the nuns had so kindly provided. "So Helene kills Sheila because of a contract dispute and tries to kill Catherine because Catherine forgot to bring enough calendars to the retreat?"

"I've heard weirder motives."

"Well, I haven't. Not weirder and not lamer. Unless . . ." I had held off as long as I could from telling Hank about the librarians' theory, the one that had what was going on at Water's Edge compared to what happened in *And Then There Were None*. If the librarians were right, more lives might be in danger, and we couldn't take the chance.

I told Hank about the book and pointed out the parallels including Richard Ward Parker and how he never could have been planning to come to the retreat in the first place.

To give him credit, he did not blow me off.

"Killed off one at a time, eh?" Hank crossed his arms over his barrel chest and looked over at the nuns. "You think—"

"I don't know what to think, I only know it's mighty peculiar. Maybe Helene really does have something against every single one of them. Maybe she arranged this whole thing, and hired somebody to leave that message that was supposed to be from Richard Ward Parker. Or maybe she's just some kind of crazy serial killer and this is how she gets her kicks. I don't know, but somebody loosened that stone and right now . . ." I dragged in a breath that made my ribs ache. "I admit it, she's looking like the best candidate."

"Wish I could get my hands on that nun," Hank grunted. His cheeks turned bright red. "You know what I mean! Nobody's seen her. Not anybody over at the ferry. Not anybody at the marina. I've talked to the cops on the mainland and I've talked to the nuns at her convent in Phoenix. There's been no sign of her."

"Well there wouldn't be, would there, not if she killed Sheila. She'd be lying low."

"And being careful not to be seen." Biting his lower lip, Hank took another look at the house. "Took us a while to get here, and there are a million places to hide in a place like this. My guys are checking out the house and the grounds now. Still . . . You were all so busy back here, she could have walked right out of the house by the front door and no one would have seen a thing."

I hated it when he was right.

Almost as much as I hated nearly being killed by a piece of falling house.

"Do you think they're in danger?" I asked Hank.

He didn't need to look at the nuns, he knew who I was talking about.

"I'll keep a couple guys here, just in case."

"And I'll be back later," I told him. "I'm going home to take a shower."

I dragged around to the front yard, wondering where I was going to find the energy to climb into my SUV, but before I could get there, something over on the other side of the house caught my attention. Just a blur moving through the trees that surrounded the far end of the house.

A familiar-looking beige blur.

"Joe! Joe Roscoe!" I called out.

The blur stopped and turned around and I saw that I was right. My B-and-B guest joined me in the circular driveway.

"Didn't want to disturb anyone," he said. "I was just coming over here to see if I could get a look at the house . . . you know, since my ancestors might have helped build it . . . and then . . ." He glanced around at the parked ambulance and the three police cars in front of the house. "What's going on?"

I assured him it was no big deal. And I managed to sound like I meant it, too. "An accident, but nothing serious. Everyone's fine."

"Except for you." Joe adjusted that ever-present cardboard tube under his arm and wrinkled his nose before he looked me up and down. "You want to drive back to the B and B with me?" he asked.

I pointed to my SUV. "I need to get it home. I'll see you there."

He nodded and watched me pull away, and it wasn't until I got to the end of the driveway and turned onto Niagara that a thought struck me.

Joe offered me a ride home.

Very nice of him.

But funny, I didn't see his car there at Water's Edge.

* * *

Meg asked if she could take dinner over to the retreat house for me that evening and as kind as that was, I refused her offer. I was a walking bundle of sore muscle, bruised bone, and abraded skin, and keeping busy might not make me feel better but it would keep my mind off the near-death experience I'd had over at Water's Edge.

Besides, I was convinced that the answers to our questions—and Sister Helene's motives for attacking her fellow nuns—lay at the retreat house.

My mind made up, I packed up the caramel chocolate brownies Meg had made both for tea at the B and B that day and for the nuns, and I was just loading them into a bag when Kate walked into my kitchen.

"I heard what happened. You should be sitting with your feet up, not cooking dinner for the nuns. I came to help."

"All done." I pointed to the one tote bag on my counter.

"So somebody's trying to kill nuns by dropping pieces of a house on them, and you're trying to kill them by starving them to death?"

I would have laughed if my ribs didn't hurt so darn much. Instead, I picked up my phone from the kitchen counter and waggled it at Kate. "Ordered six large pizzas and three big antipasto salads and I'm having it all delivered to Water's Edge. The only thing I have to worry about is getting dessert there."

"Hardly." Kate was nothing if not analytical. It's what made her such a successful businesswoman and such a challenging friend. She'd changed out of the brown tweed suit she'd had on that morning when we shared breakfast on my front porch. This evening, she was wearing khakis and a hoodie the same color as her amazing green eyes.

The sweatshirt was emblazoned with the words *South Bass* and a picture of a boat with billowing sails. She tucked her hands into the kangaroo pocket.

"You've got to worry about somebody trying to kill you, Bea."

"It wasn't me. It was Sister Catherine."

"You're sure?"

I remembered what Hank had said back at Water's Edge. "I'm sure," I said, then, in the interest of full disclosure, added, "Pretty sure, anyway. I wish we could figure out what's going on inside Helene's head, then maybe we could anticipate her next move."

Kate led the way out of the kitchen. "It's a nice evening," she said, "and I've got the top down on the convertible. I'll drive."

It was her way of telling me that she knew I was hurting, and Kate being Kate, she wouldn't appreciate it if I told her I knew what she was up to. Instead, I slid into her black BMW and rested my head back against the leather seat, grateful for the warmth of the evening, the dome of blue skies over our heads, and the fact that I had a friend who was willing to sacrifice part of her evening to help me out.

Within minutes, we were nearing the retreat house.

"I love this part of the island." We were the only car around so it didn't matter that Kate slowed down. Together, we listened to the sound of crows chattering away somewhere in the woods that bordered the road on our left. "There used to be a huge summer resort here, you know. Right here, where the state park is now."

I'd heard the stories, and of course, they sparked my already overactive imagination. "Hotel Victory, right?"

"You've been paying attention to island history!" Kate stopped the car. "See, right over there. You can see a pile of stone. It's part of the foundation of the old hotel. It burned down nearly one hundred years ago."

Together, we peered through the tangle of undergrowth and trees into what was now the campgrounds of the state park.

Those crows kept on chattering.

I guess that's why I asked, "Think it's haunted?"

She chuckled. "Leave it to FX O'Grady to ask! Except the way those birds are going at it . . ." She shivered inside her hoodie.

I peered farther into the park grounds. Or at least I tried. From where we were on the road, it was hard to see much of anything but a scramble of black somewhere in the distance that was accompanied by the rustle of bird wings.

"Honk your horn," I told Kate.

"Huh?" Like I said, she's a good friend. She might have questioned my sanity, but she played along. She gave a sharp blast on her car horn.

There in the woods, a dozen crows rose in the air like a black cloud and let us know they were not amused. Their sharp caws echoed in the evening silence.

I wondered how it was I could hear them over the sudden pounding of my heart.

"Turn the car around," I said.

Again, she didn't question me, not even when I had her drive back the way we'd come and turn into the park. We drove as far as we could, and when the paved road ended, we parked the car and got out and walked.

It wasn't hard to find what we were looking for. But then, the crows were back and we followed the sound of their squawking all the way to the abandoned swimming pool of Hotel Victory.

The birds scattered when we approached and landed

on the branches of the bare trees around us. I could feel their black eyes on us as we looked over the scene.

The first coed swimming pool in the country was dry these days, just as it had been in all the years since the biggest fire the island had ever seen consumed the six-hundred-and-twenty-five-room hotel and everything in it. The cement sides and bottom of the pool were cracked and caked with winter debris. The storm earlier in the week had left puddles here and there and in one of them—

Kate saw what I did exactly when I did, and she clutched both her hands on my arm so tight, she cut off my circulation.

"Is that . . . ?"

It was.

I stepped nearer to the rim of the pool at the same time I pulled out my phone and called Hank. While someone there at the station went to find him for me, I took a better look at the body that lay facedown in a puddle of rainwater, rotting leaves, and muck.

The jeans and sweater could have belonged to anyone, but the hair, that was a dead giveaway.

Sorry about the bad pun.

It glimmered in the gathering evening light like quicksilver.

"Hank . . ." When he finally came on the line, I had a hard time getting out the words. "I think you'd better get over to the park, Hank. We found . . ." I cleared a ball of revulsion and unspeakable sadness from my throat.

"I'm pretty sure Sister Helene isn't our killer."

❮ 14 ❯

"Somebody would have found her eventually." Hank looked over to where a couple of cops were winding yellow crime scene tape around the trees that surrounded the abandoned swimming pool, then looked back at me and Kate. "How did you two—"

"The birds." They were still flashing from tree to tree, still obviously annoyed at the interruption, and I looked up at the birds looking down at me and shivered. "We heard them from out on the road."

Hank's mouth pulled into a thin line. "It could have gotten ugly."

I remembered what we saw when we arrived at the pool. "It was already ugly."

"Yeah, but you know what I mean."

I did, but I didn't want to think about it. "Please tell me it was an accident."

He stuffed his hands in the pockets of his jacket. "I'd like nothing better."

"But . . ."

Rather than answer me, he turned to Kate, whose complexion was as green as her sweatshirt. "Why don't you go have a talk with Officer Jenkins over there." It wasn't a suggestion. Hank put a gentle hand on the small of Kate's back and gave her a little nudge. "He's going to take your statement."

I watched Kate go, her steps stiff and uncoordinated, like a person who'd been woken suddenly from a deep sleep and a bad dream.

"She can take it," I told Hank. "She's tougher than she looks."

"I know." He waited until Kate was all the way over to where the officer waited for her. "But why should she have to? Bad enough I'm going to make you listen to the details. Except from what Chandra tells me . . ." He ran a finger around the inside of his collar. "I guess you're no stranger to blood and guts, huh?"

My shoulders drooped. "She was supposed to keep that a secret."

"You know better than that, Bea. If you want to keep something a secret, you can't tell Chandra."

"I had to." It was as simple as that, and I knew it. I couldn't have told Kate and Luella the truth about my past and not told Chandra. Swimming pools, giant lampposts, and People Against Fishing Lake Erie aside, that would have been the worst sort of betrayal of a friendship. "But you're not supposed to know. No one's supposed to know."

"Yeah, Chandra said that right after she spilled the beans. That's why I'm mentioning it to you now. Thought it was important that you know that I know. Not fair otherwise. For what it's worth . . ." He knew it was the wrong time and the wrong place to smile, so he buried the expression under his usual gruff exterior. "I'm a huge fan."

I watched a couple of the birds take off from their tree branches and circle the swimming pool. They cawed their displeasure and disappeared toward the lake. "Writing about death at the hands of zombies and vampires and evil spirits is one thing," I told Hank. "It's storytelling, nothing more. It might be scary to think about, but since it can't really happen, it's a safe sort of scare, if you know what I mean. But seeing death for real, in person, that's different."

"No doubt. But the way you write about it . . ." He gathered his thoughts. "The way you describe it, it's like you've looked death right in the eye."

"No. Not really. Not until I moved here, anyway."

Hank barked out a laugh. "Except for crazy partiers, this has always been a quiet island. Until you showed up."

It was Hank's way of lightening the mood. Or at least of trying. I appreciated it and shook off the pall that sat on my shoulders. "We need to put things right," I told him and just to prove it, I went closer to where a couple paramedics were down in the empty pool with Sister Helene's body. I would like to say I strode with purpose, but my knees hurt. I'm afraid it was more of a shuffled limp.

One of the paramedics looked up at us when we arrived at the edge of the pool. "Single gunshot to the back of the head," he said.

"Suicide?" Hank asked.

The paramedic glanced around the pool. "No sign of a weapon. And not much blood. I'd guess she was killed somewhere else and the body was dumped here."

"Not an accident."

My words settled in the evening silence between me and Hank.

"How long?" I asked the paramedic.

"How long has she been dead?" He scratched a hand behind his ear. "I'm no coroner."

"Take a guess," Hank told him.

"Between the chilly night last night and the birds . . ." He made a face. "I'm guessing at least twenty-four hours."

Both Hank and I knew what it meant. "Helene couldn't have loosened the stone on the house this morning," I said. "Not if she was already dead. Someone else did."

"The same someone else who killed Sheila?"

My thoughts flashed to *And Then There Were None*. "If someone's trying to pick them off one by one . . ."

"That someone's got a long way to go," Hank grumbled. "We've still got eight nuns alive and kicking and they're supposed to leave the island on Saturday. Eight murders in three more days? I'm not buying that, and I don't think you are, either."

I couldn't. Not without losing complete faith in humanity.

"We need to tell them," I said.

"About Helene, yeah. But I'm not going to march over there and announce that someone's trying to murder them all. For one thing, we don't have anything to back up a crazy theory like that. For another, we don't need a full-scale panic on our hands."

I'd spent more time around the nuns than Hank had; I knew that with them, full-scale panic was just about as likely as all of them buying a houseboat together and moving to Key West to lounge in hammocks and sip drinks decorated with little umbrellas.

"I've got guys over there," Hank said, and I wondered if he was trying to reassure me or himself. "Two guys at Water's Edge. I'll keep a detail there around the clock until we figure out what's going on."

An hour and a half later when we arrived at Water's Edge, what was going on was the equivalent of sisterly chaos.

Those two policemen Hank had assigned to keep an eye on things were there, all right. They stood in a living room dotted with the remains of the dinner I'd sent over—pizza boxes, empty paper plates, salad bowls. The nuns were gathered around the cops, voices raised, their words washing over one another so fast, it was impossible to know what they were talking about.

"You said . . . ," I heard Sister Grace blurt out.

"You promised," Sister Francelle added.

"We can't know . . . ," Sister Mary Jean was telling the younger of the two cops.

"How are we supposed to feel comfortable?" Sister Liliosa demanded.

I pushed past both cops. "What's going on? What's happening here?"

Like I thought anyone could actually hear me above the din?

Hank took care of that when he bellowed, "Everybody shut up!"

Shut up, they did.

Hank nodded toward the nuns. "Beggin' your pardon, ladies," he said before he swung around to pin his officers with a look. "Explain," he barked.

"I was in . . . in back," the first officer said. "You know, out on the patio. And Cunningham here, he was up front. We were keeping an eye on things, Chief. Honest. Just like you said we were supposed to."

"But then the Sisters here . . ." Officer Cunningham turned pale beneath Hank's withering look. "The pizza came and they said it was time to eat and they invited us to join them and when we were done . . ."

"That's when I went up to my room for a minute." Sister Liliosa stepped forward, her hands clutched at her waist. "That's when I discovered that my room had been ransacked."

"Your room?" I couldn't help but gasp.

"All our rooms." Sister Liliosa looked to the other nuns to support the statement and they all nodded. "Sometime while we were eating dinner . . . well, there must have been somebody upstairs. By the time we realized it, that somebody was gone."

Honestly, I thought Hank's head was going to pop off right there and then. He stalked out of the room and he didn't have to say a word, those two cops followed right along. I will not report what he said to them out in the hallway word for word. I will say that a couple of the nuns blushed.

"It was Sister Helene!" Sister Grace's voice rang with certainty. "It had to be. Who else would have been so bold to walk right in here while we were all eating and go through our rooms?"

"But what was she looking for?" Sister Francelle asked. "What's she up to?"

She, of course, was not up to anything. Not anymore. Not for the last twenty-four hours.

I delivered the news with as much detachment as I could muster and watched as, one by one, the horror registered on the nuns' faces. As if they were moving in slow motion, each of them backed up and found a seat, and the silence that settled was so profound, I could hear the waves slapping the beach below the patio.

They allowed themselves a few minutes for private grief, then Sister Paul took out her rosary and began to pray and when the others joined in, I stepped out of the living room.

Hank was just coming down the steps from the second floor and he heard their prayers wafting through the air. "You told 'em, huh?"

"Sorry. I should have left it up to you, but they were sure Sister Helene was the one who'd been through their rooms and I . . ." I coughed away the tightness in my throat. "It didn't seem right letting them think that. Not considering what we found at the park earlier." I looked past him and up the stairs. "And their rooms?"

"Somebody's looking for something, all right." Hank chewed on his lower lip. "Every single room is tossed. What's going on here, Bea?"

"I wish I knew."

"Well, I've called in two more officers. And I had those two . . ." When he looked over his shoulder to where Officer Cunningham and the other policeman were coming down the steps, Hank's eyes narrowed. "These two jackasses are going outside right now to have a look around," he said. "A careful look around."

The two officers did just that.

For a few minutes, Hank and I stood listening to the sounds of the nuns' prayers. Their voices were low and soothing, their heads were bent, their eyes closed, and I stood back and watched them, drinking in the quiet solace.

Until I did some counting.

"There are only seven of them," I said.

Hank, too, had been lost in the comforting hum of their voices. "Huh?"

Just to be sure, I did another quick count. Not so hard when there were only seven nuns in the living room.

"Sister Gabriel is missing," I told Hank.

"You don't think—"

Since I didn't want to think what he thought I was thinking, I whirled toward the stairs instead. "Your guys must have checked out her room, right?"

"Well, sure. There's nobody up there." He scraped a hand through his hair. "Let's not panic if there's nothing to panic about."

Good advice.

Tell that to the sudden crazy rhythm inside my rib cage.

We stood still for a moment, me and Hank, considering our options, and it was a good thing we did. Otherwise, we wouldn't have heard a distinct thud from the direction of the library.

"Stay back." Hank waved me behind him at the same time he drew his gun, but when he hurried down the hallway in the direction the noise had come from and burst through the closed door of the library, I was right behind him.

And just in time to see Sister Gabriel freeze in place over near the wall-to-wall bookshelves on the far side of the room. She dropped the book she was holding. Her mouth fell open, her face turned as white as her wimple.

"Sister!" Hank called out at the same time Sister Gabriel stammered, "Don't shoot!"

"Oh, heck. I'm not going to shoot you!" Hank holstered his gun. "But what on earth—"

He said exactly what I was thinking.

Sister Gabriel stood in the center of what I can only describe as total destruction. There were piles of books on the floor around her and more books stacked on nearby tables. The drawers of a nearby desk hung open and their contents—from paper clips to papers to scissors and pens—were scattered all around.

"What are you doing, Sister?" I blurted out.

Now that Hank had put his gun away, Sister Gabriel regained her color. And her enthusiasm for whatever crazy scheme she was engaged in. She grabbed a thick book off the shelf, riffled through the pages, then cast the book aside.

"I'm looking, that's what I'm up to. I'm looking for the package that was supposed to have been delivered here earlier in the week. You know, those . . . those books I told you about."

"You're the one who left during dinner." She didn't deny it so I didn't feel the least bit guilty about adding, "You're the one who ransacked the Sisters' rooms!"

"Well, I've asked them like a hundred times what they did with the stupid package, and I'm not getting any answers. Not from any of them." Finished flicking through another few books, she tossed them aside. "What did you expect? I'm supposed to sit on my hands and wait?"

"Except you didn't find what you were looking for in any of their rooms, did you?" I asked and, in answer to Hank's questioning gaze, added, "She wouldn't still be looking if she did."

"That's right." Sister Gabriel kicked the nearest stack of books and sent books spinning across the parquet floor. "I haven't found a thing, and I'll tell you what, I've pretty much had it. It's important." She grabbed a book and slapped it down on the table near her right hand. "That package is freakin' important!"

Nuns in high dudgeon were obviously a little outside of Hank's job description. He took a couple steps back and left me to deal, and though nuns in high dudgeon were well out of my experience, too, I'd dealt with my share of prima donnas in my day. Actresses who'd starred in the movies made from my books. Actors who'd auditioned for the TV series that had been based on a trilogy I'd written about an evil spirit that inhabited an antiques store.

Sister Gabriel was having a diva moment.

And divas . . . I knew how to deal with divas.

"We're going to figure out what happened to your package," I assured her and I sounded so darned sincere, even I was sure of it. "But we can't do that without your help."

She wasn't sure if she could believe me. That would explain why her eyes were wild and her cheeks flooded with color.

"The house is only so big, Sister," I reminded her. "And there are only so many places a package can hide. Come on." I stepped back and motioned her toward the door. "Let's get back into the living room and we'll ask the other Sisters what they know about your package."

She pursed her lips. "I already asked."

"But that was before. They might remember something now."

She didn't look 100 percent convinced, but she didn't argue, either. With a sidelong look at Hank and that gun of his, Sister Gabriel stomped out of the library.

We followed her to the living room and arrived just as the other Sisters had finished their prayers.

"What's going on?" Sister Gabriel looked around at the somber expressions on the faces of her fellow nuns. "You're praying again. What's that all about?"

Sister Liliosa stood. "We have bad news. About Sister Helene. She's . . . Sister Helene was found dead this evening."

I'm sure that just like me, everyone else in the room remembered how upset Sister Gabriel was when Sister Sheila died. Like them, I braced myself for the waterworks. Instead, Sister Gabriel broke into a grin.

"But that's great, isn't it?" She hoped for someone to step up and agree with her and when nobody did, she peered at her fellow nuns as if they'd lost their minds. "She's the one who killed Sheila. Isn't that what you've all been saying this past week? Helene was the one who murdered Sheila on account of they were having some fight about money. And Helene tried to kill Catherine, too, and you along with her." Sister Gabriel turned my way.

"Why isn't anybody else seeing the plus side of this?" Sister Gabriel asked, tossing her hands in the air. "It means we don't have to worry anymore. Sister Helene isn't going to try and off any of us. We're safe! We're all safe!"

It was a pretty darned impassioned speech and it would have made more of a positive impression if at that particular moment, a bullet didn't crack through the living room window and miss Sister Gabriel by little more than a couple of inches.

❖ 15 ❖

By the time Hank drove me home, I was too tired to drag myself around the hulking Victorian and to the back door. I hauled myself up the front steps, got as far as the door, and grumbled a curse.

I had a rule at Bea & Bees—the front door remained unlocked until eleven. Apparently, one of my guests took that rule very seriously. It was eleven—well, after eleven—and the door was locked. Not to worry, I reminded myself, there was an extra key hidden under the multicolored rag rug between the wicker couch and rocking chair. Of course at that point, bending down to retrieve it sounded like way too much work.

Especially since Jerry Garcia was parked in the middle of the rug.

"Shoo!"

Yeah, like I actually thought that would encourage my not-so-friendly neighborhood cat to get a move on.

I put a hand to the small of my back to try to ease my aching muscles. "Come on, Jerry." I grabbed one corner of the rug and gave it a little flip in an effort to dislodge the tabby. "It's late and I'm tired and you don't belong here, anyway."

As bone-tired, tuckered-out, too-exhausted-to-see-straight pleas went, it was a pretty impassioned one.

I wasn't the least bit surprised when Jerry did not take pity on me.

What I really wanted to do was let loose my inner New Yorker and swear a blue streak, but hey, there were people sleeping inside the house, so I bit back the words, gritted my teeth, and hoped that Jerry didn't take offense (at least not too much) when I scooped him up off the rug and deposited him on my front steps.

"Go home," I told him.

He headed that way.

And though I was grateful, I am not delusional. I had not one shred of doubt that he would double back as soon as I was inside and pee on the pansies in the pots out front just so I'd have something to remember him by.

At that point in time, I was too tired to care.

I let myself in, pocketed the key, and hoped I remembered to put it back where it came from the next day. Then I . . .

Nearly had a heart attack when Levi walked out of my parlor.

"I didn't mean to startle you."

"Well, you did." Oh yeah, that inner New Yorker was aroused now. I squared my shoulders, "Why didn't I see your car? What the hell are you doing here?"

He cocked his head toward the back of the house. "I parked near the garage. You came in through the front door. As far as how I got in, those librarians are a friendly bunch. They welcomed me with open arms. Figuratively speaking, of course. And before you take it out on them . . ." I don't know why he thought I was going to. Except for the laser look of death I shot up the stairway, I was my usual cool, calm, and collected self. "Marianne was with them and she knows me and she knows—"

"What?"

His cheeks shot through with a color that matched the deep crimson in the antique Persian rug on the floor in the parlor behind him. "Well, not about that."

I didn't ask him to elaborate about *that* because for one thing, I knew full well what he was talking about and I didn't need to be reminded and for another . . .

Well, there wasn't any other.

"Marianne knows me and she thought you wouldn't mind."

I shuffle-stepped past him (sore knees, remember) and down the hallway to the kitchen. With the door closed between us and the rest of the slumbering household, there was less chance that the four-letter words that were rolling around my tongue might be heard.

I waited until the swinging door flapped shut behind him before I whirled around, my arms crossed over my chest.

"Marianne thought wrong."

Levi scraped his hands over his chin. "I figured you'd say that."

"Then for once, you were right." I backed up a step and waved toward the door.

Levi's face screwed into what I'd like to think was an expression of repentance. If I didn't know better.

"Can't," he said.

"'Can't' . . . ?"

"Leave."

"Can't or won't? There's a big difference."

"Can't and won't. If you'd let me explain—"

"I don't want an explanation. I want you out of my house."

"And out of your life."

This wasn't the time for a conversation that intense. Not when I was tired. Not when I was off my game. Not when I had so much else to worry about.

"Look . . ." I dragged myself over to one of the high stools near the breakfast counter and sat down. "It's been a really long day."

"I know. I talked to Hank."

"About what happened at Water's Edge."

"About everything that happened at Water's Edge." Trying to make sense of it all, he shook his head and a lock of honey-colored hair fell against his forehead. "Were you going to tell me that you nearly got killed today?"

I rested one arm against the black granite countertop. "No. Because I had no intention of talking to you. Not about what happened to me this morning. Not about anything."

"Not even about the body you found at the state park?"

It was an image that wouldn't fade from my imagination, not even when I shook my shoulders to try to dislodge it. "If you know about that, then you know Sister Helene was murdered."

"And that someone tried to kill another one of the nuns this evening."

Oh, how I would have loved a few hours to think through everything that had happened that evening over at Water's Edge before I jumped to any kind of conclusion! Oh, how I was convinced that with a few hours of sleep, things might look different, even though I was sure they wouldn't look better.

This wasn't the time to discuss it.

But it was as good a time as any.

"I don't think someone was trying to kill her," I said.

Levi's eyebrows rose just enough for me to know this wasn't what he expected me to say.

I wasn't sure if he knew all the details so I filled him in. "The cops say the shot came from out on the water, from a boat. What does that tell you?"

He didn't need to think about it, but then, when I heard the news, I didn't, either.

"You'd have to be either really stupid to think you could manage a shot like that, or a really skilled marksman."

"Exactly. And I don't think we're dealing with stupid."

He took another couple moments to consider what I was saying.

"So you think . . ."

"That if someone's that good of a shot, he's going to make the shot."

"And he didn't."

I thought back to the scene earlier that evening, to Sister Gabriel's shrieks when she realized what had just happened, to the way the other nuns scrambled, fear and confusion in their eyes.

"The shot missed Sister Gabriel by a couple inches, but it missed her," I said. "I think—"

"Someone's trying to send a message." Levi finished the sentence for me and for a couple heartbeats, we were back in sync, and the old feelings flooded through me like bubbly, tickling my insides and warming me through.

Until I remembered the hot sting of betrayal and came to my senses.

When Levi pulled up the stool next to mine and sat down, I made sure I turned enough on my seat so that my knees had no chance of brushing against his.

"So was that message for Gabriel?" he asked.

When I shrugged, I remembered how much my shoulders ached. "She's desperate to find a package that she had shipped to the island," I told him, because something told me Hank wouldn't have seen the incident with Sister Gabriel in the library as significant enough to mention it to Levi. I wasn't sure I did, either, but I couldn't shake it loose from my brain. "She says it was a box of books."

"But you don't believe her."

"She doesn't strike me as the type . . ." I thought about it for a moment. "She isn't scholarly, that's for sure. She isn't even all that nunly."

"Nunly?"

I ignored the glint of blue fire in his eyes.

"I'm an author," I said, my shoulders as rigid as my voice. "I'm allowed to make up words."

"So why do you think she's not nunly?" Levi asked.

"Well, she's not nearly as calm as the rest of them." If I needed any proof of that, I had only to think of the scene in the library earlier that evening. "And she doesn't seem as . . . I don't know . . . as reverent, I guess. And if I said that in front of the other Sisters, they'd be all over me about it and tell me not to judge." I drummed my fingers against the countertop. "Sister Gabriel was awfully upset when she found out that Sister Sheila was dead."

"I'm sure they all were."

"Yeah, of course. But not . . . Not like Sister Gabriel was upset. She barely stopped crying. That strikes me as more over-the-top. More personal."

"Maybe she thought someone was trying to send her a message that time, too."

"Or she thought she was the intended target and the killer got the wrong nun."

This was something Levi hadn't considered, and I couldn't blame him. Before the words were out of my mouth, I hadn't considered it, either.

"Think she's hiding something?" he asked.

I sat up like a shot. "I bet Sister Gabriel would fit into those clothes I found up in the attic."

"Then she is hiding something."

"Or hiding from someone."

"And looking to slip into that disguise and leave the house?"

"It's not a bad plan," I admitted. "And it makes more sense than if Sister Helene left the clothes there. Helene wears . . . wore"—I corrected myself—"clothes like everybody else. Regular clothes, not a habit. She didn't need jeans and a leather jacket to look different."

"Sister Gabriel is one of the nuns who does wear a habit?"

I didn't blame him for not being able to keep the Sisters straight. I nodded. "The full regalia, including the long dress and the veil and the wimple. If she wanted to look different . . ." I thought back to what I'd found in the attic the night before. It seemed a lifetime ago. "I wonder what color her hair is."

"Because if it's light, the dark hair color makes perfect sense."

Had I been plotting a new book (something I had no intention of doing anytime soon), I would have jumped right on this train of thought and ridden it to the end of the line. But this wasn't fiction, it was reality. And the reality . . .

I took off the glasses that were supposed to be part of my I'm-not-a-megafamous-author disguise and set them on the countertop. "It seems a little . . . I don't know . . . a little far-fetched for a nun, don't you think?" I asked, and even before Levi had a chance to think about it, I answered my own question.

"That all depends on how desperate the nun is, doesn't it?" I asked him and myself. "And if you'd seen Sister Gabriel in the library this evening, you'd know she's desperate. Desperate to find a package she had shipped to the island. She says it's a box of books." The words swirled around inside my head and got me pretty much nowhere. "Why would books be that important?"

"And where did the package disappear to in the first place?"

That, too, was a mystery, one I hadn't bothered to think about because it never seemed to matter to anyone but Sister Gabriel.

"Sister Liliosa says she saw the package being delivered," I told Levi. "It's got to be there at Water's Edge somewhere."

"Which means someone might have taken it and that means someone has a reason for not wanting Sister Gabriel to have it."

Instead of clearing things up, he'd added another layer to the mystery with that comment. It made my head hurt.

I rubbed my eyes. "I'm going to bed," I said, then just so we were as perfectly crystal clear as we could possibly be, I looked over my shoulder at the back door. "You're leaving."

I did my best to ignore the way Levi's grin lit up the room. "Like I told you, I can't. I'm a man with a mission."

"I don't like the sound of that."

"Don't worry, it has nothing to do with you. Or at least, not a lot to do with you." He got up and strolled toward the door. "I've got my sleeping bag in the parlor."

"Wait, wait, wait!" I waved my hands in the air to get his attention and when that didn't work and he didn't even bother to turn around, I scrambled out of the kitchen and followed him down the hallway. "This does have something to do with me. It has everything to do with me! You're leaving. No sleeping bag. No parlor. My house, remember, and I'm the one who gets to say who stays and who doesn't."

"Except when you get overruled by Hank."

The announcement left me speechless for enough time for Levi to disappear into the parlor. When I found him again, he was just unrolling a black sleeping bag on the rug in front of the fireplace.

"What does Hank have to do with this?" I demanded.

"He wants me to keep an eye on you."

"I don't need you to keep an eye on me."

"Yeah, I told him that. But then he told me how the house just about fell on you this morning."

"It was just a piece of the house. And I told Hank, I don't think that had anything to do with me."

"Well, he's not convinced." Levi kicked off his sneakers. "Hanks says he's got enough to worry about over at Water's Edge and he can't spare an officer to come over here to make sure nothing happens to you. You'll be happy to hear I'm not doing this as any sort of favor to you or anyone else. I'm officially on the town payroll, at least for as long as this assignment lasts. How could I say no? I've got to do something now that you fired Jason and he can't pay me anymore."

"If that's supposed to make me feel guilty, it didn't work," I told him.

Levi stripped off the navy sweater he was wearing and tossed it on the couch. "Not trying to make you feel guilty. Not trying to make you feel anything. Just telling you the truth. Hank hired me to watch out for you until this craziness over at Water's Edge gets sorted out."

I raised my chin. "Then it looks like I'll have to get a move on and sort it out."

He unbuttoned his green and navy plaid shirt. "Exactly what I told Hank you'd say."

"You think you know me pretty well." I sounded convincing enough. Heck, I even sounded self-assured. When he slipped out of his shirt, though, and I thought about how I'd watched him undress (heck, I'd even helped) just a few days before, I wasn't so sure how long I could keep it up.

"There's a bunch you don't know about me," I told him at the same time I whirled toward the door and hoped it looked more like a strategic move than a surrender. "Hank's going to hear about this in the morning. This may be the shortest case you've ever worked."

"Told him you'd say that, too," he called after me when I was already out in the hallway.

I refused to give him the satisfaction of a reply.

Instead, I hurried into my private suite and yes, I locked the door behind me. I was already washed up and in my jammies when I realized that though Levi claimed to know me pretty well, I apparently knew him better than he thought, too.

But then, I heard the small, shuffling sounds from out in the hallway and saw the way the light stopped filtering through the space between the bottom of the door and the floor, and I knew exactly what it meant.

He'd never intended to sleep on the floor in front of the parlor fireplace. He'd dragged his sleeping bag out to the hallway.

Levi's way of assuring my safety was to sleep on the floor in front of my door.

❖ 16 ❖

I slept through my alarm and bolted out of bed just minutes before my guests would be down for breakfast, throwing on my clothes and racing to the kitchen so fast, if Levi had still been camped out in front of my doorway, I would have tripped right over him.

But the hallway was empty; I realized that the moment my door opened without a hitch. Levi was gone, and I was glad. At least I wouldn't have to deal with any personal angst on a morning when I was sore and groggy and breakfast was bound to be late.

I breathed a sigh of relief.

And realized that the air in the house was wonderfully aromatic with the mingled scents of coffee and cinnamon.

I found the answer to the olfactory mystery the moment I stepped into the kitchen. There was a pot of coffee already made, a pan of French toast sizzling away on the stove, and Levi was spooning yogurt and fruit into parfait glasses.

I might have been grateful.

If I wasn't so annoyed.

"So now you're taking over my business as well as my house?"

He glanced up from his work. "Good morning. You look like you could use a cup of coffee."

He had it poured before I could tell him to forget it, and I had half of it polished off before I could tell myself that accepting it was tantamount to agreeing to a peace treaty I had no intention of honoring.

None of which kept me from finishing the coffee. While I did, Levi kept working. I don't know where he got a container of what looked like homemade granola, but he popped it open and layered crispy oats and dried cranberries between the yogurt and fruit.

"So how does a PI learn to be a chef?" Yeah, I know, it was too personal a question, too early in the morning, too soon after I realized that what we had of a relationship was based on lies. But I am, by nature, altogether too curious, and I simply couldn't help myself.

"One of my uncles owns a restaurant in Cleveland," he said without bothering to look my way. "I worked there when I was in college."

"So the bar was your perfect cover."

"Not completely a cover." He glanced my way, but only for a moment. "I really do own the bar. Figured as long as I had to live here, it was a good investment, and turns out, I was right. And I'm enjoying it, too. But then, there's not much call for private investigation work on an island this size."

"Unless you know a New York attorney. Or a police

chief who doesn't have the manpower or the budget to do his own babysitting."

"It pays to have connections."

I banged my coffee mug on the counter. "Good thing I moved here. Connections, that's something I've always been good at. Agents, editors, attorneys, producers, directors, actors. Lucky for me, most of them were legit and interested in bettering my career and theirs. But there were others, the ones who only wanted the connections I was able to provide." I'd been away from New York and from my high-powered, high-intensity life for a year, but even I never realized how the bitterness still lingered. "You'd be surprised how many people try to make a living by being hangers-on."

He finished filling the last parfait glass and when he laid down the spoon, the metallic clink set my teeth on edge. "That's not what I was talking about, and you know it."

"Maybe not, but it's true. Good ol' FX O'Grady! Nice to know I can still provide a public service."

He turned away long enough to give the French toast a flip and when he asked, "Serving platter?" his voice was as tight as the set of his shoulders.

It was in the cupboard just to his left, but it was too hard to explain, I mean, what with the tight ball of anger in my throat. I went over and got the platter and I held it while he scooped up piece after perfectly made piece of French toast and piled the dish high.

Domestic bliss it was not, but the mundane chore allowed enough time for both our tempers to simmer down.

"I figured breakfast was the least I could do." Finished loading up the platter, Levi took it out of my hands and set it on the countertop next to the parfaits and for the space of a heartbeat, I wondered how two people who had been so close just a short time before could suddenly find themselves acting like strangers. "To thank you for the nice, comfy place to sleep in front of your fireplace."

"Except you didn't sleep in front of the fireplace," I reminded him.

He didn't insult me by arguing the point and for that, I was grateful. If he could try to be civil, I told myself, so could I.

Maybe.

Maybe not.

"And you don't owe me any thanks," I said. So far, so good. But try as I might, I couldn't keep from adding, "You're getting paid to be here. Just like you've been paid to watch me ever since you came to the island."

He braced his hands against the breakfast counter. "I told you, coming here and keeping an eye on you, it started out as a job and ended up—"

"I'll take this to the dining room."

I grabbed the French toast and delivered it just as the librarians were piling down the steps.

"Good morning," they called out, one by one, and twittered (in the polite sort of way I expected from librarians and obviously because they didn't realize that he'd actually slept on the floor rather than in my bed) when Levi came out of the kitchen with the pot of coffee, then with the parfaits.

"We heard there was more excitement yesterday," Joyce said and reached for a piece of French toast. "Another dead nun! We never expected that sort of thing. Not here on the island."

"At least not until we thought of Agatha Christie," Angela reminded me.

"Christie . . ." I dropped into the nearest empty chair.

"What do you suppose the Christie story can tell us about what's going on over at Water's Edge?"

"That somebody really doesn't like nuns," Carole said.

"That somebody isn't what they seem," Bette added. "Because you know in the book, one of the guests is really the person who invited all the victims there in the first place. He's looking to bring the other guests to justice."

This particular bit of wisdom jibed with what Levi and I had discussed the night before. I thought about Sister Gabriel and the clothes in the attic. "But in the book," I said, "the one who isn't what he seems is also the one orchestrating the murders." This, of course, did not fit in with any theory I had because it was obvious Sister Gabriel hadn't taken a shot at herself.

What wasn't so obvious was if she might—or might not—have had something to do with both Sister Sheila's and Sister Helene's deaths.

I must have considered the possibility for longer than I thought, because when I pulled myself out of my thoughts and back to reality, I realized Levi had filled the china coffee cup in front of me. Far be it from me to waste perfectly good coffee. I took a sip and looked around the table.

"Where's Mr. Roscoe?" I wondered out loud. "And Tyler?"

Bette was working on one of the parfaits and she licked her spoon before she waved it in some vague direction. "The one man . . . the one with all the camera equipment . . . he was out early this morning. I heard him shuffling around and looked out the window just in time to see him get into his car. To tell the truth . . ." She blushed. "I was kind of grateful to see him go. He cornered me yesterday afternoon and talked birds. Birds, birds, birds. Librarians are used to that sort of thing, of course, we get all sorts of patrons who want to talk about every subject under the sun, but at least in the library, there's usually a phone ringing or another patron waiting with questions. Here, I couldn't escape."

"Out last night, too," Carole commented. She reached for the serving platter. "We were cleaning up the kitchen when he came in and that was . . ." She looked to her friends.

"Ten, I bet," Bette said.

"Maybe even later," Joyce said and added for my benefit, "We weren't cleaning up from dinner. It was like a late-night snack."

"And wine." Bette giggled.

"And that man, the one with the camera equipment . . ." Angela thought about it for a moment. "When he came in, we asked if he'd like a glass of wine, but he said he was tired, that he'd been out taking photographs of birds. What sort of pictures do you suppose a man takes of birds in the middle of the night?"

What sort, indeed.

I reminded myself to bring up the subject with Tyler when next I saw him. Until then . . .

"And Mr. Roscoe?" I asked. "Where's he this morning?"

"He was out even later last night," Bette assured me. "Him and those maps of his. Always his maps!" She rolled her eyes. "It's like those things are sacred, he never puts that tube of them down."

"Genealogists." Angela, too, must have had experience with the same types, because her voice carried just as much strained patience. "And him, I tried to have a conversation with yesterday," she added. "Asked him what his favorite sources are. You know, for research. He blew me off."

"Not like one of those roots types at all," Joyce said.

"They're usually more like that birdman. Always yapping about family and research sources."

"I get the feeling he's not finding everything he thought he'd find when he came to the island," Carole said. "When I asked him yesterday how his search was going, he said he was having no luck at all. He's probably just embarrassed. You know how genealogists love to show off their research skills."

I was sure she was right, and I didn't worry about it. There were other things on my mind.

I left the ladies to their breakfast and went into the kitchen to start cleaning up.

"You're going out?"

Something about the speediness of my work must have alerted Levi.

"I thought I'd go over to Water's Edge."

"I'd like to go with you."

I snapped the lid on the container of granola and set it aside. "You don't have to."

"I do if I want to get paid."

"Of course."

"Look . . ." I had the carton of yogurt in my hands and he took it away from me before he continued. "As long as we have to do this—"

"But we don't, do we?"

"We do because Hank says we have to, and as long as we have to, let's try to make it as painless as possible."

It was the grown-up thing to do.

Tell that to the teenaged voice of unreason inside my head.

Luckily, before it had a chance to talk, my phone rang.

I checked the caller ID and told Levi, "It's Hank," before I answered.

Hank started talking the moment I said hello, and he didn't give me a chance to get a word in edgewise. By the time I hung up, Levi was eager to know what was going on.

"Hank's over at Water's Edge," I told him. "Those clothes that were up in the attic are missing. And so is Sister Gabriel."

I can't say Water's Edge was in an uproar by the time Levi and I got there because let's face it, *uproar* and *nuns* are not two words that are generally used in the same sentence.

There was a buzz in the air, though, and it was one more of anxiety than excitement.

"We've looked everywhere," Sister Catherine told me the minute I walked in the door. "She's nowhere to be found."

I threw Hank a look. If he was smart—and I had no doubt that he was—I knew he hadn't said a word to the nuns about the clothes missing from the attic. The nuns were worried about Sister Gabriel's safety. Hank, though, had other things in mind.

I waited until Sister Liliosa gathered all the nuns into the living room before I closed in on Hank.

"Took a powder, huh?"

Levi stood to Hank's left. "Remember, that's what you thought about Sister Helene, too. And she wasn't as missing as she was dead."

It made sense in a terrible way. Except for the missing disguise.

"You've checked with Jayce?" I asked Hank.

His curt nod told me all I needed to know. "Already been four ferries over to the mainland this morning. She could have been on any one of them. Out of her habit and with her hair colored, there's no telling what she looks like."

It was an innocent enough comment and I knew Hank was right. Yet something about what he said awoke the memory of another throwaway comment someone had made about that big dinner party back in New York.

"There's no telling what she looks like," I mumbled, and when both Levi and Hank looked at me as if I'd started speaking Chinese, I explained, "The dinner in New York, Sister Gabriel had the flu. She wasn't there."

To his credit, Levi caught on right away. Believe me, I did not attribute this to the fact that our psyches were working as one and our heart beating in sync. I'd never felt more disconnected from anyone in my life. But remember, Levi was a PI and the way I figured it, a PI has to think a whole lot like an author does. Take a situation, turn it on its head. Take what looks like a simple fact and look at it in a new light.

We'd been using the light of reason when maybe we should have shone the big, bright spotlight of suspicion on the situation.

"What Bea's saying," Levi said for Hank's benefit, "is that none of these nuns have ever seen Sister Gabriel before."

Hank wrinkled his nose and scrunched his eyes. At least for a moment. Then the truth dawned on him and his eyes got wide. "You're telling me that the Sister Gabriel who was here—"

"Might not be Sister Gabriel at all," I said. "It's like *And Then There Were None*, the man the other guests thought was just one of them was really the killer."

"And you think—"

"I don't know what I think, Hank," I had to admit. "But

it is an interesting possibility, isn't it? Sister Liliosa has all the nuns' contact information," I told him even though I was pretty sure he remembered.

Hank went into the living room and both he and Sister Liliosa came out again in a bit and headed upstairs. When he came down again, he had his phone up to his ear.

"I appreciate your help, Sister," Hank said. "No, no, there's nothing to worry about. I just wanted to clear up a few things." He listened for a few moments. "Sister Sheila? Well, of course you heard about that, didn't you? The story is all over the news. Yes, she was attending the retreat here. Yes, yes. Sister Helene was, too. But those questions I asked you, don't worry about them, Sister. What I was asking about and what's happened here, it's probably not connected at all. Thank you, Sister. Yes, God bless you, too."

He ended the call and tapped the phone against his chin.

"You were right, Bea," he told me. "Sister Gabriel did miss the dinner in New York. Sick as a dog and her doctor refused to let her go. But I guess you can understand that. The poor dear is eighty-six years old."

My mouth fell open. "Our Sister Gabriel was, what? Maybe thirty-five?"

"If she was a day."

Before we had a chance to figure out what it might all mean and how it related to the murders, Sister Francelle poked her head out of the living room doorway. "We're ready, Chief," she told Hank and when he walked into the room and didn't tell us to wait, Levi and I followed.

I wasn't surprised to find Sister Liliosa at the center of whatever was going on. She stood in front of the fireplace, her hands clutched at her waist. "We've taken a vote," she told Hank, and then because it was apparent neither Levi nor I knew what she was talking about, she looked our way.

"When the chief arrived here this morning," Sister Liliosa said, "he informed us that we might all be in danger. Yes, yes, I know," she added before Hank could interrupt. "It's a long shot, but it's a possibility. Kind of like dying and going to hell. You're pretty sure you're safe, but there's always that little chance. So the chief here, he told us there's a possibility that Sister Gabriel is somehow involved in all this, in the murders and the attempted murders, though how she took a shot at herself . . ." Sister Liliosa and Hank had obviously been at odds over this not-so-little detail. That would explain why, for a second, her expression soured. "Anyway, the chief told us he thought it might be best if we all left here and went back to our own convents."

"And we've talked about it," Sister Mary Jean put in.

"But it didn't take us long to make up our minds," Sister Grace added.

Sister Liliosa took a step forward. "We're staying. And before you can argue the point, Chief, hear me out."

Yeah, like anyone would dare not give her the chance!

"It's already Thursday," she pointed out. "And we're all scheduled to leave on Saturday, anyway. That's only two more days and if your officers can't be with us the entire time—"

"They'll be here," Hank assured the nuns even before Sister Liliosa could finish.

"Our other objection to leaving is far more practical. If we change our airline tickets, our convents are going to have to pick up the bill. We're not willing to put that kind of financial burden on each convent's budget."

"So we're staying." Sister Grace stood up and walked to Sister Liliosa's side. "Besides all that, there's the question of justice to consider. We need to help you find out what happened to Sister Sheila."

"And to Sister Helene," Sister Mary Jean joined them.

"And to Sister Gabriel," Sister Paul said, stepping up.

"And it's not like we think we're professionals or anything," Sister Catherine said. "Not like all of you. But we have to do what we can to make sure the person who did this answers for it. And we've got God on our side, remember." When Sister Catherine stood shoulder to shoulder with her fellow Sisters, her eyes gleamed.

The rest of the Sisters followed suit, even Sister Margaret, whose head seemed a little higher and whose eyes didn't look nearly as rheumy when she joined the group.

Faced with the determination of the seven of them, Hank had no choice but to give in.

"But you'll stay in the house," he said, wagging a finger in their direction. "And nobody goes anywhere alone."

"Agreed," Sister Liliosa said.

Hank's phone rang. He picked up the call and listened for a moment, held up a finger to tell us all to hold on, and stepped into the hallway and though I tried to eavesdrop, it was impossible to hear anything but the low rumble of his voice and a couple words here and there that pretty much amounted to *you're kidding me* and *you think it's true?*

By the time he stepped back into the room, he was shaking his head.

"That was the chief of police over in Sandusky," he said, then explained for the Sisters who weren't familiar with the area. "It's right across the lake on the mainland, not that far away. They've got our Sister Gabriel in custody. Seems she ran a red light in a stolen car this morning and since we had an alert out on her, the cop who stopped her paid attention."

"Well, that's wonderful!" Sister Grace clapped her hands together. "That means the mystery is solved!"

"I'm afraid it's not as easy as that." Thinking it over,

Hank chewed on his lower lip. "See, they got Sister Gabriel in custody over at the station, and they asked her about the dead nuns and the attempt on her life. She's not talking."

"But she did admit killing Sister Sheila and Sister Helene, right?" Sister Paul was sure of it. "She must have! She couldn't hide a secret that terrible. Did she say she was some sort of hit man?"

"Well, that's the thing, isn't it?" Hank scratched a hand behind his ear. "About the hit man, see. She says she's got nothing to do with killing anybody. In fact, she swears the reason she sneaked off the island is because somebody is trying to kill her!"

❖ 17 ❖

I stared at the mirror and the reflection that stared back at me—a woman who was vaguely familiar, and vastly different.

The eyes were mine. The nose was the same one I remember my college friends once telling me was perfect: short, slim, turned up just the slightest bit at the tip. The cheeks looked a tad pudgier than I liked to think was possible, and I blamed that on the white linen cap that covered my head and completely hid my hair and the wimple over it where Sister Liliosa was just finishing pinning one of her black veils.

She stepped back and beamed a smile at me. "You look good."

"Do I?" We were in Levi's living room in front of a full-length mirror that we'd hauled over from Kate's, and

I couldn't help but take another gander. I turned to my right. I pivoted to my left. "I look—"

Sister Liliosa laughed. "Like a nun! Just like you're supposed to look."

I checked out the long black habit I was wearing, the sturdy and sensible black shoes, and the silver crucifix that hung on my chest and caught the light when I whirled to try to see the back of my outfit.

"It's amazing," I said.

"I'll say." Levi was in the kitchen doorway, his arms crossed over his chest and a gleam in his eye that I decided right then and there to ignore. He looked from me in my traditional habit to Kate, who was wearing one of Sister Catherine's short, gray habits and half-veils, to Luella in jeans and a red sweater much like the one Sister Helene was wearing the day I first met her. Chandra was down at the end of the line, also in a traditional habit, and when Levi glanced her way, he broke into a smile.

Another thing for me to ignore—that smile and all the warmth it sent flashing through my insides.

Then again, that wasn't exactly too hard when I took a look at Chandra, too.

Her veil sat at a slant on her head, giving her a dashing, jaunty look I was pretty sure nuns weren't supposed to have. Her habit was bunched up at the back to reveal the purple capris she wore underneath. And something told me that the sandals with the sparkling, beaded toe band would have to go.

The nuns—the real nuns—gathered around Chandra to get her costume in order just as Hank marched in, a coffee cup in his hand and a look on his face that reminded me of the thunderclouds that built over the lake in hot, summer weather.

"I still don't like it," he grumbled.

I shot him a look. We'd had this same argument earlier in the day out of earshot of the nuns, and I didn't want to bring it all up again when they were around. I moved toward the kitchen, remembering only after it was too late that my habit brushed the tops of my shoes and that I'd need to learn to maneuver in it if I wasn't going to look like a complete phoney.

"Don't make them feel guilty," I mumbled when I breezed (okay, so it was more like stutter-stepped) past Hank and into the kitchen, kicking the long skirt of the habit out in front of me so I wouldn't trip. I made sure I kept my voice down so the nuns—real and fake—in the living room wouldn't hear. "I told them that I was sure this was going to work."

"Well, I don't like it," Hank muttered.

"That makes two of us." Levi joined us over near the kitchen sink, though the way I remember it (and believe me, I remember it very clearly) I had not invited him or asked for his opinion. "It's dangerous."

"Not with Hank's guys there." This, too, was something I'd pointed out a couple dozen times over the course of the last few hours. "You'll have guys out on the water, so we don't have to worry about any potshots from boats—right, Hank?"

He nodded.

"And you'll have guys stationed out front and in the back garden at Water's Edge and inside the house, too."

This, too, was what we'd planned so he didn't bother to confirm.

"So what can possibly happen?"

I didn't give either one of them a chance to answer. I was a fiction writer at heart, after all, and given enough time to noodle the situation, I could think of a million things that could go wrong, each more complicated—and gruesome—than the last.

This, I should note, is exactly why the League of Literary Ladies had offered its services.

"We can't let something happen to another one of the nuns," I reminded them. "We've got to draw out whoever it is that's after them. And we can't use them as bait. We all agreed on that. That would be dangerous and it would be wrong."

"Any more wrong than using you four as bait?" Levi asked.

"I can defend myself pretty well," I said, and left it up to him to remember the time he'd once followed me down a dark street and I didn't know it was him. Years of self-defense classes back in New York had paid off; I'd taken him out with a well-placed punch in the nose.

Maybe he did remember. Maybe that's why he sounded so prickly when he pointed out, "And Kate, Chandra, and Luella?"

I glanced into the living room where the nuns were gathered around my friends, fussing and fidgeting, making sure that their habits looked just right and giving them last-minute advice.

My heart squeezed, and my voice caught behind a ball of emotion in my throat. "You know I'm not going to let anything happen to them," I said.

Hank gave me the briefest of nods. It might have been subtle, but I knew what it meant—he was done trying to reason with me, and he was finally okay with that. It was time for action and now that he'd committed, he'd do everything in his power to make sure that my plan went off without a hitch.

"We've got the property covered from all sides," he said and as he had done earlier after I presented my plan and we hustled the nuns out of the retreat center and over to Levi's, he pointed to the piece of paper on the kitchen sink and the rough drawing of Water's Edge. "I've got men here, here, and here." He poked a finger against the parts of the drawing that represented the garden and at various other places around the property. "And like you said, men out on the water. They're going to be fishing. Like they belong there, so we don't give anything away."

"If there is anything to give away." From the start, Levi had been even more opposed to the plan than Hank. Some little part of me said it was because the whole thing was my idea. But the kinder, gentler me (the one that didn't remember what a treacherous snake he was) said he was honestly concerned.

"We don't even know if she's telling the truth." He threw his hands in the air. "You've heard it a dozen times today, Bea. The cops over in Sandusky are talking to Sister Gabriel . . . or whoever she really is. They don't know if she's lying. All she'll say is—"

"That someone's out to get her." I nodded.

"So she could be making the whole thing up."

"In which case, nothing ventured, nothing gained, and I've got my Halloween costume worked out for this year." I ran a hand over the skirt of the habit. "But if she is telling the truth—"

"This could work. This could flush out our killer." I had to give Hank credit, he didn't want to admit it, but he manned up. "If our guy doesn't know this Sister Gabriel is already on the mainland, he'll still be around here, still looking for her."

Levi leaned back against the kitchen sink. "Well, for the record—"

"You think the plan stinks," I said.

"I think the plan's dangerous," he snapped back.

"So noted," Hank grumbled. "Again."

"And I think," Levi said, "that if anyone's over at the retreat center with the Ladies, it should be—"

"You need to stay here with the nuns." It had been a sticking point from the moment I proposed the plan; I should have known Levi wouldn't give in without a last-ditch fight. I told him what I'd told him before. "If we're going to make this work, we've got to keep them safe."

Levi shot a look into the living room and grumbled enough of a *harrumph* to let me know he was surrendering. "Me and seven nuns. Who would have thought!"

Hank clapped him on the back. "The only way up here is through the back door. It's a perfect place to keep an eye on them and a perfect place to make sure no one comes at them. The living room curtains are closed, right?" He leaned backward to look that way just to be sure. "You tell them to stay away from windows and they'll be fine."

Levi sighed with exasperation. "What are we supposed to do all night, watch *The Sound of Music*?"

The nuns had other ideas. I heard the ruffle of playing cards and Sister Francelle called out, "Five card stud, deuces wild. You in, Levi?"

By the time seven o'clock rolled around, Luella, Kate, Chandra, and I had pretty much gotten used to jumping at every little noise and gasping at each breeze that billowed the curtains in the living room of Water's Edge. By eight, we'd settled down to watch a movie, though I have to admit, I was so uncomfortable in my hot, scratchy habit and so attuned to hyper-listening for each and every telltale sound in the house, I didn't pay much attention to what was on the screen.

I'm pretty certain it wasn't *The Sound of Music*.

At ten, Chandra suggested we conduct the book discussion meeting we'd missed on Monday and then again on Wednesday when we said we were going to have our makeup meeting, but I knew from the start that was a no-go idea and Luella and Kate agreed. It was quiet at Water's Edge. Peaceful. But that didn't mean we weren't all fidgety. Too nervous to think about George Eliot, that's for sure. Too antsy to do anything other than sit and wait and wonder what we might be waiting for.

Chandra was seated near the fireplace, and either she wasn't feeling the same tension in the air as the rest of us, or she was a really good actress who got big points for trying to keep our minds occupied.

And not-so-big points considering what she tried to get us to think about.

She stuck a finger under her wimple to scratch her forehead. "The landscapers are coming tomorrow. They're going to take the final measurements. You know . . . for the pool." She glanced my way before she turned to Kate. It must have been the habit and the veil that added such an air of innocence to her wide-eyed look. "And the lamppost."

A muscle jumped at the base of Kate's jaw.

"Another movie?" I suggested.

"Nothing about wildlife." The way Chandra jiggled her shoulders made the crucifix she wore on a gold chain around her neck jump. "I can't stand it anymore. I can't stand to think how we're mistreating Mother Earth. You know, with hunting." Her look at Luella was as pure as the newly driven snow. "And fishing."

Luella slapped the arms of her chair, but before she could say a word, Kate had already popped out of her seat.

"What on earth is wrong with you?" she asked Chandra. "Are you trying to pick a fight?"

"Me?" Maybe Chandra could pass for a nun. In some alternate universe. She certainly had the whole guiltless look down pat. "I don't know what you're talking about. I'm simply expressing an opinion. We're all allowed to do that, aren't we? We're all allowed to have opinions."

"We are," Luella told her, "but not when your opinions trample on other people's rights."

"I wouldn't dream of it," Chandra assured us. "Besides . . ." She pleated the skirt of her habit with busy, nervous fingers. "I'd think you'd all be happy for me. I made some money last summer. You know, with my tarot card and crystal readings. And now I'm going to use that money to beautify the neighborhood."

"Only what you have in mind isn't going to beautify the neighborhood." Kate's voice was as tight as the fists she pressed to her side. "It's going to make the neighborhood look hideous."

Chandra tossed her head and her veil twitched. "Beauty is in the eye of the beholder. Maybe you just need to see the pictures again. Then you'll remember how lovely it's all going to be." She stopped and thinking about it, she wrinkled her nose. "The drawings are in my purse. I left my purse back at Levi's. But I'll show you tomorrow. I'll show you how gorgeous that lamppost is going to look. Then you'll change your mind."

"Not a snowball's chance in hell," Kate grumbled.

Chandra wagged a finger at her. "Is that any way for a nun to talk?"

Luella sucked in a breath.

Kate shot toward Chandra.

I jumped out of my chair just a second before Kate could wrap her fingers around Chandra's neck.

"This is not good," I told them, but I swear, at that point, no one was listening anyway.

Kate tossed her hands in the air. "I'm not going to stand here and listen to this nonsense," she said. "And you, Chandra . . ." She drew in a breath that was just as shaky as the finger she pointed at Chandra. "You're going to hear from my attorney in the morning."

The self-satisfied smile Chandra responded with did nothing to calm Kate.

"Really?" Chandra was more used to flowing clothes and long skirts than I would ever be. When she rose from her chair, she almost made it look easy. "Bring it on, Kate. Because you know as well as I do what your attorney is going to tell you. My property, my business."

"Your property, our business. The whole neighborhood's business. Isn't that right, Bea?" Kate looked to me for support.

"It's not going to help to fight about it," I reminded them both.

But it was too late for that.

Kate is shorter than Chandra, and when she got up in her face, I was reminded of a small gray mouse trying to intimidate a large black bear. (Only don't tell Chandra that in her habit, I thought she looked like a large black bear.)

Kate wagged a finger under Chandra's nose. "You're not going to do this," she hissed. "You've spent years trying to mess with the neighborhood. You and your stinky full-moon bonfires. You and all those creepy people who come to your house so you can scam money out of them with all that loony tarot stuff. I've put up with a lot from you over the years, Chandra. But I'm not going to put up with some gigantic, ugly lamppost that's going to be so bright I won't be able to get a wink of sleep. And I'm not going to keep quiet about it, that's for sure. I'm going to the newspaper. I'm going to the village council. We're going to court. And you'd better be prepared for the fight of your life!"

Kate turned on her heels and headed for the door. "I'm going up to bed," she called.

"Don't forget to lock your door," I reminded her.

Done with pushing Kate to the edge, Chandra apparently decided it was time to see how far she could get with Luella. And me.

I knew Chandra pretty well. At least I always thought I did. The Chandra I knew back when I moved to the island wouldn't care a fig what Kate or I or even Luella thought of her. But the Chandra who'd been our friend for the last year, I thought she'd be more worried that she'd upset the applecart of our friendship.

Which, I suppose, is why I bristled when I saw her smile.

"I'm assuming you two ladies will be doing the same thing," Chandra said. "Taking me to court? You'll try to stop the swimming pool, won't you, Bea? But I'm telling you, it's not going to happen. My property, my pool. They're going to survey tomorrow and then they can start digging, and there's nothing you can do about it. And Luella . . ." For a second when Chandra turned to her, I swear her eyes got dewy and her smug smile sagged. Maybe it was just a trick of the light, because the next second, she threw her shoulders back, grinning again.

"I think it's only fair to let you know, Luella, that there's going to be a rally at the marina tomorrow morning, then more rallies all summer long. The local chapter of People Against Fishing Lake Erie is all set to go. We even made signs. *Swim Free and Never Get Caught!* You're the one who came up with the slogan, Luella, and PAFLE is forever grateful." She wrinkled her nose and looked down at her habit. "Speaking of getting caught, you think we'll nab our killer before then, Bea? Because I've got to be down at the marina at nine and I sure can't go dressed like this."

Under normal circumstances, I would have reassured Chandra. Of course we'd wrap up our case by then! Of course she wouldn't have to continue in her undercover nun capacity after tonight! Of course she was free to be herself so she could lead the hordes of PAFLE in their campaign!

But these weren't normal circumstances. Not when Luella's jaw was clenched tight and her breaths were coming hard and fast.

Chandra either didn't notice or didn't care. She breezed right on. "I'll be right up at the front of the crowd tomorrow. My sign is neon orange. I'm hoping it will look good for the TV cameras. I did tell you we called all the local stations on the mainland, didn't I? We've got to raise awareness. We've got to get our voices heard. People Against Fishing Lake Erie is going to do whatever it takes to—"

"Not listening!" Luella pressed her hands over her ears and hurried out of the room. "You've lost your mind, Chandra, and I'm not listening to any of this."

She managed the steps faster than any woman her age should have been able to and within a minute, I heard the thump when she slammed her bedroom door shut.

"So . . ." Chandra threw me a look. "What about you?"

"What about me?" I wasn't sure I looked sisterly when I stepped back and folded my arms over my chest, raised my head, and stuck out my chin. At that point, I didn't much care. "You want to pick a fight with me, too?"

"I don't want to pick a fight with anyone. I'm just looking

out for myself. And hey, when my friends aren't there, you can always come over and use the pool!"

I guess she thought this was a good thing, because Chandra was smiling when she, too, went upstairs to bed.

"Use the pool!" I grumbled the statement along with some choice words more appropriate to a misplaced New Yorker than to a nun and wondered what on earth had caused Chandra to lose her mind—and her common sense. Now that she knew who I really was, I would think she would have realized that I could and would fight this crazy project of hers from now until forever. I could afford it. I could afford to tie her up in court forever.

Another thought hit, and my shoulders slumped.

As soon as I found a new attorney.

Between thinking about Jason (and thus, thinking about Levi) and thinking about how my plan to flush out the person who'd been after Sister Gabriel was obviously a bust (and thus thinking about Levi, since thinking about the nuns made me think about how they were over at his place), I'd pretty much had it. I turned out the lights and left the living room, going over the apology in my head, the one I'd make to Hank in the morning for tying up so many hours of so many cops' time with the crazy plan that obviously didn't work.

I knew there was a cop staying up on the third floor and of course, that made me feel safe, but on my way upstairs, I checked the front door anyway.

Locked and secure.

I'd already turned to head upstairs when I remembered those wet footprints I'd found inside the kitchen door that night that seemed a lifetime ago.

That door, too, would be locked. I was sure of it, but I went into the kitchen anyway.

And stopped dead in my tracks.

Which, come to think of it, was a really poor choice of words. A single light had been left on over the sink, but the rest of the room was lost in shadows. I saw the hulking shape of a man in the darkest corner of the room.

"Who are you? What are you doing here?" I didn't need to try to sound indignant. There was something about wearing a habit like those of the confident, committed ladies over at Levi's that gave me courage. "You need to leave. Right now."

The shadow separated itself just a bit from the inky blackness around it, but I refused to step back when the man stepped forward. "Where's Ginger?" he growled.

"Ginger." It took no effort at all to pretend I was confused. "Who's Ginger?"

His chuckle was anything but pleasant. "Sister Gabriel. That's what she's calling herself. Where is the little bitch?"

This was exactly what I'd planned when I came up with the plan to flush out the person menacing the nuns, wasn't it?

So why had my feet turned to blocks of ice and my tongue to sand?

I scrambled to remember every shred of the plan that had seemed so easy and so brilliant such a short time before and counted on the fact that if I couldn't see the man completely, then he couldn't see me well, either. Beneath the white wool panel that topped my habit, my fingers flew over the keyboard of my phone, speed-dialing first the cop upstairs (who didn't pick up), then Hank (who did). I didn't disconnect the call.

"I need an answer, Sister, and I need it fast." The shadows quivered when the man took another step in my direction. "She's got something that belongs to my associates and I need it. Now."

It took a moment for my brain to catch up. "The package of books! Sister Gabriel, she said—"

"Where is it?" The man lurched forward and when he did, he stepped into the circle of light thrown by the lamp above the sink. That's when I noticed two things about him:

He had a gun pointed at me.

And he was—

"Joe Roscoe!" I was so surprised, I closed my hand over the crucifix I wore around my neck, as if that would keep the world from tipping on its axis.

He peered through the darkness at me and grumbled a curse. "What the hell are you—"

I tried for a smile. I did not even try to explain the habit. "Just visiting."

With the gun, he motioned me closer. "Well, that's too bad for you now that you've recognized me."

My body stayed put. My brain, on the other hand, whirled out of control. "That explains it," I blurted out. "The beigeness! You wanted to blend in with the scenery. You wanted to be so bland and boring that no one paid any attention to you. You . . ." I hoped he didn't hear the panic in my voice when I gulped. "You're a professional. That explains how you got in here, too."

"You mean how I got past all those cops outside?" Joe chuckled. It was not the warm and friendly sound I'd expect from a genealogist. He twitched the gun toward me again. "I'm a pissed professional. Get moving. Let's get outside so we don't wake up whoever else is around."

"Sister Gabriel . . . er . . . Ginger isn't. She's on the mainland. In police custody. She told them everything."

"This, I doubt. Ginger doesn't have the brains to get in out of the rain."

"But she did have the package." The lie fell so easily

from my lips, even I nearly believed it. "She left it behind when she ran off this morning and the other nuns . . . they, they gave it to me."

"I don't believe you."

"You can take that chance . . ." I slewed to my right and the deeper shadows over near the island in the center of the kitchen. "But if you and your associates . . ." There was something about the word that made my spine tingle. "If you want it back, then you'd better believe me. I'm the only one who knows where the package is."

"Then you'd better start talking." When he raised the gun, the barrel glinted in the light.

I didn't have a moment to lose, no weapon to speak of, and nothing to go on but instinct and instinct alone. I groped a hand across the island and grabbed onto the first thing my fingers touched. It happened to be a stainless steel bowl, and I winged it at Joe Roscoe. It clunked him in the side of the head just as the gun went off and I ducked behind the island.

As Fate would have it (thank you, Fate!) that was the exact moment Hank and a SWAT team burst through the back door.

18

"I have to admit, the first thing I thought of when I watched the cops arrest the guy was if it meant he didn't have to pay for his room."

Honestly, I wouldn't have admitted it if I didn't think Sister Catherine would understand. I guess she did because she laughed. "That just means you've got a good head on your shoulders," she told me. "And what was the second thing you thought of?"

I laughed, too. "The second thing was that if he didn't pay, I could take the amount he owed me and write it off my taxes as a business expense."

This, too, she thought was pretty funny. But then, I couldn't blame her for laughing at my lame jokes. It was Friday morning, less than twelve hours since Hank and his crew had swept into the house and hauled away the man I thought was bland-as-toast genealogist Joe Roscoe.

We were all in pretty good moods that morning. So much so that Sister Catherine had volunteered to bake what she called her Official Special Day Hallelujah Celebration Cake, a dessert that she traditionally served at the shelter in Philadelphia when one of the women there achieved some milestone like finding a job or starting back to school.

I had offered to help, not because I'm especially good at baking, but because the cake—a chocolate chiffon confection iced with salted caramel butter cream frosting—sounded so scrumptious, I had to see how it was made.

Sister Catherine and I had already been to the grocery store that morning and we had our ingredients lined up on the island that—so few hours before—had provided me shelter when Joe took a shot at me.

"Joe." I grumbled the name and didn't bother to apologize. "Imagine the nerve of the guy pretending to be a regular guest over at the B and B."

Sister Catherine cut parchment paper to fit into the bottoms of three round cake pans. "The police still aren't sure who he is?"

I'd been given the task of getting the salted caramel icing started and I measured brown sugar, salt, and cream into a saucepan. "They're sure they'll know soon enough. After they run his fingerprints. I'd bet anything that he's a professional hit man." I shivered at the very thought.

"Sent to retrieve whatever it was that Sister Gabriel . . . or whoever she is . . . had sent here." Sister Catherine shook her head in wonder. "How are they going to make sense of it all?"

"It would help if we could find that package." Thinking, I drummed my fingers on the countertop. "Sister Gabriel . . . or Ginger Mancini . . . or whoever she is . . . she's not talking and our hit man isn't, either. What do you suppose happened to it?"

"The package?" Sister Catherine shrugged. "Sister Liliosa swears it was delivered."

"And Ginger obviously never found it. Something told me if she had, she would have cut and run even sooner. Instead, she waited around and searched for it, and my guess is she only decided to get out of Dodge when she realized someone was after her. By then, she didn't care if she had the package or not, she just wanted to make sure she got off the island alive."

"Can't say I blame her."

"Me, either."

"But why have something sent here anyway? Why not just bring it along?"

This was something that hadn't escaped my attention, and I told Sister Catherine the theory I'd come up with during the night when I couldn't get a wink of sleep and I found myself pacing and sipping the last of that Château Lafite Rothschild 1996 in an effort to calm my nerves.

"It was something she couldn't get caught with," I said, sounding for all the world like I knew what I was talking about rather than just speculating. "Not by the cops and not by whoever it is who sent Joe Roscoe to find her."

"Drugs?"

"Maybe."

"But why pretend to be Sister Gabriel?"

This was the easy part. "The cops have talked to the real Sister Gabriel. Ginger Mancini is her great-niece. Ginger must have known her great-aunt was invited to the retreat and she must have known that Sister Gabriel— the real Sister Gabriel—was too sick to go to the dinner in New York. She knew no one would recognize her. Why, even in that article in the *New York Times* about all of you, there was no picture of Sister Gabriel, not from the front. The photo they ran of her showed a nun kneeling in front of an altar. It was taken from behind."

"So the Sister we thought was Sister Gabriel—"

"Was using a very clever disguise. She didn't count on the determination of whoever it was Joe called his associates." The very word made a tingle creep up my spine. "She sent the package along, thought she'd meet it here, and my guess is that's why she stashed the disguise in the attic. As soon as the package showed, she planned to ditch her habit behind and leave South Bass."

"But Joe showed first."

Another cold chill reminded me that we'd all been very lucky.

Well, not all of us.

I drummed my fingers some more.

"It doesn't explain Sister Sheila," I said, just like I'd said to myself a dozen times the night before. "Or Sister Helene."

"Maybe they saw something. Maybe they knew something."

"But it doesn't explain how Sister Grace nearly tripped and fell down the steps here in the house, or how that piece of the exterior stone fell on top of us."

"Maybe Joe just made a mistake," Sister Catherine said. "Maybe he wasn't sure which of us was Ginger Mancini. I suppose to the untrained eye, one nun looks like any other."

"I suppose," I admitted. "Anything's possible. Chances are, the cops aren't going to get much out of Joe, not for a while, anyway. Hank tells me Joe asked for his attorney. It's some high-powered guy from Chicago and he's on his way to the island now."

"Friends in high places." Sister Catherine rolled her

eyes toward the ceiling, then made a face. "That poor, young policeman who was upstairs!" Not that she could see him, but Sister Catherine turned her gaze heavenward. "He ended up with quite a bump on the head."

"Joe . . ." The very name tasted sour in my mouth. "Knocked him out with one whack," I said. "Officer Jenkins will be fine. I think he's embarrassed that he never knew Joe was already hiding upstairs when he got there. But then, like I said, I'm betting Joe is a professional. That explains why he was confident enough to take a shot at Sister Gabriel . . . cr . . . Ginger from a boat. Nobody but a very skilled marksman would even have attempted it. It also explains . . ."

I was trying my best to be objective, and doing a pretty good job of it, but it was hard not to be creeped out when I remembered what Hank had told me the night before.

"That cardboard tube, the one Joe always carried with him, the one he said was filled with maps of the island and his family trees." The tingle along my spine intensified. "That tube had a high-powered rifle in it. That's what he used to take the shot at Ginger. It takes a mighty cold man to do that sort of thing."

Sister Catherine mixed oil and egg yolks and added vanilla and sugar. "Well, all's well that ends well," she said.

The little sniffle at the end of her sentence didn't exactly go along with the chipper statement.

I'd just taken the saucepan with the beginnings of the icing in it to the stove, and I turned and found her wiping the back of her hand over her cheeks.

"Hey, it's all right," I told her. "Like you said, it's over now. We'll find out the truth about Sister Sheila and Sister Helene. And Ginger Mancini, no matter what she's up to or what she's trying to hide, she's safe. We're all safe now."

"It's not that." She set down her mixing spoon so she could dab her teary eyes with the corner of the white apron she wore over her gray habit. "I was just thinking. That's all. About the cake."

"You cry when you think about cake?"

This got a watery little laugh from her. Just as I intended. "It's my Gram's recipe," she said.

I suddenly felt like an idiot. "Your grandmother, the one who's sick. I'm so sorry, I—"

"Nothing to be sorry about!" Sister Catherine smiled through a fresh cascade of tears. "I talked to her this morning and she's hanging in. That's certainly a blessing. And the memories . . ." She sniffled. "The memories are what get us through after someone's gone, aren't they? Whenever the good Lord decides to take Gram . . . well, I'll have the memories." She grinned. "And her secret recipe for this chocolate cake! She made it for special occasions when we were kids— birthdays, holidays. She's the one who christened it the Official Special Day Hallelujah Celebration Cake and thanks to her, so many women who've come through the shelter have taken that happy memory away with them. I'm going straight to see her when I leave the island on Saturday." Sister Catherine's grin was infectious.

"I called my brother this morning and he wasn't around, but he called back and left me a message a little while ago . . ." For a moment, her expression clouded and I thought she'd start crying again.

Instead, she twitched her shoulders. "I think he said he'd meet me at the hospice center."

"You think?"

"It was so hard to hear him. There was an awful lot of noise in the background. I don't know what it was, but it practically drowned him out. I'll try him again later and tell him I think we're close to the end. It would be nice if we could both be there with Gram when the Lord takes her. It would give her great comfort."

I thought of my own grandmother who lived in a mansion overlooking the Hudson River and spent her days running other people's lives. "She's a gentle woman?" I asked Sister Catherine.

"But no pushover," she said. "You know, when we were kids . . . well, I was an angel. That goes without saying." She smiled in a way that said she was teasing. "But Michael . . . Gram had her hands full with him. Drugs, some minor brushes with the law. He's straightened himself out," she added quickly as if I might criticize. "Thanks to her iron fist and a whole lot of prayers. I think it would be good for Gram to see him one last time. That way, she can remember what a fine job she did raising him. The three of us haven't been together since that dinner in New York."

It was a nice thought, and for a few minutes, we let it settle between us while we worked at our tasks. I heated the mix of brown sugar, salt, and cream, then let it cool while I beat some butter to add to the icing.

Sister Catherine sifted flour and beat egg whites.

"He's nice," she said after a bit.

"Your brother, Michael? I'm sure he is."

Sister Catherine laughed. "Not my brother. Well, he's nice, too, but he's not who I'm talking about. You know who I'm talking about."

I didn't.

At least not for a couple heartbeats.

My shoulders sagged. "Look . . ." I set down the mixer so I could give Sister Catherine my full attention. "You've got the wrong idea."

"Do I? Then I apologize. I can only say that Levi was

chomping at the bit to get over here last night. He was sure something was going to happen to you and as it turns out, he was right, wasn't he? I got the feeling he would have given his right arm to make sure you stayed safe."

I slapped the mixer back in the bowl with the butter.

A little too hard.

Before I could continue, I had to clean up the splats of melted butter all around.

I grabbed a cloth and wet it at the sink. "He's getting paid," I rumbled and when Sister Catherine didn't respond, I was sure to add, "Hank was paying him to keep an eye on me. So really, it's nice to know he's so conscientious, but believe me, it had everything to do with a paycheck. And nothing to do with me."

"If you say so." She busied herself mixing cake batter. "He's a lousy poker player."

Not a comment I was expecting from her, so my head shot up.

"He's a lousy poker player," Sister Catherine reiterated. "Can't maintain a poker face. His left eye twitches when he's holding lousy cards."

Since I wasn't planning on playing poker—or anything else—with Levi anytime soon, I filed this bit of information away in the interesting but pointless category.

"Of course, it didn't help that he was sitting next to Sister Margaret." Sister Catherine laughed softly. "The poor dear nattered on and on all through the card game and I kept wondering how Levi could think straight at all. One moment Sister Margaret was peeking over at his cards and upping the ante, the next she was talking about some fertilizer delivery she couldn't find. Said she was sure it had come, but she couldn't remember what she'd done with it."

"She talked about fertilizer the day I saw her in the

greenhouse," I mentioned in passing. "There must be some connection to something she's doing back home. She is a sweet woman. I'm only sorry she doesn't remember what she did with—"

I froze.

"What is it?" Sister Catherine asked. "You've thought of something."

"Sister Liliosa said Ginger's package was delivered."

Sister Catherine nodded.

"And Sister Margaret said she got a package of fertilizer."

Sister Catherine's eyes went wide. "You think—"

I wiped my hands against the white apron I had looped around my neck. "Ginger looked everywhere. She rummaged through all your rooms and every other room in the house. But I bet she never looked—"

"In the greenhouse!" Sister Catherine was right behind me when I raced out of the kitchen.

We found our way to the greenhouse and I paused just inside, trying to picture Sister Margaret as I'd seen her the day the piece of the house came down and nearly clunked me and Sister Catherine in the garden.

"She was over there," I said, and led the way to the potting bench. The terra-cotta pots that Sister Margaret had been organizing were still stacked into neat piles. I stood where she'd been standing and Sister Catherine stopped to watch me, not far from where I'd stood when I talked to Sister Margaret that day, my hands automatically flying over the flowerpots, just as Sister Margaret's had.

"What if she thought her fertilizer order had come?" I asked Sister Catherine and myself. "What if she scooped it up off that table where Sister Liliosa said the delivery guy had left it? She could have brought it here and—"

I looked at the two shelves below the potting table and sucked in a breath.

So did Sister Catherine when I retrieved a package and set it on the potting table. It was addressed to Sister Gabriel Hyland.

As it turned out, it was a good thing we didn't open the package. Evidence, and all that.

When Hank did and peeked inside, he let out a low whistle and slid the contents out on the potting table and even later, after a team of FBI agents arrived to take over, I still remembered the tingle of excitement I felt when I saw what was inside the package.

Stacks of fifty-dollar bills.

Lots of stacks of fifty-dollar bills.

We were back in the house, and Hank was just finishing up with the team of feds. "It was the consecutive numbers on the bills that gave them away," he told me and Sister Catherine. "They were taken in a bank robbery in Denver."

"Denver, where the real Sister Gabriel lives," I said.

Hank nodded. "And where her great-niece, Ginger Mancini, also lives. The feds here are on their way to Sandusky now to talk to Ginger, but I think we can guess what happened. She was probably supposed to hold on to the money from the robbery."

"And she took off with it instead. Disguised as a nun so no one would recognize her." I had to admit, it was ingenious. Or at least it would have been if it had worked.

"Somebody wasn't happy with Ginger," Hank said. Understatement. "She should know—"

"No honor among thieves," Sister Catherine said.

Hank headed for the door. "You've both given your

statements to the FBI?" he asked, even though he knew we had. "Well, good." He clapped his cap on his head. "Now that all this craziness is taken care of, maybe things can get back to normal around here."

We waited until he'd gone before we looked around the kitchen.

"Think we can salvage your cake?" I asked Sister Catherine.

She grinned. "I think they don't call it the Official Special Day Hallelujah Celebration Cake for nothing! You pour the batter into the cake pans. I'll preheat the oven."

I got to work, only half listening when the oven click-click-clicked in response to Sister Catherine turning it on.

That is, until the oven whooshed, belched, and exploded.

◈ 19 ◈

I went airborne for the space of a couple rib-hammering heartbeats. That is, before I slammed into the kitchen cupboards.

My head hit first, then I collapsed like a rag doll on the floor, but thankfully, I didn't black out. If I had, I never would have seen Sister Catherine's dove-gray veil catch fire.

I guess if I was thinking more clearly, I would have screamed for help, but the way I saw it, I didn't have time. My legs shaking, my blood racing, and my ears ringing like I had first-row seats at a heavy metal concert, I hauled myself to my feet and lurched across the kitchen.

Sister Catherine lay facedown on the floor, her arms splayed out at her sides and her legs at funny angles, and I yanked the flaming veil from her head and tossed it into the kitchen sink. A flare of orange flame shot up nearly as high as the light fixture over the sink. The fire consumed the fabric in an instant, signaling that the veil was completely annihilated with a puff of black smoke that trailed through the air and wrapped me in acrid fumes.

I gulped down the sick feeling in my stomach; I didn't like to think what would have happened if the veil had still been on Sister Catherine's head.

That was the moment when . . . well, I was going to say all hell broke loose, but I guess it's more accurate to call it holy hell.

The nuns converged from all corners of the house and above their startled cries and the high-pitched ringing in my ears, I heard one of them say she'd already called 911.

Hey, by this time, we should have just put the cops on speed dial.

The thought hit just as I took the time to take a careful look at Sister Catherine. She wasn't moving and I knew better than to flip her over and risk making any injuries she might have even worse. As it turned out, I never had the chance. I pitched toward the kitchen island, one hand out to keep myself upright, and kicked Sister Catherine's phone. It must have fallen out of her pocket when she was blown back from the oven, and before anyone else could trip on it, I picked it up. By the time I tucked it away in the pocket of my jeans and steadied myself again, Sister Francelle was already kneeling on the floor. She put two fingers to Sister Catherine's neck.

"It's weak, but she's got a pulse." Sister Francelle sat back on her heels and let go a breath of relief. "She's alive!"

"Don't you worry about her." Gentle hands clutched my shoulders and turned me away from the scene.

Too disoriented to question what was happening, I was cradled in Sister Liliosa's arms and marched into the dining room before she plunked me down in a chair.

"We've got to make sure nothing's wrong with you." She bent down to look me in the eye and spoke slowly.

"But—" I was already halfway up and out of the chair when she pushed me back down.

"Sister Catherine is in good hands," Sister Liliosa assured me. "And listen, the ambulance is almost here."

I would have to take her word for it, I couldn't hear the siren, not above the never-ending buzz between my ears.

But not so impossible to miss Hank and the crew of paramedics when they burst through the front door and made a beeline for the kitchen. A minute later, Hank stalked into the dining room.

"What happened?" he asked me.

At least I was pretty sure that's what he said.

"Ears." I pointed to each in turn. My own voice sounded like it was muffled beneath a thick down pillow and I had a feeling I was talking too loud, but I couldn't help myself. "The stove blew up!"

Hank nodded. "I know that. But how?"

I shrugged, then added, "Old," in case he'd forgotten what the kitchen looked like.

I was convinced I was right and wished Hank looked like he was convinced, too. I tugged on the sleeve of his jacket.

"You don't think . . . Joe Roscoe? Could he have—"

The way Hank shook me off, I wasn't sure if he was telling me I was right. Or that I was way off base.

I didn't have time to find out, either. One of the firefighters who'd just arrived at the scene ducked into the dining room and pulled Hank out into the hallway.

I grumbled a curse and wasn't even sorry. After all, if I couldn't hear it, maybe Sister Liliosa couldn't, either.

"Not to worry." When she patted my shoulder, I figured

it was Sister Liliosa's way of forgiving me for my language. Instead, she added, "You stay put. I'll do a little eavesdropping." She tiptoed to the doorway and paused there. A second before Hank reappeared in the doorway, she gave me the thumbs-up and scooted back my way.

Hank waved toward two paramedics who walked into the room behind them. The emergency crew was beginning to look way too familiar. "They're going to check you out," he said.

"And Sister Catherine?"

Even as I asked I saw another paramedic team wheel a gurney out of the house.

Sister Catherine was flown to the mainland for treatment at a hospital there, and even by the time the plane took off, she was still unconscious and she couldn't speak up for herself.

I had no such problem.

I was thoroughly checked by the paramedics, but since they didn't find any obvious damage and I promised I'd see a doctor about my hearing as soon as possible, there wasn't much they could do. Besides, Dorothy was right when she said there was no place like home. The librarians were off somewhere with Marianne, and Tyler was, no doubt, in hot pursuit of warblers; my home was blessedly quiet that early afternoon.

That is, until Kate, Chandra, and Luella arrived.

I'd been sitting in my private suite, but that wasn't good enough for them. Within thirty minutes of their arrival, I had my jammies on and my feet up on the couch. I was covered with a plaid wool blanket even though I wasn't cold, there was a cup of tea at my elbow even though I wasn't thirsty, and Chandra had just brought me a bowl of tomato soup and a bag of those little crackers shaped like fish.

No, I wasn't hungry. But who can resist that sort of pampering?

"You're going to need to scoot around." While Chandra stood by with the soup and crackers at the ready, Kate grabbed my feet and gently moved them from the couch to the floor. "She can't hold that soup bowl in her lap," she told Chandra and really, I thought that was the end of that.

Until Chandra set the bowl on a nearby table, spooned up some soup, and stuck the spoon in my mouth.

It wasn't like I had much choice so I swallowed dutifully. "Really . . ." Before she could get another spoonful into me, I waved away her ministrations. "I can do that by myself. I'm fine."

"Lucky to be fine." Luella eyed me from the other side of the room. "Someone wanted you dead."

"Someone was the someone—" Another spoonful of soup cut off my protest. I gulped it down. "Someone was the someone who built that stove about a million years ago," I told Luella. "Come on, there was a reason Elias didn't want us cooking over at Water's Edge. It—"

Chandra popped two goldfish crackers in my mouth.

I chewed and swallowed before I said, "Now we know why he wanted us to do all the cooking here. It's my fault. I should have told Sister Catherine that she couldn't bake a cake at the retreat center. We should have come here after we were done at the grocery store and she could have used my kitchen. Sister Catherine . . ." When Chandra came at me with another spoonful of steaming soup, I turned my head and put out a hand. "What's the latest word?"

Kate sat down on the couch next to me. "No word. Not

yet. Hank promised he'd call us as soon as he knew anything."

"And it isn't your fault."

We all jumped at the sound of a fourth voice and, as one, turned. Sister Liliosa stood in the doorway to my suite.

"I hope you don't mind I let myself in the front door," she said.

"Of course not." The nun's arrival was just the excuse I needed. I waved away Chandra and her spoon and her crackers. "Please, come sit down."

Luella grabbed the chair from in front of my desk and dragged it over and Sister Liliosa sat. "I wanted to call," she said, "but I remembered what you said. About the ringing in your ears."

"It's better," I told her and didn't bother to point out that *better* is a relative word. The high-pitched sound coming from somewhere inside my skull was just about driving me crazy. "How did you get here?"

Sister Liliosa arranged the skirt of her long habit. "I took one of the golf carts, of course. The retreat center is in such an uproar, I doubt anyone's even noticed that I'm gone. And really . . ." Her cheeks, already pink, flushed cherry red. "It really was wonderful tooling around the island with the wind in my face."

"You haven't heard—" I was afraid to finish the sentence.

"About Sister Catherine? No. Not a word from anyone. We're praying. For her. For the doctors and nurses who are helping her at the hospital."

There was silence for a minute and I was grateful for it. Without the added voices muddling up whichever of my senses had been scrambled, the ringing toned down a bit. I sighed and reached for the cup of tea, sniffing it carefully before I took a sip. It was strong, black tea laced with milk, the drink I'd learned to love in England and not one of Chandra's stinky brews.

"You didn't come all this way in a golf cart just to see how I was doing," I said to the Sister.

"Of course I did. You saved Sister Catherine's life, and besides, we've all come to depend on you and care for you." She scooted forward in her chair. "But that's not the only reason I came. I had to tell you what it was the police chief and the firefighter were talking about. You know, back at the retreat center."

The memory rose from my brain through a fog—Sister Liliosa listening in at the door between the dining room and the hallway.

"That firefighter had already given the stove a quick look and he told Chief Florentine what he'd found."

"Bea says the stove was old," Chandra commented, and since I'd refused any more of her crackers, she popped a few down. I wondered if she realized they were shaped like fish and hoped her friends from the morning's protest at the marina didn't catch wind of her treachery.

"Well, it was obviously old," Sister Liliosa agreed. "But the firefighter said that as he was examining the stove, Sister Paul stepped forward and made a confession."

I put a hand to my suddenly hammering heart. "Sister Paul? You can't mean that she admitted that she—"

"Messed with the stove? Of course not!" Why did I have a feeling that if Sister Liliosa had had a ruler, I would have gotten my knuckles slapped? "What she confessed was that she'd used the oven. Late last night. After all the commotion and the arrest of that man who tried to shoot you. She said she was too keyed up to sleep so she went downstairs and rewarmed some of the leftover pizza from the other night."

"And the oven worked just fine." Even if my ears had been working at 100 percent, I knew my voice would have sounded leaden. But then, some realizations just sort of have that effect. "That means—"

Sister Liliosa nodded. "The firefighter confirmed it. He said that sometime between yesterday when Sister Paul reheated the pizza and this morning, the gas line had been tampered with."

My stomach went cold.

Luella was right.

Joe Roscoe might be in custody, but that didn't change a thing.

Someone still—someone else—wanted us dead.

❦ 20 ❧

It was Friday afternoon before everyone finally decided I could actually be left on my own for a while. Sister Liliosa returned to the retreat house to await word about Sister Catherine. Kate had to check in at the winery, and promised she'd be back in a couple hours. Luella had some work to do on her boat, but she said if everyone else would pitch in with side dishes, she'd provide the main course for the night's dinner. She'd caught some walleye that morning and with a defiant look at Chandra, she promised to fillet it and debone it and sauté it and she assured me it would taste like heaven on earth. Chandra, it should be noted, turned a tad green at the very thought, but that didn't stop her from taking that bag of fish-shaped crackers with her when she walked out the door.

I was too tired to sleep and far too worried about Sister Catherine to keep still. My knees felt like Silly Putty, but

I didn't let that stop me. I went into the kitchen, made some coffee, and realized that besides those few spoonfuls of soup and those couple crackers, I hadn't eaten a thing since early that morning. I grabbed a yogurt and sat down on one of the high stools near the breakfast counter to try to figure out what the heck was going on.

Maybe the noise in my head would block out the distractions of the day and help me concentrate.

It didn't block out the sound of someone rapping on the back door.

I'd already called out, "Come in," before I saw that it was Levi.

"You okay?" At least he had the sense to stay back near the door, but still, I could see the shimmer of genuine concern in his eyes.

I waved it away with one hand. "I'm fine. Well, except for my ears. Sister Catherine—"

"Hank says she's still in surgery. I thought you'd want to know."

"Thanks." I meant it and figured I should show my appreciation. "Coffee?"

He crossed the kitchen. "It smells great. You want a cup?"

It was the first I realized that though I'd brewed a pot, I'd never poured a cup for myself.

Levi brought one over. "You're not going to eat yogurt, are you?" he asked. "After a day like you had?"

"After a day like I had, what am I supposed to eat?"

He scooped the carton of yogurt off the counter and put it back in the fridge. While he was on the other side of the room, he grabbed a mixing bowl. "Scrambled eggs," he said, plunking the bowl down on the counter near where I was sitting. "You drink too much the night before, you eat scrambled eggs the next day. You're worried or nervous or you're trying to make some big decision in your life, scrambled eggs clear your head and make things better every time."

"You know this for a fact?"

Rather than answer, he went and got the eggs, expertly cracked them into the bowl, and found a whisk. Realizing he was familiar enough with my kitchen to find all that and a pan without asking brought a pang to my chest, so I concentrated on my coffee and didn't watch him cook.

A few minutes later, he slid a plate of perfectly scrambled eggs in front of me and put a fork in my hand. "You're joining me?" I asked him.

"Absolutely." He got another plate of eggs for himself and sat down next to me. "You want hot sauce?"

I never ate hot sauce with my eggs, but there was something about having the world blown out from under my feet that made me think maybe this was the time to start. Levi sprinkled hot sauce on his eggs and passed the bottle my way.

"So . . ." With his fork, he pointed toward me so that I knew I had to take a bite before he would, and I dutifully obeyed. The first forkful was drizzled with hot sauce and I sucked in a breath.

Levi was apparently an old pro when it came to hot sauce. He chewed and swallowed. "Where are we on the case?"

I wanted to say *we* weren't anywhere, but I didn't have the energy.

"Joe Roscoe was in police custody when the stove was tampered with," I said instead.

"I know that."

I shouldn't have been surprised.

"So Joe couldn't have messed with the gas line."

Levi knew that, too, which explained why he kept on eating and didn't say a word.

I followed his lead and finished my eggs.

"So what are we going to do?" he asked.

I knew he wasn't talking about a second helping of eggs.

I drummed my fingers against the black granite countertop. "I think Joe Roscoe was working alone." Truth be told, this hadn't occurred to me until that very moment. "I mean, if he's a professional hit man, he would be, wouldn't he? It's not exactly a business where you share what you're doing with other folks."

"True." Since I'd finished my coffee, Levi got up and refilled my cup and got another cup for himself while he was at it.

"That means there's another bad guy."

"That's got to be true, too." He set the coffee in front of me. "So who is it? And what is he after?"

"That's the million-dollar question." It was the first I realized the ringing in my ears had gone from a gong to a muted knell and I smiled. Maybe Levi was right about scrambled eggs and how they could cure anything. "So maybe Joe isn't the one who killed Sister Sheila or Sister Helene."

"He swears he's not."

"So let's pretend for a minute that he's telling the truth. That means Joe was here simply to recover the money from the bank robbery from Ginger Mancini and that he was willing to do anything like take a potshot at her to scare her and make her give him the money. And our other bad guy— we'll call him Bad Guy Number Two—he's the real killer."

"But why kill two nuns?"

The question was at the heart of our mystery, and I knew

until we found the answer, we'd never find the person who was responsible.

"Let's think about who died," Levi suggested. "First Sister Sheila. What do we know about her?"

"She was a musician and she might have been a little unstable, I mean, if you believe what Sister Helene said about her and about how her behavior was always a little erratic."

"And the other dead nun?"

"Sister Helene. Also a musician." For one brief shining moment, a feeling very much like hope lifted my spirits, but a second later, it burst like a pinpricked balloon and my shoulders sagged. "That certainly doesn't explain why anyone would attempt to kill Sister Catherine. She runs a women's shelter. She has nothing to do with music."

"So what the nuns do for a living might not be the connection. What else do they have in common?"

"They're nuns." Levi didn't laugh, but then, it wasn't much of a joke. I sifted through the bits and pieces of the week that felt as if they'd been scattered when the oven went blam. My mind drifted over the scene.

Sister Catherine, facedown on the kitchen floor.

Just like Sister Sheila had been facedown in the lake when I found her.

Facedown, her dove-gray habit ghostly in the twilight.

"They dressed alike," I blurted out and in answer to Levi's inquisitive look added, "Not Sister Helene. Sister Helene wore street clothes. But Sister Sheila and Sister Catherine . . . Sister Catherine was the one who said it, I think. Earlier in the week when we were talking about what might be going on over at the retreat house, she was the one who said that to a lot of people, all nuns look alike."

I knew exactly when what I was saying clicked in Levi's brain; his eyes shone. "And Sister Sheila and Sister Catherine would have looked alike, at least from the back."

"Their dresses were the same. Only their veils were different. And if the light was bad, and it was because it was evening—"

"And someone came at Sister Sheila from behind—"

"Catherine might have been the target all along!" Back when I was writing, the feeling was second nature to me— that moment when the plot points came together and the denouement to a convoluted story line made so much sense, I sometimes jumped out of my desk chair and shouted, "Hallelujah!"

This was one of those moments!

Or at least it would have been if another thought hadn't hit me.

Before the *Hallelujah* had a chance to escape my lips, I sighed. "It's a great theory, but it doesn't explain Sister Helene. She didn't wear a habit. No one could have mistaken her for Sister Catherine."

"You got that right." Levi tapped out a rhythm against his coffee cup. "But when that piece of the house came down—"

"Sister Catherine was there."

"And the oven, of course."

"Sister Catherine again. But how could anyone have known we were going to bake a cake? And now poor Sister Catherine is in a hospital over on the mainland and—"

Now that the ringing in my ears had toned down, maybe my mind was clearing because a new thought hit me.

"Do you think anyone called her family?" I asked Levi.

His shrug pretty much said it all.

The thought still simmering, I went into my suite and

dug through the pocket of my jeans for Sister Catherine's cell phone.

"She said her brother left a message this morning," I told Levi, but when I checked, the only call that had come in that morning was listed as restricted.

"I need to listen to her messages. Maybe he left a number where she could get ahold of him."

If I'd been with just about anyone else (except maybe the Ladies of the League, who were getting pretty darned good at investigating), they would have reacted like normal people and been outraged that I'd even think to snoop so blatantly.

But Levi wasn't other people. Snooping was the name of his game.

"You're going to have to figure out her password," he told me.

But I was one step ahead of him.

I keyed in "Gram" and was into her voicemail in an instant.

The only message in it was from her brother, Michael.

I listened to the message for just a second and made a face. "She was right," I told Levi. "Sister Catherine said there was so much noise in the background, she could barely understand what her brother was saying." I listened some more and I guess I knew when my mouth fell open because Levi popped out of his chair.

"What?" he asked.

I waved a hand to tell him to keep quiet and listened until the end of the message before I jumped out of my chair, too, and told him, "We've got to go see Hank."

By dinnertime that night, the news was all over the island— Sister Catherine Lang had died on the operating table. I felt awful about it, and more determined than ever to find justice for the murdered nuns.

I kept the thought firmly in mind as Levi and I drove back home from the police station.

We were just in time to find Tyler Stevens packing his camera equipment into his car.

It took me an uncomfortable moment to drag my aching body out of Levi's Jeep, but that didn't much matter, Levi had parked right behind Tyler's rental car; he wasn't going anywhere.

"You're leaving?" I asked him.

He poked a thumb over his shoulder. "I left you a note on the hall table, and the rest of the money I owed you. I'm not having any luck at all with the warblers and well . . . I don't mean to make you feel bad or anything. You've got a lovely home and I hope to come back some day. But I heard the news. You know, about the latest nun who was killed. It's just really too much. I've got two more days of vacation before I have to get back to work. I have to go somewhere that doesn't have a black cloud hanging over it. I need to clear my head. I think I'll have a better chance to do all that on the mainland."

"Well, then I'm glad I caught you right in time." I hooked an arm through Tyler's and turned him toward the Jeep. "Levi and I were just over on the other side of the island. We saw them! We saw warblers."

"No, no, no." Tyler shook me off. "There's no way. I've been looking for them all week. There's no way an inexperienced birder would have—"

"Small songbird, yellow underparts with an olive green back, right? That's what you told me, Tyler. You said warblers have black sideburns down the side of their faces and throats and yellow stripes around their eyes, like glasses."

"Black sideburns, yellow stripes." He considered the possibility. "Yes, it sounds like a warbler, but—"

"And their song. It's *cheery, cheery, cheery*, right?" I put a hand on Tyler's back to usher him into the Jeep.

He locked his knees. "It does sound like a warbler, but—"

"Then you don't want to miss it, do you?"

"I don't, but the ferry—"

"It's Friday," I reminded him. "There will be a late ferry tonight. You'll see your warbler and then you can be off."

I mean, what could the poor guy say?

He smiled and climbed into the Jeep, but truth be told, he didn't look very cheery, cheery, cheery.

Tyler's mood did not improve when we pulled into the driveway at Water's Edge. He glanced around. "You saw warblers? Here? I'm sorry, Bea, I know you're only trying to help, but it seems an unlikely place. I searched all over this part of the island and I never—"

"Nothing ventured, nothing gained, right?" When Levi stopped the Jeep, I hopped out (yes, I winced doing it) and opened the back door so Tyler could get out, too. I led the way into the house, Tyler trailing behind me and Levi right behind him.

I walked into the living room and stopped near the windows. It was a mild evening and the windows had been left open. A soft breeze moved the curtains to the tempo of a heartbeat and brought with it the scent of damp earth and new life.

"Right out there." I pointed toward the garden. "Levi and I, we were here earlier. That's where we saw the warblers."

"Three of them," Levi added. "Right there near those rose bushes."

Tyler narrowed his eyes and scanned the patio and frowned. "Well, they're not there now."

"That doesn't mean they might not come back." Levi took a step nearer. "You should watch for a few minutes. You never know. That's the whole thing about being a birder, isn't it? Patience. It's all about patience."

"Patience." I spoke the word on the end of a sigh. "But that's not something you have a whole lot of, is it? If you did, you wouldn't have been so anxious to kill Sister Catherine."

I didn't need to look Tyler's way, I felt the change in his body. He flinched, then went rigid, and I knew in my gut that he would have recovered in an instant and taken off for the door if Levi wasn't right behind him.

"You didn't think you could actually get away with it, did you?" I'm not sure how I managed it, but I kept my voice light and even when I pointed toward the garden. "Look, a cardinal. They're such beautiful birds. But then, you don't care much about birds, do you? The birding thing, that was just a cover. Like genealogy was for Joe Roscoe."

Tyler might not be able to step back, but that didn't mean he couldn't edge to his left, a little farther away from me. "I . . . I don't know what you're talking about."

"I'm talking about how to a lot of people, all nuns look alike. But the truth is . . ." I waved toward the doorway and when I gave the signal, the nuns marched into the room.

Sister Liliosa and Sister Margaret led the way. Sisters Paul, Grace, Francelle, and Mary Jean were right behind. When I'd stopped by earlier in the evening and told them what I had planned, they had agreed to line up in front of the fireplace. I bet when they did, they didn't picture themselves as I saw them now, like a gleaming army of angels, their heads high and proud, their eyes shining.

"These nuns don't look alike, though—do they, Tyler? I mean, not like Sister Sheila and Sister Catherine did."

He sniffed. "I told you, I don't know what you're talking about."

I shook my head. "If I were you, I'd work on a better defense. *I don't know what you're talking about* isn't going to hold much water in court. Why don't you try something like this . . ." I strolled around to his left so that I could turn and face him. "You thought you'd killed Sister Catherine the first night the nuns were here. That's why you went back to the mainland the next day. You figured you'd done what you came to the island to do. But then you saw the news, right? You saw the news, and realized you'd killed the wrong nun. They did look alike, didn't they? The light was fading and their habits were the same. You came up on Sister Sheila from behind. It must have been quite a surprise when you heard who she really was."

He shook his shoulders and I suspected he'd offer another lame excuse, so I breezed right on. "You couldn't come back right away because the weather was bad and the ferry wasn't running. But you showed up again when it was. You said it was because somebody told you there were warblers. And when you got back, that's when Sister Helene was killed."

When I moved to stand in front of Tyler, Levi had moved, too, and now, he was stationed in the doorway, his arms crossed over his broad chest and his feet planted. "That part didn't make any sense. I mean, Sister Helene being killed. But really, the truth of the matter had been staring us in the face all along. See, both Sister Catherine and Sister Helene were at that dinner back in New York. They . . ." I stepped nearer to the man who'd registered at my B and B as Tyler Stevens. "And their families."

"Now, Sister Helene, she went to look around the island on the morning she died," Levi added. "And if she just so happened to meet someone she recognized—"

"She would have had to be silenced. And you see," I added, "that's what had us confused. Because there didn't seem to be any connection between Sister Sheila's and Sister Helene's deaths. But of course there was, because Sister Helene recognized you, Michael."

Tyler's face went pale, but I knew from experience that that didn't mean a thing. Who wouldn't be a little off their game with accusations coming at them from all sides? "I don't know who Michael is," he stammered. "And even if I did—"

I perched myself on the arm of the couch. "Michael is Sister Catherine's brother. And you know what we found out today? That when Michael and Catherine's grandmother dies . . . and unfortunately that looks like it's going to happen soon . . . Sister Catherine's shelter back in Philadelphia is going to inherit all of Gram's money. I didn't realize how much there was of it. Not until just a little while ago. A few million is going to do a whole lot of good at the shelter. A few million . . . it's also as good a motive for murder as any I've ever heard."

"Killing for money." Sister Liliosa was so incensed, her shoulders shook. "It's terrible."

"It's ridiculous, that's what it is." Tyler . . . or I should say Michael Lang . . . swung around to take us all in. "You're all talking crazy. I don't know who this Michael guy is and I certainly am not related to any nun, dead or alive. I'm leaving, and I'm leaving the island, but you can be sure I'm going to contact my attorney about all this when I get home. You can't just fling around accusations and say that I'm someone I'm not. You can't prove it. Not any of it.

Now . . ." He sniffed, raised his chin, and stepped up to the doorway. "If you don't get out of my way," he told Levi, "I'm thinking some slick attorney can get a kidnapping charge added to the suit I'm going to file against you all."

Levi didn't argue. But then, he didn't need to.

He stepped out of the doorway to reveal who'd been behind him the entire time.

Sister Catherine.

❮ 21 ❯

Of course Hank had been nearby the whole time and as soon as we picked Michael Lang up off the floor where he had fallen into a swoon when he saw the sister he thought was dead, Hank read him his rights and hauled him away, and the nuns surrounded Sister Catherine like a host of ministering angels and helped her to a seat on the couch.

"That was so brave of you," I told her.

She smiled through the tears that streamed down her cheeks. Sister Catherine's left arm was in a sling, her hair had been shaved, and her scalp was slick with salve to ease her burned skin. There were cuts on her cheeks and both her eyes were black and blue.

"I can't believe it," she whimpered. "My own brother." She'd been reluctant to believe me from the moment I suggested what might be going on, but now she'd seen it with her own eyes and she couldn't deny it. "He dyed his hair," she said. "He's not a redhead, he's a blond like me. Even so, we sat at the same table with Sister Helene and her family at that dinner in New York. There was no way she wouldn't have recognized him."

"And he couldn't risk her coming back here and telling you she'd seen him." Someone had the good sense to bring over tissues, and I plucked one from the box and handed it to Sister Catherine.

"But how . . ." She blew her nose and looked at Levi. "How did you know?"

"That was all Bea," he told her.

The nuns gathered around and I explained. "It was his voicemail. You were right, Sister. It was nearly impossible to hear him. That noise in the background? I recognized it right away. It was the blast of a ferry horn. Of course, that doesn't mean anything. There are plenty of ferries in plenty of places in the world. He could have been calling from anywhere. But I listened really closely and that's when I knew that he was at our marina, because in addition to the ferry horn, I heard something else."

Sister Catherine sniffled and dabbed at her nose. "There was chanting in the background, like a crowd."

"A crowd of protesters," I told her. "And there was no way you would have recognized it because, really, it's so silly, it must have sounded like nothing more than a jumble of words. But I knew what they were saying—swim free and never get caught!"

Sister Catherine shook her head. "It's so sad. All this time, I thought Michael had turned his life around. But I guess he never did. He never stopped wanting more and now that Gram is near death . . ." She sobbed.

"But how . . ." Sister Liliosa stood behind the couch and she patted Sister Catherine's shoulder. "How could he have possibly known? About the oven?"

That was an easy one, and I let Sister Catherine explain. "It was the Official Special Day Hallelujah Celebration Cake, of course. Once Joe Roscoe was arrested and we thought we were all safe, Michael knew I'd make it. It was the recipe we used to celebrate every . . ." She sniffled. "Every special occasion."

"And what about putting out word that Sister Catherine was dead?" Sister Francelle asked.

Since it was my idea, I explained. "I figured it was one way to see if we were on the right track," I told the nuns. "Once Michael thought he'd done what he came to the island to do, he'd leave. I was right. We caught him just in time."

"It's all so very sad," Sister Catherine said, and though I knew she was right, I also knew that we all needed the kind of catharsis that would only come from recognizing that we'd gone through a tough time together and come out on the other side stronger than ever.

"You still have the recipe for Official Special Day Hallelujah Celebration Cake, don't you?" I asked her.

"I don't need a recipe," she said. "I've made the cake so many times, I could bake it in my sleep."

"Then let's get going." I stood and helped her off the couch. "If ever there was a time we needed Official Special Day Hallelujah Celebration Cake, it's now!"

That night we were all gathered in my dining room—the nuns, the librarians, every police officer Hank could spare, the firefighters, Levi, and of course, the League of Literary

Ladies. We let Sister Catherine do the honors, and she sliced thick pieces of the Official Special Day Hallelujah Celebration Cake we'd spent the last couple hours making.

The cake wasn't just delicious, it was fabulous, and a couple bites worked miracles all around. By the time Chandra, Luella, and Kate helped me pass around coffee, we were all smiling and chatting.

Well, except for Levi. He finished his cake, set his plate on the table, and quietly moved toward the door.

I could have pretended I was so busy talking to Hank that I didn't see him making his exit, but let's face it, that would have been immature, not to mention unworthy of me.

I made my apologies to Hank and caught up with Levi in the kitchen just as he was about to go out the back door.

"Thanks for your help," I said.

He paused, his hand on the doorknob, and glanced over his shoulder at me. "You think we'll work together again?"

"I can't say."

He turned to face me, but he kept his place near the door and I was glad. I stood firm, too, near the breakfast bar, far enough away to signal that for now, the best thing we could do was to keep our distance.

"I'll see you again?" he asked.

"You willing to risk getting whacked with a wet mop?"

He grinned. "You're worth it," he said, and he walked out the door.

The nuns left the next morning with the promise that they would return someday. I was glad. These were women I was proud to know, and I wanted the chance to talk to them when we didn't have to worry about houses falling down on us.

The librarians, too, headed back to where they'd come

from and once they were gone, it was just me, Chandra, Kate, and Luella. We sat on my front porch and enjoyed the silence.

That is, until Luella spoke up. She looked across my yard toward Chandra's. "I thought you said the surveyors were coming."

Chandra pursed her lips and looked up at the ceiling. "They'll be here," she said. "They've been busy . . . uh . . . doing . . . uh . . . you know . . . surveying stuff."

I had had a week of mysteries and investigating. I wasn't exactly in the mood to try to figure out what Chandra was up to, so I asked her point-blank, "What's going on?"

Her cheeks turned the same cherry red as the T-shirt she wore with her yellow capris. "They're going to be here," she said, lifting her chin and tossing her head so that her blond bob wiggled. "And they're going to build the biggest pool and install the biggest lamppost this side of the Ohio mainland."

My ears had stopped ringing that morning—thank goodness—and apparently, the silence had cleared my head. I pinned Chandra with a look. "That's a lot of baloney!"

Kate sat up straight on the wicker couch next to me. "What are you talking about?" she asked me.

But Luella was more perceptive. "What are you up to?" she asked Chandra.

Chandra picked at an invisible piece of lint on her capris and her determined expression collapsed. "I just thought . . ." She burst into tears.

Pools and lampposts and fishing protests aside, there is nothing like tears to bring out friends' loyalty. We got out of our seats and gathered around where Chandra sat sobbing on the wicker rocking chair.

"I tried to stay strong," she sobbed. "I thought I could pull it off. But . . . but after everything that happened this week and those poor nuns who died and those other nuns who were so brave and so loyal to their friends . . ." Her wail startled the gulls on the strip of grass across the street and they took off over the lake. "I can't lie to you anymore! There is no pool! There is no lamppost and Luella . . ." She reached for Luella and squeezed her hand. "There aren't going to be any more protests. I promise, I promise, I promise!"

Kate, Luella, and I exchanged looks. "Want to explain?" I asked.

Chandra nodded and we all returned to our seats and gave her a moment to compose herself. After a whole lot of sniffling, she did, and looked at each of us in turn. "Don't you realize it's been a year?" she asked, her voice watery. "It's been one whole year since Alvin Littlejohn sentenced us to be a book discussion group. And because of that—"

"We had to meet for one full year," I said. The truth dawned on me and I would have slapped my forehead if I wasn't afraid my ears would start ringing again. "Chandra, were you trying to get us to take you to court? So Alvin would sentence us to another year in the League?"

She nodded, and cried and after a minute of taking it all in and realizing what it meant, I have to say, there were tears in all of our eyes.

"It doesn't take a court order!" Kate plumped back in her seat and crossed her arms over her chest. "Even if we weren't forced into the book discussion group, we'd still be friends."

"I doubt it." I looked around at my friends' horrified expressions. "But I'm glad we are and as far as the League of Literary Ladies . . . Chandra, it's your choice. What book will we be reading next?"

If you enjoyed this book, try a taste of

IRISH STEWED

the first book in Kylie Logan's
Ethnic Eats Mysteries!

*Coming soon
from Berkley Prime Crime*

❰❖ 1 ❖❱

"I can explain."

At my side, Sophie Charnowski pressed her small, plump hands together and shifted from one sneaker-clad foot to the other. The nearest streetlight flickered off, then on again, and in its anemic light, I saw perspiration bead on her forehead. "It's like this, you see, Laurel."

"Oh, I see, all right." Good thing I was wearing my Brian Atwood snakeskin ballet flats. In heels, I would have tripped on the pitted sidewalk when I spun away from the building in front of us and the railroad tracks just beyond. When I pinned short, round Sophie with a look, I meant to make her shake in her shoes, and it gave me a rush of satisfaction to realize the ol' daggers from my blue eyes still carried all the punch I intended. Sophie flicked out her tongue to touch her lips, then swallowed hard.

While she was at it, I stabbed one finger toward the

train station and the sign hanging above the door that declared the place "Sophie's Terminal at the Tracks."

"This wasn't what I expected," I said.

Sophie rubbed her hands together. "I know that. Really, I do. I can only imagine how you must feel."

"No." I cut her off before she could say anything else ignorant and insulting. "You can't possibly imagine how I feel. I just drove all the way to Ohio from California. Because you told me—"

"I wanted it to be a surprise." Sophie was a full eight inches shorter than my five foot nine, and as round as I am slender. She had the nerve to look up at me through the shock of silvery bangs that hung over her forehead. Believe me, the hairstyle wasn't a fashion statement. When I picked Sophie up at her small, neat bungalow so we could drive across Hubbard and she could show me the restaurant, I had the distinct feeling I'd just woken her from an after-dinner nap. "I knew once you saw the place—"

"Once I saw the place!" Was that my voice echoing against the old train station and bouncing around the semi-gentrified neighborhood with its bookstore, its coffee shop, its beauty salon and gift boutiques?

I was way past caring. "Sophie, you told me—"

"That I'm having my knee replaced tomorrow. Yes." She took a funny sort of half step and pulled up short, one hand automatically shooting down to her right knee. She kept it there, a not-so-subtle reminder of the pain she'd told me was her constant companion. "And that I need someone to help out while I'm laid up. Someone to run the restaurant."

"Which isn't the restaurant it's supposed to be."

"Well, really, it is." A grin made her look so darned impish, I almost forgave the lies she'd been feeding me for years.

Almost.

"The Terminal at the Tracks has been a neighborhood gathering place for going on forty years now," she told me, and don't think I didn't notice the way she rushed to get the words out before I could stop her cold. "I always loved it here. We used to stop for breakfast on Sunday mornings after church. And after our Tuesday bowling league, we'd always get a bite to eat here. Only these days . . ." This time when she caressed her knee, she added a long-suffering sigh. "Well, I'm not doing very much bowling these days. But that doesn't change how I feel about this neighborhood. It's got the feel of history to it, don't you think?" Instead of giving me a chance to answer, she drew in a long, deep breath and let it out slowly while she swiveled her gaze from the train station to the tracks behind it and the boarded-up factory beyond.

"When I had the opportunity to buy the Terminal fifteen years ago, I just jumped at it. So there's my name up there on the sign." Sophie made a brisk *ta-da* sort of motion in that direction. "And here I am." She pointed at her own broad bosom. "And now . . ." It was spring and almost nine, which meant it was already dark. That didn't keep me from seeing the rapturous look that brightened Sophie's brown eyes and brought out the dimples in her pudgy cheeks. "And now here you are, too. So you see, everything is just as it's supposed to be."

Really? I was supposed to buy into this philosophical, all's-right-with-the-world horse hockey?

My pulse quickened, and my blood pressure would have shot to the ceiling had we been indoors instead of outside in front of the long, low-slung building with a two-story section built in the middle above the main entrance. When that street-light went off and on again, it winked against the weathered yellow paint and the dark windows of the restaurant.

I hardly noticed the sparkle of the light against the glass.

But then, I was pretty busy seeing red.

I would have leveled Sophie right then and there if she wasn't thirty years older than me, and limping, to boot. Instead, I followed along when she hobbled to the front door.

"What you did was low, underhanded, and dishonest, Sophie," I told her.

"Yes, it was." She didn't sound the least bit penitent. She stuck her key in the front door. "But now that we're here, you'll look around, won't you?"

I should have said no.

I should have put my foot down.

I should have opened my mouth and, as so often happens when I do, I should have let what I was thinking pour out of me like the lava that spews from a volcano and incinerates everything in its path.

Why I didn't is as much a mystery now as it was then. I only know that when Sophie pushed open the front door and stepped inside the Terminal at the Tracks, I followed along.

"Welcome." She touched a hand to a light switch and the fixture directly over our heads turned on.

I was just in time to see Sophie beam a smile all around.

I did not share in her enthusiasm. In fact, I took one look around the entryway of the Terminal at the Tracks, and a second, and a third.

That's pretty much when I had to remind myself to snap my mouth shut.

What I could see—at least here in the fifteen-by-fifteen entryway where customers waited for their tables—was a mishmash of kitschy faux Victorian, everything from teddy bears in puffy-sleeved gowns to posters advertising things like unicycles and moustache wax.

And then there was the lace.

Doilies and rickrack and bunting.

Oh, my.

Brand-spanking-new, it would have been overblown and downright dreadful. With fifteen years of service under its belt, the lace was yellow and bedraggled. The teddy bear propped on the old rolltop desk that also served as a hostess station looked as if it could use an airing, and what had once been a magnificent floor made of wide hardwood planks was scratched and dull.

"I knew you'd love it as much as I do," Sophie purred.

Fortunately, at that moment a train rolled by, not twenty feet from the back of the restaurant, and the place shook the way L.A. had in the last earthquake I remembered. My sternum vibrated. My bones rattled.

When the train was gone and my body was done with its rockin' and rollin', I pretended I didn't even remember Sophie's last comment.

"There's something special I need to show you." She latched on to the sleeve of the silk shirttail I wore with skinny jeans and tugged me toward a glass counter with a cash register set on it.

"Right here." Sophie said, and tapped the glass next to the cash register. That's when her smile fell and her silvery brows knit. "Well, it was here." She chewed her lower lip. "It's always here. I must have left it . . ." She waved in some indeterminate direction. "In the office. I must have left it in the office when I took the day's receipts in there to file. You know, on Saturday, the last day the restaurant was open before I had to close." Another puppy-dog look. "Because of my knee, you know. And my surgery tomorrow."

Sophie gave the counter another pat. "The receipt spike," she finally explained. "You know, the thin, pointy thing where we stick the receipts—"

"After they're rung up on the register." I'd worked in enough restaurants in my day; I knew exactly what she was talking about.

"This one is special," Sophie confided. "About yay high . . ." She held her hands ten inches apart. "And made completely of brass. It was Grandpa Majtkowski's. From his bakery shop in Poland. He brought it with him when he came to this country back in 1913. Imagine that: He came with one suitcase, one change of clothes, and less than twenty dollars in his pocket, and he still thought it was important to bring that receipt spike with him. And no wonder! It was all he had of home, all he had of the business he worked so many years to build, and—"

A tap on the front door saved me from any more of the history lesson.

Sophie didn't seem to mind. In fact, when she looked toward the front entrance, she grinned.

"It's Declan!" Quicker than a woman with a sore knee should have been able to move, she scooted over and opened the door. "It's Declan," she said again, and she moved back to allow a man to step into the Terminal.

Let's get something straight here: I had spent the last six years of my life working as a personal chef to Meghan Cohan. Yeah, that Meghan Cohan, the Hollywood megastar. I wasn't just used to catering to the culinary whims of the Beautiful People, I was comfortable rubbing elbows with them. When she was working on a film, I traveled with Meghan. All over the world. When she was bored, she'd take me along when she jetted to her place in Maui. Or the one in Tuscany. Or the villa in the south of France. I was in charge of Meghan's diet regimen, and her parties, and the late-night soirees that sometimes ended up getting talked about in *Vogue* or *Elle* or *Cosmo.*

Meghan was powerful. She was gorgeous. And she allowed only powerful and gorgeous men into her circle.

I wasn't sure who this Declan guy was, but I knew that one look, and Meghan would have welcomed him with open arms.

Tall.

Dark.

I won't say handsome because let's face it, that's a cliché, and Declan's looks put him far beyond platitudes.

His hair was a little too long and tousled just enough that had we been back in L.A., I would have suspected he'd just come from some tony salon. He had an angular face defined by a dusting of dark whiskers, and he wore jeans and sneakers and a black leather jacket over a red-plaid flannel. Untucked. All of it was casual enough, while at the same time it sent the message that whatever else Declan was, he was comfortable in his own skin.

None of which mattered in the least bit.

Not to me, anyway.

No matter how handsome the locals might happen to be, I'd already decided there was no way I was staying.

Declan came inside the Terminal and closed the door behind hm.

"I saw the light on," he said to Sophie. "And no one's usually here this late at night. I just wanted to make sure everything was all right."

"Aren't you just the best neighbor ever!" Sophie twinkled like a teenager. "Declan's from the Irish store." She looked out the window, and I saw the lighted windows of the gift shop that was across the street and catty-corner to the restaurant. From here, it was impossible to see exactly what was in the display windows on either side of the front door, but there was no mistaking the crisp green colors touched with a smattering of orange, or the wooden sign that hung above the front door—a gigantic green shamrock.

"Of course, everything's fine. I was just showing off the place." She closed a hand over the sleeve of his jacket and piloted him nearer. "Declan Fury, this is Laurel Inwood."

Add a thousand-watt smile to that description of Declan. And a handshake that was warm and firm enough to send the message that he was no-nonsense, practical, and far more sure of himself than 99 percent of the actors (yeah, even the ones who play tough guys in the movies) Meghan had introduced me to over the years.

"So, you're finally here." Declan had a baritone voice that managed to caress even the most ordinary greeting. "I know your aunt's been looking forward to your arrival."

I'm afraid my smile wasn't nearly as broad as his. Or as genuine. I refused to look at Sophie when I said, "She's not really my aunt."

"Oh." Declan pulled his hand back to his side, not as embarrassed as he was simply curious. "I guess I'm confused because Sophie always refers to you as her niece."

This time, I did take a second to slide Sophie a look. I wasn't surprised to see something like contrition in her pursed lips and her downcast eyes.

Which didn't mean I believed it was genuine.

"That makes me wonder why Sophie was talking about me at all."

Contrition be damned! Just like that, Sophie was back to her ol' grinning self. "You know we're all just as proud as punch of everything you've accomplished." She patted my arm. "Laurel's famous," she told Declan and then, because she apparently saw the sparks shooting from my eyes, she was quick to amend the statement to: "Well, practically famous."

Maybe Declan was also a better actor than most of the ones I'd met out in L.A. He pretended not to notice the undercurrent of annoyance and avoidance that flowed back and forth between me and Sophie. In fact, when he turned back to me, it was with a smile sleek enough to send prickles up my spine.

Not that it mattered, I reminded myself.

Since I wasn't staying.

"Well," he said, giving me a quick once-over from toes to top of head and apparently approving of what he saw since his smile stayed firmly in place, "it's nice to know there will be a practically famous chef holding down the fort while her aunt is in the hospital."

He had a short memory.

And he smelled like bay rum and limes.

I shook away the thought and the way the scent always made me think of tropical islands and warm sea breezes.

"Sophie's younger sister, Nina, was my foster mother for four years," I told him. "So you see, Sophie and I, we're really not related."

"Except you don't have to share DNA to be family, do you?"

"I'm just showing Laurel around," Sophie said, and she wound an arm through mine. "You know, because I'll be gone six weeks and someone needs to run the place."

"That doesn't mean that someone is going to be me." I untangled myself from Sophie's grip when I said this, the better to look her in the eye so she knew I meant business.

"We obviously need to talk, me and Laurel," she told Declan. "There might be some rocky road ice cream in the freezer, and I don't know about you, but I think heart-to-heart talks always go better over rocky road."

Declan stepped toward the doorway that led into the main part of the restaurant. The woodwork around it was painted dusty blue, like the trim on the outside of the station, and there was a lace curtain in the doorway that was tied back on either side with purple ribbon. He poked a thumb over his shoulder into the darkened room. "If you like, I can take a look around before you settle down for your heart-to-heart."

"No need!" Sophie's warm laugh bounced up to the ceiling fans that swirled overhead. "You know this is a safe neighborhood."

Declan leaned forward just enough to take a peek beyond the entryway and into the pitch-dark restaurant. "Maybe so, but it is late and—"

"And you need to get back to whatever it was you were doing before you took the time to come over here and check on an old lady like me." Sophie led him back to the front door. "A good-lookin' guy like you, you must have better things to do on a warm spring night."

Declan tipped his head and when he smiled, the air between us sizzled. "Then good night, ladies."

"Isn't he the dreamiest?" Sophie giggled once he was gone.

Her back was to the door. Otherwise, I wondered if she'd still think he was dreamy when she realized that Declan didn't go across the street to the Irish store. In fact, he walked along the front of the Terminal, turned at the far corner, and headed into the side parking lot.

Once he was out of sight, I turned back to Sophie and was just in time to see her shuffle her sneakers. "Rocky road?" she offered.

I let go a sigh of pure frustration. "You're not going to bribe me with ice cream, Sophie. I told you, I don't appreciate being lied to. All those years, you came to California to visit and you showed me and Nina—"

"Pictures of the restaurant." She looked up at me through those unruly bangs. "Yes, I know."

"But it wasn't this restaurant."

Sophie's cheeks flushed pink, but I wasn't about to let that keep me from saying my piece.

"You showed us photographs of a lovely place out in the country. Linen tablecloths, soft lighting, a fabulous wine cellar. That's the place I thought I was going to be helping out with while you were recuperating. This place—"

"This place is all I have."

Yes, her comment would have tugged at my heartstrings.

If I had heartstrings.

Unfortunately for Sophie and luckily for me, I didn't.

That didn't mean I was a complete philistine. "I said I'd take you to the hospital tomorrow morning, and I will," I told her.

"And you said you'd be running the restaurant after that."

"It's not going to work."

Her shoulders drooped. "I know. I guess I knew all along. But still, you're here. Let me show you around." Her limp more pronounced than ever, she walked through that lace-curtained doorway and turned on the lights in the main dining room.

What I saw was pretty much what I expected.

Five, six, seven, eight . . . I counted . . . tables lined up against the far wall next to the windows that looked out over the railroad tracks. None of them covered with linen. Four tables to my left and two doorways, one marked *Kitchen* and the other *Office*. To my right, six more tables, more lace, more kitsch, and once I skirted the jutting-out wall that marked the back of the waiting area, windows that looked out at the street and gave a bird's-eye view of the light that shone on that green shamrock across the way.

And one customer.

I froze and looked at the man lying facedown on one of the tables.

"Uh, Sophie." She was already shuffling back to the kitchen in search of ice cream and when I called out, Sophie hitch-stepped back the other way. "There's a guy here."

"A guy? That's impossible. That's—"

She got as far as where I stood and she froze, too, looking where I did, at the table against the wall where a man in a brown jacket was slumped, his head on his arm.

And that receipt spike of Grandpa Majtkowski's sticking out the back of his neck.

"Oh, my goodness!" Sophie wailed.

If I didn't act fast, I knew I'd have another problem on my hands, so I pulled over the nearest chair and plunked Sophie down in it before I dared to close in on the man in the brown jacket.

From this angle, there wasn't much to see. In the light of the faux-Tiffany chandelier directly above the table, his neck looked as pale as a hooked fish. Well, except for the thin river of blood that originated at the spot where the receipt spike was plunged into his spine.

I dared to put a finger on his neck, but even before I did, I knew I wouldn't find a pulse. His skin was ice, and there were tinges of blue behind his ears and on the fingers of the hand that hung loosely at his side.

I fumbled for the phone in my pocket and dialed 9-1-1,

hoping that when the dispatcher answered, I could make the words form in a mouth that felt suddenly as if it had been packed with sand.

And all I could think was the one thing I knew I wouldn't dare say to Sophie or to the cops—this gave a whole new meaning to the word *terminal*.